# TO THE END OF THE DAY

## Eve Bonham

Book Guild Publishing

Sussex, England

First published in Great Britain in 2011 by
The Book Guild Ltd
Pavilion View
19 New Road
Brighton, BN1 1UF

Typeset in Baskerville by
Ellipsis Books Limited, Glasgow

Printed in Great Britain by
CPI Antony Rowe

A catalogue record for this book is available from The British Library.

ISBN 978 1 84624 582 4

*For Julie*

*Chapter One*

A woman is watching the birds. She is envious – she was once free like them. The house martins arrived a month earlier and have nearly finished constructing their precarious nests underneath the eaves of the old house. Soon it will be dusk and their swooping, darting and wheeling will cease as darkness overtakes the garden. Anna loves to see the small birds as they fly in carefree circles and shriek like schoolgirls showing off in a playground. She can hardly believe that they do not collide with one another as they tumble about the sky, and wonders how it is she now seems unable to avoid collisions.

A man is watching her from the house. He sees her slight figure standing on the grass, an almost ethereal silhouette against the pale yellow sky. She is gazing upwards at the circling birds, the cloud of her pale hair blurring even further the outline of her head.

This is his woman and his house and his garden. Youenn feels just a little alienated from her with her preoccupation with the circling birds, and suppresses an unworthy prickle of anxiety.

The woman turns back to look at the house. She observes the familiar brooding figure sitting in a tall-backed chair illuminated in the light of the lamp by which he has been reading. She can see that he is looking out towards the garden and realises with dismay that he has been watching her. For a few motionless seconds they stare at each other dispassionately and then she raises one arm in a placating gesture – a wave to him. The man looks down at his book again, affecting unconcern, pretending to be absorbed in the words on the page.

Anna sighs and, with a last glance at the sky, she turns and walks back up the garden, across the terrace and into the house. The large room within is both kitchen and dining room and, together with the sitting room beyond, where there is a preponderance of dark wooden furniture, it is known as the *séjour*. At the end furthest from the cooker, and beyond the dining table, there is a large chair on which her husband sits to read or contemplate. She looks at the clock on the wall and then opens the door of the oven to check that the *blanquette de veau* is simmering correctly, before putting on a pan of water to boil. She walks across to the old wooden sideboard; this is a large solid item of furniture, the necessity for which seems to be endemic in Breton dining rooms. Anna has a theory that they are given as wedding presents and remain as a kind of family heirloom which gets passed on to one of the children. She finds the heavy reproduction pieces hideous – though at least Youenn's is scratched with age and use, and therefore more acceptable.

As she pulls opens the heavy lopsided drawer containing the cutlery, she notices the gaunt boniness of her fingers. She has convinced herself that her scrawny hands are the only visible sign of her weight loss and hopes their condition can be accounted for by the physical assault she inflicts on them with her gardening, cooking and housework. These are new occupations which she would have scorned and avoided in her younger years, but which now give her some sort of pattern and solace.

She starts to set the table for four people, and has a warm sense of anticipation of company at a meal. For a few years now, since Youenn's children left home, there have been only two places at the table, as her husband rarely invites guests to dine with them any more. He has become more reclusive with age.

They will start with a fish pâté she has made earlier in the day with some *pain campagne*, which she buys from the family *boulangerie* up the road. She quite enjoys cooking and is not unskilled, but realises that as an Englishwoman in France she will never be accorded any acclaim for her culinary proficiency. To her neighbours the explanation is simple: she isn't French and therefore she can't cook. Brittany is naturally superior to Britain – a country that can never be allowed any accolades. The locals share in the national blindness which makes many French people think that it rains all the time in England, that it is impossible to get a good meal there, and that the English have no passion or finesse. They just aren't as perfect as the French – and are to be pitied for it. She finds these simple convictions and opinions, though misguided, both amusing and irritating. She does not, of course, tell her neighbours this – she would not wish to increase her sense of alienation by criticism, knowing that a rebuttal of their provincial views would provoke strong disapproval. The Englishwoman has never felt she is accepted here, even after five years. She feels her difference and knows she is, and will always be, foreign to them.

She glances across at her husband, who is an educated man who would, she had once believed, disassociate himself from these parochial views. Now she is not so sure that he does. He did not utter a word when she came in from the garden, though he has since put down his book and she is aware that he is watching her moodily as she walks back and forth in the large old kitchen. He coughs and she then looks at him.

'You're getting too thin,' he remarks in French. He comments on things he can see, finding it uncomfortable to discuss those he cannot. He is a man of few words. It is safe to talk about appearances; what lies behind can be uncharted waters and he has become wary of his wife's tendency to indulge in embarrassing emotional revelations if she is given the chance.

Anna is unsurprised that he has noticed her loss of weight – he spends much of his time observing others. She smiles and replies in his language, 'Better than too fat.'

'Not necessarily,' he grunts. 'Do your friends speak French?'

'Yes, rather well. But probably not up to your exacting standards.'

Youenn gets to his feet – he is a tall, angular man with thick white hair – and walks towards the window, where he stares out at the untidy red sky. The sun is filtering weakly through the fir trees on the left as it passes downwards into the darkness of their tangled lower branches. He accepts natural beauty with a calm detachment, and is slightly contemptuous of those who express their enthusiasm. It is there; it happens; that is good. Nothing needs to be said about it.

'And this Lizzie, whom I have never met – you are very good friends?' He speaks with his back to her, his hands folded across his chest. He coughs again.

'Lizzie is more than a friend – she's more like a sister,' says Anna. 'We don't see each other often but we're very close.' This is an inadequate explanation for the complex interwoven nature of her relationship with Lizzie, but Anna does not feel that it would be wise or useful to elaborate any further. Youenn would not understand and he is not genuinely curious about the matter. Her past does not interest him – as nothing does that is not relevant to him. There was a time when he was less self-centred and more outgoing but it has long passed. He is a man with an inward soul, engrossed in himself and his place in the world.

'I think I'm getting a cough,' he says leaning against the door frame, watching her but making no effort to help prepare their evening meal.

'Poor you,' Anna murmurs with not quite enough sympathy.

'What time are they arriving?' Youenn asks, feeling hungry and not wanting to delay eating too much longer.

'Soon,' says Anna. They ought to have been here by now. Please don't be too late, Lizzie, she pleads silently.

Uncannily, the doorbell sounds at that moment. Anna pulls off the cloth she has wrapped round her skirt and pushes past her husband who has made no move to answer the summons. That is his way. Delay in reacting to outside intervention is a positive ploy and not the result of shyness. She crosses the hall and, finding that Youenn has for some perverse reason shot the bolt on the heavy front door, she struggles to push back the stiff metal before she can open the house to her guests.

Two figures stand in the dusk outside, and Lizzie's warm voice says, 'Locked up for the night already, Anna? You *are* expecting us, aren't you?'

'Of course we are!' says Anna, throwing her arms round Lizzie. She looks over her friend's shoulder at the other guest, Lizzie's husband, who is standing a couple of yards away smiling at the women's genuine demonstration of affection for each other. 'How good to see you both!' she exclaims, drawing away from Lizzie and giving Paul a kiss on the cheek. He puts his arm round her and gives her a hug. Though the light is fading, as she glances back at her friend she observes that beautiful Lizzie is less slim that when they last met.

'Yes, I know. I've put on a few pounds – or kilos,' says Lizzie with a smile. 'It's happy fat.' In their embrace, she has felt Anna's hard bony shoulders and registers the fact that the other woman is now a lot thinner than her. It used to be the other way round. 'You've lost weight, my dear,' she murmurs.

Paul looks across proudly and affectionately at his wife, who appears exotic, sleek and beautiful in the light coming from the hall, and then follows her gaze and looks at Anna, who has, he perceives, lost her delicate beauty and now merely looks fragile.

And older.

As the two women calmly and without embarrassment examine each other, Paul says, breaking into the long moment, 'Car all right here?' He is drawing attention to a beautiful old Bentley which is obviously his other pride and joy. The motor car has warm golden bodywork and it glows metallically in the dying evening light. He walks round to the rear of it, takes two small elegant cases out of the boot and places them on the ground before the lid is closed with an expensive subdued click.

'Your wonderful car!' responds Anna, who is familiar both with the Bentley and with Paul's affection for his old model. 'Yes, leave it there. My neighbours will be curious in the morning. They'll never have seen anything like it before in this village, I'm sure.'

The three of them become aware that Youenn is now standing in the doorway and looking beyond them at the car. He is mesmerised by it, and can hardly bring his eyes back to the faces of his guests when Anna introduces them to him.

Because he is aware that Lizzie is a very old friend of Anna's, he kisses her ritually once on each cheek (twice is formal here; four times is the norm when greeting close friends and family), leaning down to do so. He then shakes hands firmly with Paul, who says in fluent French that he is delighted to meet Anna's husband after so long, and that he is happy to be visiting them in their home. Though he is not a tall man himself, Paul usually finds that he looks down on most Frenchman, whom he considers are usually either rotund or diminutive or both, so he is surprised at Youenn's gaunt height.

'Good car, that.' Youenn speaks for the first time – in French, of course.

'Yes, it's a splendid machine', responds Paul, again in good French, and since Youenn is not looking at him but staring at the car, he transfers his gaze from his host to his vehicle. 'It's an S Type Continental, and this one is an S2 with six cylinders.'

'How old is it?' the Frenchman asks, his eyes still on the gleaming bodywork.

'It was built in 1962. There were lots of them made, but I think it's rare now to find one in this condition. I've owned it for over twenty years.' His tone is light – Paul is proud of his car but affects a modest indifference.

'Come on in,' says Anna, slightly embarrassed by Youenn's fascination with the Bentley, in stark contrast to his austere greeting of her friends. 'We've been standing out here long enough.'

They all enter the house and Youenn reluctantly closes the door. The car stands silently and majestically outside, the streetlamp casting a soft light on the golden sheen of the long bonnet, an image of which is imprinted on Youenn's inner eye.

*     *     *

They have finished dinner and are drinking coffee whilst sitting in the high-backed chairs looking out over the silent garden and the dark fields beyond. It has been a pleasant evening. Anna is relieved that Youenn has after all made an effort to be sociable and he has been unusually attentive to his guests. He has proffered some excellent wine and Paul has praised it. He has also complimented Anna on the delicious meal. Lizzie has been entertaining them with stories and anecdotes told in her erratic and delightful French with its English accent, and Youenn has clearly found her charming. He is unusual for a Frenchman in that he likes English women and finds it refreshing that the ones he has met talk to men unselfconsciously and without overt flirtation.

Lizzie and Paul are now telling Youenn about one of the hotels in the Auvergne where they stayed during their tour of the region, and about the conical hills there known as *puys*. 'We decided,' Paul says, 'to take a very leisurely two weeks driving round slowly and without any specific plans, staying where we ended up each night.' His French is very precise and correct, and he speaks in a slow genial way. It is almost as if he is on his best behaviour.

Lizzie takes over, speaking French imperfectly but without embarrassment, explaining that the holiday in their sedate car has been so very different to their normal racy lifestyle, where everything is pressurised and organised to the last detail, with no time to spare. 'What is life if full of care,' she says theatrically in English.

She then pauses, looking at Anna, who quietly finishes off the quotation, 'We have no time to stand and stare. This might be true for you, Lizzie,' she continues, 'but these days I have rather too much time on my hands. The Breton life goes at a much slower tempo. I've taken up gardening, which is both satisfying and time-consuming.'

Her reply in English has displeased Youenn, who switches the conversation back into French, asking Lizzie what restaurants they have eaten in and which ones were superb and which merely fine. There is no question of a French restaurant being less than good.

There ensues a lively conversation on the merits of French cuisine and the undesirable qualities of many English efforts. Paul and Lizzie are not rocking the boat and play the usual game of over-praising French food and rubbishing English fare. This view is the expected one and, because they know it will please their host, they choose to perform. But when the conversation moves on to politics, the discussion is more balanced and less simplistic. Paul and Youenn enjoy arguing about Europe, and the problems and possibility of political and economic union. They are wide apart on many issues and indeed would prefer to disagree as this makes for a better discussion. But the one thing they find they have in common is scepticism in relation to the future of the European Union.

Anna sits back in her chair and looks at them affectionately. She is pleased that they seem to be getting on so well. This is what she wanted and hoped for, but did not expect. Youenn has been so dour and so antisocial recently. He does not like retirement − he is an active, intelligent man now separated from his former associates and occupations. But tonight he is like his former self. He is almost ebullient. It is as if the handsome car in which his English guests have arrived has given them a glamour and a glow which has brightened up his taciturn disposition and temporarily dispelled the surliness which is now usual with him.

While the men argue desultorily about taxes, corruption and racism, Lizzie and Anna, sitting opposite each other, talk in English about mutual friends, exhibitions they have seen, and books they have read. Youenn suddenly laughs delightedly and leans across to shake the other man's hand. Paul has promised to take him for a short drive in the Bentley before he and Lizzie depart in the morning to drive to the coast for their ferry across the Channel. Anna knows that both men will enjoy that. Paul extends the invitation to her but she declines, explaining that she has to leave early in the morning and so cannot be included in the excursion. In any case, she has been in the Bentley before and cars do not really interest her. The topic of the motor car now takes over and Paul tells Youenn about its history.

Anna quietly gets up from the table to clear away the coffee cups. From the kitchen she looks through the open doorway at the oval dining table, where three candles illuminate the faces of those sitting round it. Youenn is clearly in a good mood, for which Anna is thankful – he is smiling his rare and rather rapacious smile, showing his crooked teeth; there is a glint in his eye as he listens. He is a good-looking man who has not gained weight with age and whose tanned face with its dark moustache makes him look a decade younger than he is, despite the almost white hair. In contrast, Paul is rotund beneath his well-cut linen jacket, his genial face is clean-shaven and his greying hair is neatly combed. He is not an imposing man, but he looks distinguished and his urbane manners are impeccable. This is someone who is at ease with the spruce image he intentionally portrays to the world. Youenn's appearance, about which he is unconcerned, is, in contrast, always just a shade dishevelled. Anna prefers men to look wind-blown or casual. She finds Paul just a bit too neat. He is laughing – but not unrestrainedly – at something Lizzie has said, and his teeth are white and even.

Anna pauses in the kitchen doorway, covertly examining

10

Lizzie, who is trying to describe in French an encounter with a *gendarme* who had stopped them to get a closer look at their grand car. She has always been quite an extrovert and has grown even more confident over the years. During dinner, her French accent has improved but her grammar has deteriorated with the relaxing effect of the wine and the ambience. Anna thinks her friend is looking quite disarmingly beautiful. She is wearing the clothes she has arrived in – a soft yellow wool dress, with one of her elegant silk scarves thrown round her neck – and looks remarkably fresh considering she has been driving for some hours. Although he showed his guests their room, Youenn did not allow them any time to wash or unpack, launching into aperitifs immediately and sitting down to eat soon afterwards. Youenn is always hungry for his evening meal and he dislikes any delay. The couple though, have shown no indication that they thought this discourteous. Lizzie's face is full of good humour and contentment, and her skin glows softly. I must not be envious, thinks Anna. The light from the candle flame dances in her friend's glossy dark hair. Perhaps it is dyed – she might be going grey by now as I am. Lizzie has put on weight but it suits her – she was far too thin for too many years. We're the same age but she looks a lot younger than me. I'm fifty-two but I know I appear older, Anna admits to herself.

Lizzie suddenly turns and looks directly at Anna with a generous smile, as if to say, 'I know you've been looking at me and I don't mind, but I'm just the same old Lizzie who loves you.' What she actually says is: 'Come back to the table, Anna – leave all the clearing up – we'll do it later.'

Anna smiles at her friend, and walks back to the table. Lizzie is asking Youenn if he speaks any English, and when he shakes his head and says, 'No, I cannot at all,' in stilted English, she says she doesn't believe him. Sensing that her guests are not yet ready to go to bed, and wanting some conversation alone with her old friend, Anna suggests that Youenn and Paul might like a game of backgammon – she remembers that she had taught them both to play the game – at different times and in different countries. Paul sets out the board while Youenn gets them each another digestif.

It is a warm May evening, and Anna asks Lizzie if she would like a stroll in the garden. Both women feel the need to talk together out of earshot of their men. 'I'll lend you a shawl,' she says. Anna puts on a old cardigan and while she searches for her new pashmina, Lizzie looks around the large living room which has an open fireplace and rather austere chairs around it. The dining area is hemmed in by a large, heavy provincial dresser and a huge bookcase crammed untidily with books, and the main staircase leads off it. It's so French, she thinks. And Youenn is so Breton. But, Lizzie observes astutely, Anna – in spite of having lived in France for ten years and having learnt to speak French fluently – is so very English.

She sees Anna descending the stairs at the far end of the living room and notes again, with a concern which she does not show on her face, that Anna is too thin – almost gaunt. On their last encounter, Anna was overweight, so by contrast the change is more noticeable. Her friend is a good-looking woman with prominent cheekbones and expressive eyes, but her copious fair hair, Lizzie notes, is sprinkled with grey. Why doesn't she dye it like the rest of us?

Anna hands her the pale apricot woollen shawl. Lizzie throws it round her shoulders and they both pause to watch their men playing backgammon at the table. Youenn is throwing the two dice with impatient panache, and as they hit the side of the board and bounce back, he swears softly, 'Merde,' and leans across to make his move. The Frenchman plays by sliding the pieces sharply and slamming them into place on the appropriate 'point'. Paul throws in a controlled fashion and then leans back to contemplate the board before he makes his move. He then picks up the counters and places them carefully and precisely where he wants them according to what the dice throw up. Having given their men the illusion that they are interested in the contest, the two women then walk outside into the cool darkness. They link arms automatically and unself-consciously without either one of them suggesting it, and walk down to the far end of the garden, where they stand together and look out over the countryside. The fields are grey dark and the trees dotted on it are black dark, whilst above them the stars shine more distinctly in the absence of the moon.

'It's so good to see you,' Anna begins. 'Tell me, how's life treating you?'

'Oh, everything's fine now. I got over my little problem last year and I've been given a clean bill of health. I feel marvellous. And Paul and I have had such a lovely relaxing few days. I don't know when we last had such an uncluttered time together – we both had a chance to completely unwind. It's been such a change from our normal hectic life.'

'Well, you look marvellous,' says Anna sincerely and admiringly. 'And Paul seems fine.'

'Yes, as always, he's in great spirits – he's so fit and active – for a man of sixty-odd. We get on just fine these days – he assures me that his little fling in Japan has never been repeated. I'm not sure I believe him, but I'm old enough to turn a blind eye these days. I try to make life comfortable and fun for Paul – we have more similarities than differences, and I'm sensible enough to steer clear of issues that might cause discord. I don't rock the boat, so our marriage stays afloat. So many of my friends have recently broken up and although they all swear they're better off on their own, I'm not so sure. Most of them are lonely in spite of all their gung-ho girly suppers and outings. I'd rather have a man than not, and at my age I'm getting too old to embark for a second time on life as a divorcee. I've been through all that before and I didn't like it then. Anyway, Paul's devoted to me – I suit him. And he suits me, warts and all.' As usual, Lizzie has gone straight to the heart of things.

She then switches her analytical spotlight onto Youenn, whom she has met tonight for the first time. She realises that Anna has not yet mentioned him, so she says, 'Tell me about Youenn. What an attractive man: tall, dark and moody!' She says this with a raised eyebrow and a slightly teasing intonation.

Anna is not yet ready to talk about Youenn, so ignores the comment and changes the subject. Lizzie knows from this that she needs time to work up to revelations.

'How are Ralph and Katrina? I haven't seen them for years.' These are the children from Lizzie's first marriage. Anna remembers them as teenagers and is unable to imagine how they might be now in their mid-twenties.

Lizzie accepts Anna's usual initial reticence on the subject of her own emotional life, knowing that later on she will open up, and answers, 'Ralph's fine – still in Hong Kong and still in banking. He loves it over there. I don't think he'll ever want to live in the UK again.' There is a hint of disappointment in her voice. 'Katrina got married in San Francisco two years back – you know she's been working over there for five years now? The wedding was a small affair which Paul and I flew over for.' She says this quickly to avoid explanations as to why Anna hadn't been invited. 'Kat doesn't say much about her life with Anton, but I'm a little concerned that things may be a bit rocky. She's such an independent woman – well, almost selfish – that I think she may find marriage cramps her style a bit. I worry about her, but she's chosen to live halfway round the world from me, so it's hard to do the motherly supportive act.'

Anna is silent. Lizzie has never been the maternal supportive type, and they both know it. In the past they have often commented to each other that the one who chose to remain childless would have been the better parent than the one who embarked early on motherhood. Lizzie, who is quick at picking up unsaid things, laughs and says ruefully, 'Well, maybe I've never been too good at that role. Far too busy playing other ones.'

This is a reference to the fact that Lizzie used to be an actress – and at one time had a lot of work in the theatre. 'In fact, I've finally decided that I no longer like treading the boards,' she admits. 'I kept getting the warm-hearted middle-aged or earth-mother roles, and they don't suit me. The commercial work tailed off – probably because my agent doesn't push me enough any more. So I've got a job assisting a casting director. It's just up my street – I've loads of contacts and it seems to be going well. The guy I work for is very laid back – quite amusing, but distinctly unattractive, so Paul isn't jealous. It's hard work but fun and I'm busier than ever.'

'And Paul is still in the mercantile world, I assume,' says Anna. Paul has been involved in many diverse things, including importing olive oil from Italy, running an up-market travel company and trading in precious metals in the Far East. He considers himself a cultured man who likes music, art and drama, whilst rarely finding the time to attend concerts, go to exhibitions or see plays. Lizzie has reformed him somewhat, now that she has at last learnt to be an appreciative theatre-goer with no wish to perform herself any more. Paul works industriously and successfully; his income allows them to indulge in acquiring art, and they both enjoy visiting galleries together and buying contemporary paintings if the mood takes them and their tastes coincide.

'Yes, of course. It's a very competitive world, but he's always had a flair for business. He still travels a lot and often I go with him. He's doing well and likes the buzz – and the profit – that he gets from a good deal. He's also prepared to take risks. Recently he's become an angel – you know, someone who backs theatrical productions financially. A friend of ours is a producer, and he's cast his net over Paul.'

'He certainly looks very angelic,' laughs Anna, thinking what an apt description it is, with his round face and deceptively innocent smile. 'Does he polish his halo in the mirror?'

Lizzie giggles – they can laugh about Paul's vanity. Again she realises that all the conversation has been about her side of things, and being genuinely curious to know, in her direct way she asks Anna again: 'Are you and Youenn happy?'

Anna is silent for a moment, which tells Lizzie more than any words, and then says, 'I'm not sure what happiness is any more. I used to aspire to it. When I was young it was always just out of range whilst appearing to be there for the taking if I could only grasp it. But as the years pass, it seems less possible to ever reach it. That's what I think. I can't speak for Youenn. Ask me an easier question.'

'How did you meet him?'

'We met in Paris, when I was living there. He rarely goes to the capital – he doesn't like crowds and noise. He was on a visit to see his son – he's been married before and has three children. The other two are much younger, and when I first came here, they used to live with him though now they've moved on.'

The women have wandered over to stand beneath a walnut tree, and Anna's face is in full shadow – though their eyes have become accustomed to the dark.

'This is rather a change isn't it?' Lizzie can't resist observing. 'From the bright lights of Paris to the quiet of rural Brittany.' She cannot understand why anyone would want to bury themselves in the middle of nowhere in preference to Paris, that beautiful, exciting, sophisticated city. She is thinking of the Champs-Elysées, the Rue de Rivoli, the Opéra district.

Anna, however, is recalling her time in the Marais near the Place des Vosges. The appeal of her tiny apartment in one of the old passages was considerable, but the lure of a decisive man had been stronger. 'I did love Paris – and in particular the old quarter where I lived and worked. But just at that time I needed a change. My teaching job was proving duller than I had expected – English as a foreign language has its limitations. I had foolishly become involved with one of my students, an attractive young man – amusing and sexy, but much too young, raw and insecure.'

'Are we talking about Malo here?' says Lizzie, who well remembers that week in Paris some seven years before, when she was working on a commercial and when she met up with Anna and her young lover Malo. 'Your toy boy, your impulsive impatient student lover.' There is no note of disapproval in Lizzie's voice – quite the opposite, in fact – she had admired Anna's raven-haired Apollo.

Anna laughs and does not contradict the description or deny the relationship. 'Of course – I remember now, you met him when you were filming that advertisement for some perfume, and staying at the Stendhal Hotel. Yes, Malo – that over-emotional madcap – only twenty-two – he was half my age. He was searching for an older woman to have an experience

17

with, and I must have been searching for my lost youth.' She laughs with some self-reproach and a hint of regret. 'He was amusing, though very engrossed in himself – but he was so romantic – he used to buy me flowers – tiny violets one day and tall sunflowers the next. Up and down. Unreliable, uncontrollable, passionate, wonderful. It could never have lasted. And it didn't. Along came Youenn.'

Anna remembers the day she first met Youenn. She had arranged to meet Malo at the Café de l'Industrie for a drink after her evening lessons had finished. The sun had just reappeared after a short but heavy rain shower. She had lost her umbrella – the third one which the Métro had claimed as a result of her inattentiveness to personal possessions – and so she arrived with her wet face shining in the watery sunlight, her hair in lank tendrils dripping down the front of her soaking linen jacket, and with waterlogged shoes. Malo was there – at a small table, with an older man who looked vaguely familiar. She was shivering. Her lover had jumped up waving his arms at her bedraggled appearance and, without introducing his companion, had started to dab ineffectually at her hair with his scarf. The older man had risen to his feet, silently picked up his long black overcoat and put it proprietorially round her shoulders. Then Malo had made the introductions.

Anna sighs and turns to Lizzie, who is standing under the tree and moving her arms to pull the shawl closer round her. 'Are you cold? We can go in if you like.'

'No, no, I can't wait to hear more.' Lizzie recalls meeting Malo and Anna at the Musée de Cluny on the left bank, and her envy at her friend's freedom to live in Paris, take young lovers and live the bohemian life. In the dark, unseen by Anna, she winces with a twinge of guilt. She remembers the old mansion where Malo led them round a series of exquisite tapestries entitled 'The Lady and the Unicorn', representing the five senses, and that he had held Anna's hand all the while.

Then Anna puts her hand on Lizzie's arm and says, 'What you don't realise, Lizzie, is that Youenn is Malo's father.'

Lizzie is astounded – and almost annoyed. She had no idea. She has always liked intrigue and secrets, but prefers to be privy to the inside information. She reflects that she does not like revelations which she feels she has had a right to know beforehand and which come too late to savour. Anna and Youenn have been together now for some years, and though Lizzie has always been curious about him, Anna has failed to invite her and Paul over to meet him before now. The two women are not as close as they once were; their homes and their minds are further apart. Though Anna has, over the years, written to and kept in touch with Lizzie, she has never before mentioned the connection between her two French lovers.

'I had no idea,' says Lizzie slowly. 'You kept that quiet.' A thought strikes her. 'I suppose this means I shall have to reciprocate and reveal one of my secrets this evening.'

Anna says lightly, 'Yes, indeed you will.' She knows what the other is talking about – their lifelong pact that they should be open with each other and occasionally each reveal a secret or confess a misdemeanour. At school they had made three 'sacred' promises – to both share their important possessions freely, to always tell their secrets to each other and to no one else. If they had to part for a time, they were never to look back but had to remember the other until they met up again. There were to be no regrets and no reproaches. These childish pledges had been carried over into adulthood and had become a light-hearted code of behaviour with them. They usually affected to laugh at the pact, and joked about it between themselves, but in reality both adhered unswervingly to their self-imposed rules.

Expanding on her disclosure, Anna then tells Lizzie the story of how Youenn stole her from his own son. 'He was a man – not a boy – and his confidence and experience were that much greater. Though less worldly than Malo, Youenn was more intelligent and quietly compelling.' Physically taller and emanating a sense of control and potency, the older man was aware of his attractiveness and had ruthlessly deposed his son within a few short and exciting weeks. Finding him more of a challenge intellectually and his overt sexuality tantalisingly difficult to ignore, Anna transferred her love and commitment to him.

It was only later, Anna explains to Lizzie, that she realised that the father and son were fiercely competitive. When he was eighteen, the young man had broken away from home, left Brittany and gone to Paris, where he worked in a bookshop by day and studied English in the evenings. Youenn had been jealous of his youth and freedom, and it was inevitable that the father would desire what his son had and take it, given the chance. Malo was well aware of these aspects of his father's character and his rapacious attitude to anything his son possessed.

But the conquest had turned sour for the older man. Anna sums all this up by saying to Lizzie, 'When Youenn carried me off to Brittany as his prize, Malo would not forgive either of us and, when we married, he cut himself off from us and refused contact. Youenn had won a wife but lost a son.' Anna pauses at this point, initially to emphasise her rather neat turn of phrase, and then, looking at Lizzie's dark, attentive head, because she cannot bring herself to say the truth – that her husband is a lonely, passionate man who, now that he has got what he wanted, exerts pressure and control to keep it. She is not ready to tell Lizzie that she feels stifled by his possessiveness, though she is aware that the other will soon realise this. In a slightly altered tone, Anna continues, 'But he loves me – or he says he does. I've made the right choice, I'm sure. Malo's affection for me was just a passing youthful adoration – Youenn needs and loves me more – he's an intense and demanding man.'

'Out of the frying pan into the fire,' Lizzie remarks dryly.

'For a while it was a good blaze.' But Anna will not say why the flames have died down. 'Youenn is a wonderful lover.' Noticing the present tense, Lizzie's twinge of envy is momentary. In her direct way of encapsulating a problem and pigeonholing a personality, she deduces that Youenn is probably a jealous and selfish control freak. She is astute enough to realise that Anna probably concurs with this view and both of them are wise enough not to voice it.

'Why did you *marry* Youenn? Why break away from your usual pattern of having men only as lovers?' She is curious.

'Because, Lizzie, to start with, this is a conventional rural corner of France, and Youenn is not the type to cross the line by living with a woman who isn't his wife. And because it was a novelty for me, and agreeing to marriage was a way of demonstrating my commitment to him. As a widower and a solitary man, he needed that from me.' Anna touches Lizzie's arm, and asks in her turn, 'Why did *you* agree to marry Paul?'

'He asked me and wanted me to. It commits me to him, which is something I probably need.'

They look up and, from across the darkened garden, watch their two men illuminated in the room beyond the window. Paul is leaning back in his chair with a glass in his hand, and Youenn is bent over the board, probably trying to decide which of two possible moves to make. Anna hopes Youenn is winning

21

– he does not like to lose. And she knows that Paul will not mind either way; he wins against competition when it is important, but is content to gracefully concede on trivial matters.

'It's been a while since we last met,' Lizzie muses. 'When was it? Perhaps eighteen months ago when you came to England to see that literary agent, and you stayed with us.'

'Not for long, remember? You were off to eastern Europe with Paul about some business deal he had. How did that trip go?'

'Oh, fine,' says Lizzie, who cannot really recall it – there have been so many. 'I'm more interested in how your book is going, though.'

Her interest is genuine and Anna responds, 'I finished it last winter, and then revised it. The agent I met on that trip has taken me on, and she's found someone to publish it.'

'My dear!' exclaims Lizzie with real enthusiasm. 'That's wonderful! Wasn't it on Shakespeare or something?' Anna has been working on this project for some years. Her friends have for a long time regarded the epic work of criticism as a white elephant – doomed to extinction. Most of them have learnt not to ask about it any more, to avoid causing Anna embarrassment.

'Yes. It's about destiny and choice in Shakespeare's tragedies.' Anna does not expand. She has taken too long to write her book, and has learnt brevity when discussing it. She sensibly keeps quiet on all matters about which she thinks others do not really want to hear.

But Lizzie is genuine in her delight that her closest friend has at last achieved publication. 'Well done, dearest. You're far cleverer than me – far more academic. It always amazes me that anyone can find anything new to say about Shakespeare, but he's such a genius and his characters so complex that I expect there will always be something different to write about. So, when will your book come out?'

'Actually . . .' says Anna oddly hesitant, 'it's being published next week. In fact, I'm off to England tomorrow to meet my agent and the publishers and to have an interview with some magazine before publication day.'

'Tomorrow!' Lizzie is surprised. In contrast to herself and Paul, who often fly off on quick business trips or luxury mini holidays snatched in between work schedules, Anna has always been vague and disorganised about travel. 'That explains why you're leaving early. You could drive back with us – though I should warn you that we're going to take it slowly.'

'Thanks, but I've got to be in London by midday tomorrow, so I'm flying over.' She doesn't mention that she is actually going in an executive jet belonging to a company whose managing director is known to her agent. The plane has been chartered by some businessmen who are going to Nantes for a three-day conference, and Anna's agent has arranged for her to travel to England in it on its return voyage to Farnborough, when it would otherwise have been empty. She has booked a limousine to drive her from there to London. Despite Anna feeling the need to keep all this to herself, Lizzie, who has spent her life jetting around the world, wouldn't have thought her method of travel anything remarkable.

'Are you going to have a book launch?' asks Lizzie, who loves first nights and publicity events.

'Oh no, I think not,' says Anna hastily. She has always been indifferent to formal gatherings. 'It's an academic book and, I would imagine, of minority interest.'

'Is Youenn coming with you?' Lizzie already knows the answer but needs to make a point by forcing Anna to admit to the fact of her husband's selfishness.

23

'No, he's not. And I wouldn't want him to.'

They are still looking back at the house, and they see Paul rise to his feet and come to the window. At first he cannot see them because he is in the light and they are in the deep shade of the tree. He cups his hands round his eyes to shut out the lamplight and focus on the garden. To allay his uneasiness at not being able to see them, Lizzie emerges from under the overhanging branches and stands in the starlight. Paul gives her a beckoning wave and in response the two women start to walk slowly towards the house. Anna can see that Youenn is still sitting unconcernedly at the table with the bottle of calvados in front of him – he feels no need to search her out, for he knows that she will return to the house in due course. She always does.

Anna and Lizzie pause as they walk up the path to the terrace. Lizzie says, 'I'm still amazed that you never told me before about Malo being Youenn's son. It's bizarre.' She wonders what happened to the beautiful young man. She stops, makes a decision and then, turning to Anna, says, 'Well, it's my turn to reveal a secret now. Remember the rules – no remorse on my side and no reproaches on yours?'

Anna nods and thinks she knows what is coming.

'Well – I had a fling with Malo myself – we met once in Paris, and on another occasion in Bruges . . . it was a brief affair. Rather like you, I just couldn't resist him.' Anna remains silent so Lizzie blunders on. 'So that's my confession, my dear. Rather a lapse from my usual good behaviour. I should have told you that I had invoked our Sharing Pact but there never seemed to be a good moment. But it was over six years ago and you were already with Youenn. I don't regret it and, as you know, we don't do guilt.' She looks into Anna's face, trying to gauge her reaction.

Anna says, 'That's right. No guilt and no regrets.' She stops speaking, remembering a misunderstanding she had once had with Malo. She had been trying to explain to him about Lizzie and the close and serious nature of their long relationship. The moody young man had become jealous and muttered something about latent lesbians and why didn't she and Lizzie live together if they were so bloody intimate? Anna had coolly replied that she and Lizzie as adults had never shared a home or a bed. Physical desire for each other was absent. Being together all the time would be claustrophobic, and in any case they would always be inseparable even when they were apart. In a moment of irritation at his crass immaturity, she had said, 'What we do share is our minds and our men.' That must have been when she had put the germ of the idea in his head.

They resume their walk back to the house. Paul is standing just outside the garden door, and as they approach him, Anna says quietly to Lizzie, 'I knew about you and Malo. He boasted about it to me – it was after I'd run off with his father and he was trying to make me feel jealous. It really doesn't matter now.' She wants to let her friend off the hook. She was angry at the time, but her short-lived storm of jealousy has long since dissipated, and her loving friendship with Lizzie has been reasserted. She simply doesn't mind about it any more. She laughs to convey this message to her friend, and says cheerfully to Paul, 'We've been having a good natter and revealing some old secrets.'

Misunderstanding these words, Paul gives Anna an odd look, and while Lizzie is entering the house ahead of her, she frowns and gives him a minute shake of her head.

Inside the living room, Youenn puts his arm possessively round his wife's shoulders. He tells Paul that Anna needs to go to bed because tomorrow she is to have a very long and active day. He reveals the means by which Anna is to go to England to have her meeting with her publishers. He is more proud of her racy mode of travel than he is of his wife's achievement in finally getting her book published and his competitive instinct compels him to mention it, since he regards golden Bentleys and executive jets as pretty much on a par.

Paul dutifully whistles and turns to Anna, politely speaking in French to make sure that Youenn can understand. 'So, you'll be travelling in style. What else is on the agenda tomorrow?'

Anna replies in English because Youenn already knows as much as she wants him to know. 'I rarely go to England these days, as you are aware, so when I do I tend to cram in as many things as possible. I've a midday meeting with the publishers and a lunch with my agent and then an interview with a literary magazine in the afternoon. Then I plan to get a train down to the south coast to catch the ferry across to the Isle of Wight where my younger brother lives. It's his fiftieth birthday tomorrow and he's taking over some swanky restaurant on the island for the celebrations.'

'How is Gavin? I haven't seen him for years.' Lizzie's tone is breezy but her eyes soften a little as she recalls her last encounter with Anna's brother, many years before.

'He's very well – he enjoys being an islander,' Anna responds. 'It suits him. I think he's invited quite a few people to his party, so it should be fun. I'll be staying the night, and the next day I'll come home. On the ferry and train.'

'Wow, Anna,' says Paul, 'a day on the fast track!'

Anna looks at him with a smile. 'Well, you and Lizzie wouldn't find that unusual – you've spent most of your lives in the fast lane. But for little ole me, living a quiet life in rural Brittany, it's a bit more unusual. I'll probably be exhausted by the time I get to the party.'

Hearing the note of self-deprecation in her voice, Lizzie chimes in with, 'How exciting for you, Anna! It'll do you good. It shouldn't be too tiring – no driving to do – you'll be fine. You won't have time to think, but if you do, spare a thought for us spending hours bobbing across the Channel.'

'Role reversal,' says Paul, obliquely, 'is very exhilarating.'

Youenn, who has understood little of this exchange, has removed his arm from Anna's shoulder and has placed his hand on her elbow. He now exerts a bit of pressure on her arm, saying formally to his guests, 'It has been an agreeable evening, and now we shall say goodnight. My wife has to get up very early.'

He looks down at Anna and conspicuously kisses the top of her ear. He is almost flaunting his affection and desire. Anna stands passively beside him. Watching them, Lizzie feels a pang for her friend. She wonders if this man is not just a little jealous of the long conversation which she and his wife have shared outside and of the love and close relationship between them which goes back many years before he entered Anna's life. He seems to want to control situations and to assert his authority over his wife. She wonders why Anna is so submissive. It is not like her.

Paul says goodnight, thanking his host for a very pleasant evening, but Youenn is not listening – he is thinking about his wife. He is not particularly happy about his woman going away for two days, but he is confident in his magnetism and in her obedience; he knows that she will return. She loves him, he is sure. She needs him.

As Anna smilingly says goodnight, her heart sinks. She knows what the pressure on the arm means. She has a dull ache in her stomach. As she climbs the stairs ahead of Youenn, she knows what he is thinking. He has told her many times that she is frail and insecure – that she needs him to love her and look after her. What her husband fails to realise is the fact that it is her perception of his absolute need of her that keeps her with him. She loves him less than she once did. It is not insecurity but guilt that makes her stay. For her he has sacrificed his relationship with his son, so she cannot now run off causing him to lose his wife as well. This would compound her crime. He wants her with him – he may even love her. He is aware of his power to attract, but not of his need to dominate those around him. To desert him, as she once contemplated doing but then decided against, would destroy him.

The two couples retire to their separate rooms. Lizzie, who has been stimulated by memories of Malo and by Youenn's sexual overtures to Anna, entices Paul to make love to her, and afterwards they fall asleep contentedly. Anna is dismayed when it becomes apparent that Youenn wants sex, but is compliant because it is less complicated and quicker to give in than to protest. Afterwards, Youenn falls into a heavy sleep, and Anna lies awake thinking of that time in Paris, and of Malo and Lizzie. The pain in her stomach has subsided, but she is exhausted. During the day she has been occupied with making the preparations for their guests and the dinner, with packing for her trip to England, and with dealing with Youenn's moody antipathy towards both of these things. There has been the emotional upheaval of being with Lizzie again, and of sharing sympathy and revelations – this is more than she usually has to cope with in one day. For the past few days, she has been excited at the prospect of Lizzie and Paul's visit, and has also been feeling unwell and hiding both these things from Youenn. Concealment is tiring. She hears the church clock strike one o'clock. She eventually sleeps.

# Chapter Two

In May the village morning begins before dawn. Anna wakes, jolted from a restless light sleep by the crash of the municipal truck as it collects garbage from outside the shops and houses on the main street well before it is light. She feels both apprehensive and excited about her day of travel and her various meetings in London. This is interwoven with pleasure at the prospect of temporary freedom and an absence of guilt. She thinks Youenn unreasonable and oppressive with his lack of enthusiasm about her book and her visit to England. She feels she deserves a couple of days away from him, if not longer. She lies in bed, staring up into the darkness, feeling conscious of Youenn heavily asleep beside her, though she cannot yet see him. Outside, all is still and silent, though the house martins will soon commence their activity.

After an hour, as the light comes up, she quietly gets out of bed and goes to the window which looks out over the main street. The villagers are slow to wake and resume their regular business of the day, except for Rouxel's *boulangerie* in the small square, where activity starts very early, and from which baking smells emanate enticingly. After a while she sees Bruno, a neighbour who sets off for work earlier than most, wobbling down the street on his bike. As he passes their house, he catches sight of the large English car parked in the forecourt of their house and, craning to see more, swerves and bumps into a parked car. He falls off with a yelp, but being probably still a bit drunk from the night before at the Café du Centre, he picks himself up and, shaking his head to clear his brain, sets off again down the road.

Watching him go, Anna is reminded of another, more significant, collision many years before, when she and Lizzie were schoolgirls. It marked the end of an idyllic and untroubled phase in their young lives, during which they had become close friends and shared so much.

The chain of events that had ended in that horrible day of the biking accident began three years earlier, when they were both about twelve. The girls had met for the first time when Anna started at her new school, her family having moved into the area during the summer. On that first day of term, sick with apprehension, the new girl sidled into her classroom and, pretending to be unconcerned, looked around at the others. Their curious faces examined hers, cursorily evaluated her and promptly dismissed her. She was on her own.

Then a wonderful thing happened. A tall girl with dark hair in a long plait ran up to her and said, 'I know who you are – you've moved in just down the road from me!' Anna was embarrassed because she felt certain she had never met her before. The girl sat jauntily on one of the desks and chatted away, leaning towards Anna as she did so. 'I'm Lizzie. I live in India, but my parents are on leave and we have just rented a house here for three months. I stay with guardians in the village when they go back to Delhi. I noticed you outside your house the other day. My mother met yours in the village shop and they realised that you were to going be at the same school as me, so she told me to look out for you.' Lizzie then smiled at the new girl and Anna felt less nervous and very grateful.

Lizzie was open and friendly and introduced the newcomer to her best friends – Dinah, who was West Indian, and Kerry, who lived on a farm – and Anna became one of their group, although initially she felt a little on the periphery. But she soon acquired some of the glamour and confidence that radiated from the others and she rapidly became part of the inner circle, joining in with Lizzie and Dinah, who enjoyed flouting the school rules, though Anna always seemed to get caught whilst the others got away. Quite unjustly she was branded as the naughty one by the teachers. Later on she was blamed for being a bad influence on Lizzie, when it was actually the other way round. Anna did not mind this though – she was glad to take the blame for the girl who had befriended her and allowed her to join in.

Anna lived much closer to Lizzie than Dinah or Kerry, so they spent a lot of time together after school and at weekends. Their mothers became friends, so that when Lizzie's parents were due to return to India, Anna's parents offered to become Lizzie's new guardians, which would mean that she would live with them during the term time, and fly out to join her own parents in the holidays. Both girls were delighted with this plan, especially Lizzie, who had often complained to Anna about her previous guardians, who were stuffy. 'They're too boring for words and there are too many restrictions,' she told Anna. The couple were rather elderly and had found the young teenager somewhat too boisterous in their retirement, so they were pleased to be divested of their charge. After her parents went back to India, therefore, Lizzie moved into Anna's family home, and into her friend's heart.

Inevitably this brought change into the household, as Lizzie's energetic personality impacted on the family in a number of ways. Anna, who had always been quite reticent and thoughtful, became more animated and entered a more active and outgoing phase; benefiting from having a best friend with whom she could share everything. This was considered an improvement by her parents, who had been mildly concerned that their clever Anna had her head in books too often and was less sociable than they would have wished. Her younger brother, Gavin, had been the livelier and more demanding of the two children, but Lizzie's arrival shifted the dynamics of the family so that he became less selfish and more subdued, while his sister grew in self-confidence.

There was no doubt the new arrangement worked well. Anna's mother felt sorry for Lizzie, who had spent most of her childhood separated from her parents, and she overcompensated by giving her new charge a lot of her attention and time, with the result that the girl developed a strong affection for her substitute mother and a latent grudge against her real one, who was always distant in both place and manner. Lizzie also achieved an easy-going relationship with Anna's father, and was able to talk to him freely and even tease him – something she had never been able to do with her own father, who was a rigidly serious and reserved man.

Anna also began to appreciate her mother and father more when she realised, after long talks with her new friend at night in their shared bedroom, that Lizzie had been largely ignored by her own parents, spending most of her time in India at their home in the company of an ayah who looked after her, fed her and played with her. As an only child she had no other person on whom to bestow her affection, and so she had become very fond of her ayah. She was therefore devastated when she

32

returned from school in England on one occasion to find that the woman had been dismissed and that she would never see her again. Anna considered this to be an act of such wanton cruelty that she was outraged and resentful on behalf of her friend in a way that Lizzie did not seem to be.

During the holidays, Anna missed her friend and longed for the start of term, which would bring her back. Lizzie used to return from holidays in India laden with new clothes and exotic trinkets, many of which she unselfishly gave to her new 'sister'. These expensive gifts were, Anna was convinced, a way of Lizzie's selfish parents trying to buy the gratitude and love of their daughter in a way that cost them money but no time. She felt warmly happy that her own parents loved Lizzie and gave her a secure home – at least during the term time – but she did not feel threatened that this meant their affection for their own daughter was diminished in any way. She had long since worked out that parents could love any number of children equally and with impartiality.

This was something, however, that her brother had yet to learn. Gavin, less astute and more vulnerable than his older sister, was quite deeply affected by the change that had come about. Before the advent of Lizzie, his sister had played games with him and did not mind taking a subsidiary role if he wanted to control things. She often used to dispense upon him all the worldly wisdom she had gained from her vast two and a half year advantage over him. Now she had defected and Gavin felt isolated, though he managed to preserve an air of insouciance so that his parents were not aware of his sadness. Instead of being one of a pair, he now felt the outsider in an unbalanced trio. Although he knew that his sister was genuinely fond of him, whereas before he had cheerfully tolerated her occasional teasing, now he had to endure two giggling girls taunting him. At first he withdrew and quietly seethed with resentment of the intruder. But as Anna and Lizzie's bond of friendship became even stronger, he felt abandoned and jealous, though he did not altogether give up trying to fit in, and there were times when he wanted badly to please them and win their attention.

For the first year he attempted to join in, but entry into any of their games was always on their terms, and he found this humiliating. The next year, he opted out and spent much time on his own playing with construction kits and designing super cars. His parents were partially aware of what was going on and gave him support and encouragement to become involved in activities separate from those of the girls. He was growing up, they thought, and needed to be less dependent on his sibling.

In the home, Gavin achieved pleasurable revenge by barging into the girls' room and interrupting their endless conversations or sabotaging their private games. He succeeded in irritating them and bore their protests with stoic satisfaction. As far as he was concerned, any reaction, however negative, was better than no reaction at all. But it was worse when they were given the bicycles because then they were able to escape from him totally. Though it seemed to him like a disaster at the time, this turned out ultimately to be beneficial for Gavin because it forced him to try harder to make friends with some boys at his school and get involved with activities and games outside his family.

Anna and Gavin's parents had decided that, because their house was close to a main road and their financial situation was modest, the children should not have bicycles until they were a bit older. But when Lizzie had been with them for a couple of years, they received a communication from her father saying that, in addition to remitting the regular sum for the maintenance of his daughter, he would fund the purchase of a bike for her whilst she was in England. They therefore decided to buy both girls bicycles on Anna's fifteenth birthday. Anna recalls she felt no resentment that Lizzie had been given a present of that magnitude without the occasion of a birthday to justify the gift. Her parents insisted that the two girls learn the highway code and made them promise to ride safely before they let them go out on their own.

Suddenly the garden and the house were too cramped and the girls discovered the freedom of the small town and the surrounding countryside. They biked together for hours and occasionally Dinah joined them. They were often late for meals and occasionally arrived back with arms and knees grazed and bruised from falling off, which they made considerable efforts to conceal. It was speed that intoxicated them, and they raced along, calling to each other out of pure exhilaration. It was too tedious to obey strict rules that they should always wheel their bikes across main roads, and heedless of safety, they flew along like a couple of young birds soaring beyond the limits of their territory.

Lizzie and Anna treated each other like sisters, and often referred to each other as such. They wanted to experience everything together. Once when Anna had to stay behind at school for an hour's detention after lessons were over and had been told to clean the gym as punishment for some misdemeanour, Lizzie elected to stay behind too to keep her company. When Lizzie twisted her ankle and was unable to take part in the rowdy fun at break, Anna sat quietly with her although it went against her boisterous inclination. They made a promise to each other that they would always try to share everything. Realising the impracticality of dividing all their material possessions, they further defined this sharing pact as including intangibles such as success and failure, secrets and problems, as well as more practical things such as friends, books, clothes and make-up. They would help each other and participate together in what life had to offer them.

But like sisters there was also rivalry between them. Both girls were good swimmers; both were fast at freestyle. When they competed for the single place on the school swimming team, and Lizzie managed to get into the team, Anna felt upset at being passed over but was also proud of her friend's achievement. When Lizzie was disappointed with her exam results, Anna felt ashamed that she herself had done so well, and pretended that her success was just luck. The other girls at the school respected Anna for her undeserved reputation for wayward rebellion against authority and also for her quick repartee, but although she made friends, she was not really popular. Lizzie, on the other hand, had always been a favourite with both teachers and pupils, winning their trust and affection with her easy-going charm, kindness and generosity. Without intending to, she eclipsed her best friend.

The other problem between them was that although Anna was austerely attractive in a classic way, Lizzie's prettiness developed into a soft, vulnerable beauty that attracted boys. There was no need to flirt for Lizzie turned heads in her direction, and boys competed for her time and her approbation. It was hard for Anna not to feel envious. Though they paid little attention to her, she too was vaguely interested in boys. Under the terms of her pact with Lizzie, she felt she should not feel resentment and, though it was a struggle, she was pleased that she managed not to let her envy weaken her admiration and affection for the other girl. She decided that she would never let rivalry for boys come between them.

By the time Lizzie and Anna were nearly sixteen, their discovery of boys as objects of attraction was beginning to make inroads into their passion for biking. There was much discussion by girls at school of the relative merits of some of the boys in their class, and much time was spent – or wasted, as Anna thought – on exploratory flirtations, minor triumphs and rebuttals. However, the two friends still preferred each other's company to anyone else's, and often still rode off together on their bikes after school or at weekends.

One warm Saturday afternoon in spring, the girls had taken a picnic and spent the middle of the day sprawled on long grass in a field a few miles from their home. Their bikes lay thrown on the ground a little way away beside a path which led through some young birch trees back to the road. Anna lazily flicked the flies off the remains of their food and Lizzie twisted tendrils of her long dark hair round her fingers. In silent companionship, they listened to the noise of a distant motor and the sounds of birds in the surrounding bushes and trees. They had been discussing a number of important things: whether Anna really liked a boy called Tom who had asked her to go to a film with him, and whether Lizzie would let her boyfriend go 'any further' with her. They had also debated the pros and cons of changing their hair colour because Lizzie was bored with being a brunette and wanted to go blonde, and Anna wanted to see if henna would make her dusty fair hair more interesting. They were both working for exams that summer and were also faced with what choices they wanted to make for their A levels, so that needed talking over too. But these cares and concerns did not weigh too heavily upon them, and after a while they decided to ride on. Soon they were pedalling fast and forgetting caution in the exhilarating feeling of fresh wind rushing past.

An elderly man was mowing his lawn when he heard the excited cries made by the two girls on their way along the road towards his house. He watched them with a feeling of yearning as they hurtled past, freewheeling downhill. At the bottom of the incline was a crossroads. They were on the minor road, and they knew the other road was not a busy one either, so they kept going fast, ringing their bells with delight. The man saw the dark-haired girl on the red bike, who was in the lead, turn round to call something to her friend on the green bike. He then became aware of the sound of a vehicle approaching at speed, and he experienced a moment of frozen horror.

At the same instant Anna glimpsed a blur of white on the other road and yelled, 'Lizzie, look out!' Lizzie was almost at the crossroads, but on hearing Anna's cry, wrenched her handlebars round so that she skidded across her friend's path. Anna, who was already braking hard, could not stop her bike in time and with a shriek collided with the other girl. Their bikes sprawled entangled on the gritty tarmac. A large white van shot past a yard in front of them and disappeared, oblivious, into the distance.

Anna was thrown off her seat into the ditch, and Lizzie lay on the road beside her twisted bike. For a couple of suspended seconds the only sound was the retreating vehicle. Anna savoured the cool green around her, until she registered that she was being stung by nettles and, with a cry, scrambled out. Still on her knees on the verge of the road, she looked across at the closest friend she had ever had. Lizzie was lying on her stomach, quite still. For an agonising moment Anna believed the girl was dead. Trembling with shock and apprehension and unable to stand up, she started crawling towards the inert figure.

Lizzie, after a few moments of total blackness, had come to the stunned realisation that she had not hit the van and was alive, alive, alive. She moved her head and rolled over onto her side, groaning as a sharp pain shot through her left arm. She had cut her hand and blood was welling up through broken skin mottled with grit. Anna reached her and, suffused with gratitude that Lizzie was alive, cradled her friend's head in her arms. Then both girls started wailing with pain and shock lying in the road amid the broken spokes and twisted red and green wheels of their bikes.

The man ran over to help them while his wife telephoned for an ambulance. At the hospital it was discovered that neither girl had major injuries, although Lizzie had broken her arm, and had also cut her hand badly, probably from a sharp piece of metal from one of the bikes. Her thigh was very badly lacerated and it was some weeks before she could walk without pain. Anna was in shock, but only bruised by her fall and itching from the nettles that had attacked her in the ditch.

Lizzie's broken arm was set and encased in the usual plaster cast, which the girls later spent many hours decorating and getting their friends to sign. The cut on her left hand eventually healed to produce an interesting Y-shaped scar which was slightly protrusive on her skin. She took to rubbing it to see if she could reduce the puckered surface, and though this had little effect, stroking the small scar became a habit, and was something she did almost unconsciously in moments of stress or absent-mindedness.

At first Lizzie and Anna were stunned by the awful realisation that they might have been killed. They were quiet and subdued for a few days afterwards, and those around them took that to mean that the girls were so ashamed of their carelessness and so frightened from the experience that they did not want to talk about it. Gavin was at first shocked by what had happened, and then felt secretly pleased that the proud and superior pair had taken a fall. Anna's parents were both appalled by the incident and angry with the girls. Everyone was aware that the accident could have been fatal if the van had hit them. Lizzie's parents had to be informed and they too were upset and blamed the other couple for not taking enough care of their daughter. The bikes were badly damaged and no one felt any inclination to get them repaired.

However, in the privacy of their shared bedroom, the girls had discussed the accident in minute detail and had very different views about what had happened. Lizzie claimed that she had never heard Anna's warning cry but had seen the van approaching at a fast speed, and had turned her bike across her friend's to save them both.

'I saw something coming on the road ahead and realised we were going too fast to stop in time, so I decided a minor collision between the two of us would be preferable to a bigger one with the van, which might have been fatal,' she explained. 'By thinking so quickly I managed to stop us both zooming into the path of the van.'

'That's rubbish,' protested Anna. 'You weren't looking, and it was my shout that alerted you to the danger. You took evasive action and turned sharply and hit me – I was already braking and wouldn't have hit the van in any case. So it was *me* who really saved *you*.' She very much wanted to feel that it was she who had prevented a tragedy.

She also needed to talk about those awful few seconds when she thought Lizzie was dead. 'I felt this huge sense of panic and loss. It was so paralysingly awful that my legs felt like jelly and I could only crawl towards you. It was like a nightmare. I felt so guilty that I was alive and breathing while you were so still and silent. Then you moved your head and I felt a hot wave of hope wash over me, and – well, it was wonderful.'

'I don't remember the impact at all,' Lizzie told Anna. 'I just remember opening my eyes and seeing the light filter round the black surface where my face was – I suppose that was the tarmac. I felt puzzled and sort of flattened but needed to move so I rolled over on my side and that's when my arm went flop and it began to hurt like bloody hell,' she went on dramatically. 'Then you came and held my head, which was sweet, and I looked up at you and the blue sky, and I was glad, really glad, to be alive.'

In a strange way, the accident heralded a change in their young lives. It brought their phase of selfish recklessness to an end, its serious implications sobering them up. It also sharpened Anna's fear of speed and Lizzie's dread of dying. In later life, although Anna confronted her demon and became a risk taker, tempting fate by driving fast and becoming a good hard skier, Lizzie's natural cautiousness increased and she never relished travelling at speed, preferring to keep within the limits of her own fear.

In one sense the incident had brought the two girls closer together, yet in another more physical sense it caused their first separation. Lizzie's parents reacted badly to it, although they had not rushed home immediately after hearing the news – it was not convenient to do so, and anyway they had been reassured that Lizzie was all right and her injuries were healing. However, by the time they did come home on short leave at the end of the summer term, they had developed a grievance against the family with whom they had entrusted their only child. The blame lay with Anna's parents, and so Lizzie was to be taken from them.

A number of other things contributed to Lizzie's removal from the family she had grown to love, and this cruel blow was another cause of her subsequent estrangement from her parents. First, it was felt that the near-fatal accident with the bikes showed irresponsibility on the part of the guardians. Second, Lizzie was becoming more resentful and moody when she visited her home in India, and no longer bore that uncritical love for her mother and father which they had once enjoyed but never appreciated. Then one of the teachers at the school informed them that Anna was a bad influence on their talented daughter whose behaviour, in his opinion, had deteriorated considerably since the two girls' close friendship had developed. But probably the most potent reason for their decision to remove Lizzie from her term-time home was that they were jealous of the affection their girl so obviously had for her friend's parents.

Naturally, both girls were distraught at being parted. They would miss their constant companionship, their complete openness with each other, their sharing of troubles, and their mutual emotional support. Lizzie made extravagant promises that nothing and no one would ever be able to destroy their friendship and Anna devised practical ways in which they would be able to keep in touch and occasionally meet up. Anna's parents suffered too – they were very fond of Lizzie and felt that they had been judged too harshly, and that Lizzie's feelings and wishes had not been taken into account. But they had to accept her parents' decision and could do nothing to allay the two friends' resulting distress.

Lizzie's parents, in their cushioned and removed world in India, had decided to send their daughter to a new school for her sixth-form years, where she would board. She would return to them as usual during the holidays, so there would be little opportunity for her to maintain a relationship with the family who had been her only source of love and friendship for over three years. The link would thus be broken, and their daughter would be removed from the companionship of someone who clearly had an undesirable influence on her. They had made this decision without consulting their daughter.

Lizzie, returning to India with her father and mother for the remainder of the summer vacation, felt as if she had been torn in half; her protests were ignored, and her sense of insecurity increased. She never forgave them. Neither did Anna.

And I had no access to my best friend for more than two long years, thinks Anna as she recalls that traumatic summer. She shrugs to banish the painful memory. But in the end it had made no difference – they had eventually been reunited and had taken their schoolgirl friendship into adulthood. Since then, they had come together and parted so many times. Each time their old incantation would be uttered: 'Remember me.'

She is smiling as she turns from the window to face the interior of the room. She sees Youenn, lying on his back wide awake, looking at her. 'What are you thinking about?' he asks. 'You've been standing there for some time.'

'Bicycles,' she says shortly, and leaving him mystified, goes into their shower room to prepare for her day in the fast lane.

## Chapter Three

As she descends the wooden staircase, Anna can hear someone moving about in the kitchen, the clink of a spoon, the rustle of a packet. She is surprised to find Lizzie up at this early hour, although she is in her dressing gown – a Japanese kimono of printed silk which looks somewhat too gaudy and exotic in the solid dark Breton kitchen. There is a muffled bubbling sound of boiling water and a click as the electric kettle switches itself off.

'Good morning, darling,' says Lizzie, still with her back to Anna while searching in the cupboard. She recognises her friend's step – it has been pacing through her life for almost as long as she can remember. Turning round, smiling as she triumphantly holds a packet of tea bags that she has located, she says, 'I thought I'd get up and make you a cuppa before your early start.' She uses the word 'cuppa' in an almost self-conscious way to demonstrate that her roots are homely too. The flashy silk wrap-around and jewelled sandals are, as they both know, not really tasteful or appropriate; they are a masquerade – a concession to Paul, who adores Japan and who has probably brought the garment back from one of his many business trips there to give to his wife. To emphasise her distaste for its touristy garishness, Lizzie places the tea on the table and puts up her fingers to her eyes to pull the skin outwards from the corners, flattening her eyes into an oriental shape. She pouts in a way that she thinks a geisha might and says simperingly, 'You want tea?'

They both laugh. 'Yes please. That's sweet of you,' says Anna, 'though you shouldn't have bothered.' She is touched that Lizzie, who has never been an early riser, should have made the effort to get out of bed at least two hours before her usual time. She sees that Lizzie has located a couple of pottery mugs, into which she tosses two bags and pours the boiling water. The mugs are decorated with crude pictures of lighthouses and Anna, who dislikes them, is reminded of why she now has to use them. 'Sorry we don't have a teapot – it got broken last year, and I haven't got round to replacing it yet.' She opens the fridge to get a carton of milk. 'Not too much for me. I'm trying to learn to take it black.'

'Sugar? You always used to.' Lizzie waves a teaspoon at a packet of sugar she has found in the cupboard.

'I've finally given it up. All your nagging over the years must've finally done the trick.' Anna accepts the mug and sits at the table, where Lizzie joins her.

They sit side by side and look out of the window at the smoky grey dew on the grass in front of them. The house martins somersault about the sky, which is a pale lemony blue, and they both know that it will be a fine day, though neither feels the need to voice this.

'Paul still asleep?' Anna is not really interested. It is a way of starting the conversation.

'Mmmm.' Lizzie takes a sip of the tea, holding the cup in her pale slender hands with their manicured and painted nails.

Anna has always admired Lizzie's elegant hands, which contrast pleasantly with her own rather battered pair with their short nails. There had been a time when hers too had been admired for their artistic thinness and length – but now they just seem rather gaunt and lined. Anna once read an article about how hands demonstrate character and reveal experience, and she has taken note of them ever since.

'Youenn's awake.' Anna is still looking at his garden. She thinks of it as *his*, not because he does the work in it – she does – but because he has lived here all his life, whilst after only six years, she is still the newcomer. 'He's lying in bed brooding about the fact that I'm leaving him for a couple of days. He doesn't want me to go, but he can't think of a good enough reason to prevent me.' Then she corrects this by saying, 'Or rather, to *persuade* me not to.' Her voice is clear and without any note of bitterness.

'Why do you stay with him?' Lizzie is saddened by Anna's remarks and, concerned that their conversation might be over-heard, is almost whispering.

'Because he needs me, and because there's no one else who does.' Anna is talking in her normal tone – there is no need to talk quietly because Youenn would not understand them even if he could hear them.

'I need you.' But not as much as I used to, thinks Lizzie.

'You've got Paul.'

There is a pause.

'Youenn is an attractive, sensual older man,' Lizzie says softly.

'Oh yes, he is that.' What he is not is left unsaid. Anna is reticent.

'Too possessive?' prompts Lizzie.

There is another pause, during which Anna decides to revert to her old habit of confiding in Lizzie, though she is out of practice. They seldom see each other these days, and recapturing their earlier trust and frankness takes time.

'On a simple level I suppose you could say that. But it's also to do with his need to control everything around him. It makes me want to break out, but not enough to actually break up. Sometimes I get so desperate that I think I must leave the man. But then I realise I'm just following a pattern – I always leave men. To go is a cowardly, easy way out – and it would be just another failure on my part. It's much harder to remain and I really am trying. Love is too fragile and serious to smash it up so recklessly.'

'Do you love him, Anna?'

'In my own way, I do. Do you still love Paul?'

'I've grown used to him – and he loves me, even if he isn't always faithful.'

'At least I haven't any problems on that score with Youenn. He may flirt with women – as he did with you last night – but he's the obsessively loyal type. His focus on me is unwavering – dauntingly so. His intense commitment is flattering, but it often feels like a burden. I feel guilty that I don't appreciate his devotion more.'

'I feel the same about Paul,' says Lizzie with a laugh.

'You're lucky. He's kind and thoughtful and he knows how to please you. Youenn is more selfish and often seems abrupt and dour. But I suppose that's just his way.'

'He's more macho than Paul – I'll bet he's good in bed.'

Anna does not reply. She is slightly bothered by the note of envy in Lizzie's voice. Is it distaste she feels, or anxiety?

Paul is not asleep. Lizzie has left the bedroom door ajar, and as he lies in bed he can hear the faint murmur of the two female voices as they talk below in the echoing kitchen. He is somewhat uneasy. These are two women whose bond he is well aware of. They are almost like sisters. They do not talk trivia or swap banalities with each other, nor do they bicker as other siblings do. They are both clever – Anna is a serious and direct woman, and though his wife is occasionally frivolous, she is never silly – and she is always perceptive. He finds their affection for each other rather unsettling. And in view of the various disagreements and noisy quarrels they had had in the past, he finds it puzzling. Paul is a man who underestimates the unswerving nature and strength of women's reciprocal forgiveness.

His thoughts turn to Youenn, whom he finds easier to contemplate. He rather likes the chap – he seems to him to be pleasantly uncomplicated, though a bit aloof and stern. Paul has been flattered by the man's admiration of his car and his wife, and he now looks forward with pleasure to the short drive around the village in his Bentley which he will have later this morning with Youenn. The Frenchman will probably be ecstatic in his praise of the classic English car. Paul feels faintly superior to him because of his ability to speak the other's language, which gives him an advantage that makes him feel comfortable. He is unaware that his host has absolutely no feelings of inferiority over his lack of English – quite the reverse, in fact. Youenn is proud to be French and even prouder to be Breton, and he has no desire to acquire the language of a country he does not really care about, however much he might be attracted to its latently passionate women.

Paul, on the other hand, likes to acquire assets – whether they be in the form of education, languages, property, money, or the appreciation of fine art, beautiful women, good food and wine. Success is another of these assets. He has achieved that too, but not without a lot of hard work. He thinks complacently but realistically of all that he has accomplished, and feels content with his present situation. He has earned it, and is prepared to relax a little now and enjoy the fruits of his labour. There are still some things that he would like to do – own a Ferrari, walk in the Himalayas, and better understand the complex nature of the woman he has married. He hopes that there will opportunities to do all of these, and feels that since he is only in his late fifties – though sixty looms uncomfortably close – there is still plenty of time. He is not given to depressing thoughts about his own mortality, and has still managed to retain some shreds of a youthful delusion that he will live forever. He plans ahead but not too far, and long ago decided to take each day as it comes, placing his triumphs and disasters in the perspective of a long life of overall satisfying attainment. As he says to his younger colleagues, in an effort to impress them with a modern catchphrase, 'I don't do disappointment.'

He picks up his book, *The Seven Pillars of Wisdom* by T. E. Lawrence, and feels its weight in his hand. He is nearing the end of this massive work, and enjoying it thoroughly; the magnificent descriptions of the desert are compelling, though he finds Lawrence's introspections somewhat too intense. He will also enjoy telling his friends he has read the whole thing. So many people he meets say regretfully that they have not yet managed to get through it but they hope to find the time one day. That he has actually read it all will give him at best an edge, or at least a topic of conversation. The work is beautifully written, and Paul considers himself an educated man who can appreciate what is good and what is not. It is part of the secret of his success. He begins to read.

Downstairs, Anna has been telling Lizzie about Youenn's two younger children by his first marriage, the topic of Malo having been exhausted the previous evening.

'The trouble was that they had been living here all their lives, on their own with their father since the death of their mother, and they resented my intrusion hugely. At first they were shocked that Papa had married an Englishwoman whom he had known for only a few weeks, and then they were angry and jealous because they felt I had supplanted them in their father's affection. I tried so hard to be a friend to them and not a substitute mother, but it didn't work. Loïc left first – to go and work in Lyons. His younger sister, Cécile, is now at university in Metz, and she usually stays with Malo in Paris for the vacations. Malo, who is still there, working in advertising, is happy to offer his sister a place to stay because he knows it will irritate his father. She does come home here from time to time, but when she does she makes a point of spending long evenings out with her old school friends, so she doesn't have any time to spend with us.' Anna gets to her feet and picks up the empty mugs.

'Surely Youenn must be upset by all his children's desertion of him.' In her mind Lizzie is comparing how she thinks Youenn would have felt with how she reacted when her own children went off to live overseas. She knows she ought to feel sad and abandoned and is faintly worried by her lack of concern. She says, 'He probably misses them now they live in another part of France.'

Anna ponders this. 'Oddly, he doesn't seem as upset about this as I would have thought. I think he's still distressed by the estrangement between him and his eldest child, but he seems to have just accepted the departure of the two younger ones. After all, they *are* young adults now – nineteen and twenty-three – so you'd expect them to leave home. And he has me as a consolation. And his faith.' The last three words are said with a hint of contempt.

51

'Of course, he's a Catholic. As I am.' Lizzie says this firmly, rattled by the scornful note in Anna's voice. All her life she has been convinced of the existence of God, and she decided to adopt Catholicism in her late twenties. Anna has an aversion to religion in all its forms, so it has been a taboo subject ever since her discovery of Lizzie's traitorous conversion. But Lizzie is not ashamed of her faith and does not think, as Anna does, that she has compromised her intelligence.

'Everyone round here is Catholic, or professes to be,' Anna tells her. 'Churches are often full – and if you never go then you don't ever really fit in.' She has tried hard to adjust to life in a small Breton community that is not tolerant of outsiders who don't conform or pretend to conform, but she has no time for God, regarding belief in him as a refuge for cowards who cannot face up to a world which is not controlled by a Deity. It is her uncompromising decision not to hide her atheism which upsets Youenn, rather than her lack of faith. Anna is prepared to flaunt her unbelief and this intransigence hinders her acceptance by the community.

'So you don't really feel you belong here? That's sad. It's such a peaceful place,' Lizzie says softly.

'You know that I'm never really at peace. I don't even know what it means!'

'The peace of God passes all understanding.'

'Please Lizzie, don't preach. You may have been converted to Christianity but don't try to subvert me. It won't help. It won't change things. I make my own decisions. You believe you can leave everything in God's hands – which means you don't have control over your life. It's pathetic; it's pitiful.'

'You always criticise things you don't accept yourself.' Lizzie is annoyed but speaks quietly. 'You insult people who merely hold differing views to your own – now *that* is pitiful.'

'On the contrary, I admire people who have strong views. I even rather admire your touching faith – though I feel it's misguided. A belief in God gives a false sense of security – you think there is someone out there who will ultimately look after you. You've always needed a carer, Lizzie. First it was my mother, then me, and now God.'

'It's too early in the morning to have an argument about the existence of God,' Lizzie says wearily, wondering why she has allowed herself to be drawn into a dispute on a subject they have agreed never to discuss. 'Neither of us is going to change our views at this stage in our lives. Once people reach their fifties, they're less likely to alter their convictions. They become more set in their ways.'

'Speak for yourself,' Anna says airily. 'I might decide to set off on a new path. I still have options and the ability to change my situation.' She has an uncomfortable feeling that this claim may be mere bravado on her part, and says in a more conciliatory tone, 'But you're right. For once, let's part without cross words. That would be a novelty.'

While speaking, she has been gathering up what she needs to take with her to England: a book to read during the flight, an apple to eat in the car, her wallet and her glasses. It is nearly time to go.

'You've got your passport?' asks Lizzie, knowing the question is unnecessary but feeling the need to show her concern, as well as to bring a bit of mundane reality back into the conversation.

Anna nods, and checks she has her credit card and diary tucked in the side compartment of the small overnight bag she packed yesterday. She has not liked carrying a handbag since the day she had hers snatched in Naples a number of years ago. She remembers her companion running fruitlessly after the two youths who had ripped it off her shoulder as they sped past, laughing, on a scooter. Her companion, Mario – or was his name Marco? – had been very upset – almost more than her, since it was his own countrymen who had done this to his friend. He had waved his arms excitedly and had been extravagantly apologetic about the incident, almost as if it had been his fault. That was when Anna had decided that she preferred Frenchmen.

'When are you leaving?' Lizzie has seen Anna glance at her watch.

'Just before eight – a friend is going to drive me to Nantes. She wants to go there for a day's shopping. I can catch the bus to the airport from the city centre. Youenn wouldn't want to drive me there himself – it's nearly an hour away.' Anna sees the look of disapproval in Lizzie's face as she registers another instance of Youenn's selfishness. 'Anyway, he says he wants to repair the garden fence. He might even do it. You never know,' she adds with a smile.

'Are you going to eat something before you go?'

'No, I shan't bother. I rarely eat much at this time of day. But Youenn will go out and get bread. If you ask him nicely he'll get some croissants too, or brioche, but he won't think of it if you don't mention it. I can hear him moving around upstairs – he'll be down soon.'

'In that case, I'd better get dressed.' Lizzie gets to her feet and wraps the gaudy kimono round herself. 'I'll say goodbye now, then. It's been so good to see you, Anna, and to meet Youenn. One evening together isn't enough and it's over much too quickly.' After these platitudes Lizzie pauses, then puts her arms round Anna's thin shoulders and hugs the woman who means more to her than her own husband. She says with great seriousness, 'You know you can always come to stay with us in London – for as long as you want. I mean it.'

'I know you mean it.' But Anna also knows that too often the house in Highgate stands empty, as they work away from home so much. She shivers inwardly with a faint feeling of apprehension: when she arrives in England, Lizzie will not be there – she will still be in France. She returns her friend's embrace and then gently releases herself. 'Say goodbye to Paul for me.'

'You'll be all right, won't you? You've got it all organised – your hyperactive day? You won't get too tired?' Lizzie has sensed Anna's hesitation and doubt and is now feeling anxious on her friend's behalf.

'Of course I will, and yes I am all organised, and no I won't get tired,' laughs Anna. 'My dear, please don't worry about me. I'm a capable woman!' She forces herself to speak calmly, and to reassure herself that she is, of course, capable of anything. She pauses and then utters the incantation agreed between them so many years before and repeated since on many partings: 'Until we meet again, remember me.'

The noisy birds outside distract her and she glances out of the window at the garden and the field beyond. The tree under which they talked the night before is bright in the sunlight, but it casts an oblique shadow across the grass in the early morning sun. Anna remembers one of her favourite short poems by Emily Dickinson: 'Presentiment is that long shadow on the Lawn'. A slight coldness comes over her but she shrugs it off – she has experienced so many farewells before.

Lizzie regards Anna with a worried frown, which she swiftly erases as the other woman turns to face her. 'Bye then,' she says cheerfully, 'I must go and get dressed.' She pauses and woodenly recites her repetition of the familiar exit line, 'Until we meet again, remember me.' Then she turns and walks upstairs, feeling just a little less buoyant than when she descended earlier. She knows that Anna is watching her, but she does not turn round. That too is the arrangement – the one who walks away does not look back. It is also understood that they do not mention the pain that either of them may be feeling at their impending separation.

Anna hears the bell in St Pierre's clock tower start to toll eight o'clock as Youenn enters the kitchen. They exchange no words. They often don't. She places a cup of coffee in front of him and when he is seated she leans over from behind and puts her arms round him. He grunts, accepting the reassurance he thinks she is trying to give him.

When the doorbell sounds, Anna kisses his cheek and, picking up her bag and coat, walks through to the hall. He remains where he is, watching her. She is wearing a pair of black trousers with a camel-coloured jacket; he prefers her in skirts. She stretches up to unbolt the door, exposing a thin wrist, and murmurs goodbye to him as she slips outside. She closes the door firmly behind her and steps away from the house, leaving inside all that she loves in the world. Youenn hears a car door slam and a few seconds later the sound of the engine revving up and then receding. A minute later he feels a slight sense of alarm because he has just registered that what Anna said was 'adieu' instead of 'au revoir'.

It is an hour later. The remains of the baguette and the brioche are lying on the table beside the apricot jam and the fruit bowl. Lizzie is in the kitchen on her own, sitting on one of the upright wooden chairs and thinking. They have finished breakfast – there is no butter in the house – often the case in French homes – but the coffee, prepared in silence by Youenn with considerable care, was excellent. He served it in large ceramic bowls and only after drinking his did he start to make conversation.

Coffee is clearly his kick-starter to the day. Shortly afterwards, he reminded Paul of his promise to take him for a drive in the Bentley, and they went off together.

Lizzie, having packed up their small suitcases and tidied up the guest bedroom, has been having a thorough look round the house whilst they are out, but is now having another cup of coffee, and feeling no guilt at all about her curiosity. Anna shares her inquisitiveness and would know that it represents not intrusion but affection – the desire to know more about each other and to appreciate their individual tastes. If you love someone then you are curious about their life and home, thinks Lizzie, and she knows that if the situation were reversed, Anna would be just as interested in exploring the London house.

She looks around her. She is surprised by the heavy wooden furniture and the lack of comfortable chairs downstairs, and thinks that this style is probably traditional – she remembers how often she finds French homes to be quite formal and not very relaxing. But although the uncompromising Youenn might not be one for soft sofas, she would have thought that Anna might have prevailed upon him to have one as a concession to her tastes. She reflects that Anna used to love lying full length on her threadbare red sofa in Paris reading her book or listening to music. Youenn has made no adjustment for his wife's comfort. And the bedroom – the marital bedroom – surely it need not be so spartan and unfeminine? Downstairs there are few pictures on the walls, blinds instead of curtains, and no rugs on the cold flagstones or on the plain wooden floors. The fact that there are no family photographs is not surprising – Anna never bothered with them either, and presumably Youenn does not choose to be reminded about children whom he rarely sees and who ignore him and his new wife.

What is strange, Lizzie thinks with slight anxiety, is that there is little evidence of Anna's flamboyant love of colour and her eclectic taste in art, no indication of Anna's former predilection for the bohemian and the unusual. There is no harmony, no originality – everything is too hard, conventional and tidy. Anna never used to care if a place was in a muddle – casual disarray was the hallmark of her living spaces. Perhaps Youenn could not tolerate her clutter or has Anna changed and decided to be neat and organised instead? If so, she wonders why.

She is perturbed by the lack of Anna in the house – it is as if her friend has made no effort to stamp anything of her personality on Youenn's home. Of course, her many books are here, shoved untidily and at random into a large wooden bookcase against one wall, and on shelves to the right of an open fireplace. And in front of them stands one of the few other items that she recognises as belonging to Anna – her desk, that had once belonged to her father and, as far as Lizzie can remember, has always been in poor condition with a scuffed surface and pieces of veneer missing. She is relieved to see that the top of the desk is characteristically untidy. This is clearly Anna's domain and Youenn is wise enough to leave it well alone. Various papers are heaped on the top around a metal table lamp, a jam jar is stuffed with pens and pencils, and a wooden bowl is crammed with paper clips, rubber bands and other odds and ends. A battered notebook balances on a large dictionary, and Lizzie has resisted the temptation to open it. There are a few brochures, still unopened in their plastic sachets or envelopes, thrown into an overflowing waste-paper basket beside the desk. Anna loathes unsolicited junk mail and, in her usual uncompromising way, doesn't even bother to open it before discarding it. She is less curious than Lizzie, who always opens everything that arrives in the post to see whether it might be of interest before she jettisons it.

The proportions of the rooms are attractive and decorated in a provincial French style with thick wallpaper and unpainted wooden doors. Lizzie knows that Anna dislikes busy wallpaper, but clearly she hasn't bothered to persuade Youenn to change it. Surely, she thinks, after five or six years there should be more of Anna's influence here? With the exception of Anna's bookcase and the desk, it is all somewhat severe and disciplined and – masculine! Lizzie picks up her coffee cup and walks across the kitchen to put it on the draining board. She has been sitting with her back to the window, but now, as she looks out at the garden, it suddenly occurs to her that this is Anna's territory.

French gardens tend to be either formal and geometric or neglected and dull; but what she sees here looks different – the chaotic profusion of spring flowers and unkempt shrubs growing in various beds of no particular shape and pattern makes it look more like an unkempt English cottage garden. It is May, and a wide variety of flowers and plants of different colours and heights jostle for position and prominence in the morning sunshine. Undoubtedly this is where Anna has imposed her personality and indulged her taste for colour, excess and disorder. Though seemingly random and natural, clearly a lot of work has been done to make this small Breton garden really beautiful. Yesterday evening, in the dark, Lizzie had not realised how lovely it was, and she now regrets that she has not complimented Anna on her creation. The glowing garden softens the impact of the austere house.

Turning back to the interior, she catches sight of a sculpture on a small table in the darkest corner of the room. She goes across to it and knows instantly that this belongs to Anna. It is a small bronze figure of a young man leaning on a rock looking upwards, and it reminds her, as it surely must remind

59

Anna, of Adam. She runs her finger across the cool metal and wonders where Anna acquired it. The youth is finely wrought but Adam was more beautiful, and she wonders where he is now. She sighs and wanders through to the front hall, where a large wooden wall clock is ticking loudly. She listens to the muted sounds of the village as the day gathers momentum and people arrive in their cars from the outlying smaller hamlets to do their shopping.

Lizzie hears the low, controlled growl of the big car as it stops outside, and then the double slam of two doors, so she retreats into the kitchen. Youenn gives a loud bray of laughter as the two men enter the house, and the sound rebounds off the stone floor. Lizzie suspects that laughter is a rarity in this house and finds this sad because Anna used to have such a sense of fun and always laughed uninhibitedly.

She looks up as the men enter and smiles at their obvious mutual camaraderie. Paul, who has slept well, is good humoured and relaxed. Youenn's dark face has a look of undisguised gratification – he knows he has been seen by many of the villagers driving round in what, in this part of France, is a most unusual and valuable car. His enjoyment of this simple vanity has for the moment eclipsed his uneasiness following his wife's departure an hour earlier.

His guests are about to leave to drive up to the Channel port from where they are to catch their ferry in a few hours' time. As they are putting their overnight bags in the boot of the car and preparing to set off, Youenn talks to Paul about the route and how long the journey might take. Paul is smiling and nodding, but not actually listening – he knows that Lizzie will sort all that out in the first few minutes of their drive. She is more organised than she cares to show to the world. Both of them are aware that her affectation of feminine muddle

60

and seeming inefficiency will endear her more to others than ordered calm and business-like competence. It is a lesson the intelligent Anna has failed to learn.

The couple say goodbye to their host and thank him with a formality that seems appropriate. The Englishman watches as Youenn politely and courteously kisses Lizzie's hand and then solemnly opens the car door for her, closing it carefully after she has seated herself. Then Paul salutes the Frenchman and lowers himself into the driving seat, closes his door, which makes a muffled click, and starts up the engine with a muted roar. With an imperious toot, the Bentley turns out of the drive into the street. Lizzie leans out of her window and waves goodbye as Youenn stands unsmiling and erect framed by his doorway, still watching as the car drives slowly and regally down the main street of his village. When they are out of sight, his back sags slightly as he slowly turns and goes back into his house.

As there is plenty of time before their ferry departs, the couple have decided to meander north on minor roads, taking a slightly longer but more picturesque route. Once they have left the village and joined their chosen road, Lizzie puts away the map she has used to get them on the correct route, leans back in the old leather seat and sighs.

This is a signal for Paul, driving confidently and sedately, as he usually does in this car, to begin the conversation.

'Youenn seems nice enough,' he says genially. 'What do you think – is he good news for Anna?'

'No, I think he's probably very bad news for her. He's obviously a control freak. I think she's lucky that he's let her go on this swift visit to England. He'd chain her up if he could. It's just as well he didn't understand when I invited her to come and stay with us in London sometime soon. I should think the chance of his allowing her to go away without him for a week would be remote.'

'Come off it, Lizzie – he's not that bad. He's really quite charming.'

'Oh, he's charming all right, in a kind of wolfish way, but I think he might have a bit of a temper if you crossed him. He's obviously of the opinion that a wife should obey. He's the kind who exerts pressure on his woman to get what he wants.'

'I'm not sure I agree with you.' Paul is often defensive of male dominance, though he doesn't behave that way himself. 'But even if what you say is right, Anna can surely stand up to that sort of emotional bullying. She's quite tough really – or she used to be.'

'I don't think she's as resilient as she once was,' Lizzie says slowly, remembering how gaunt her friend has become. And more subdued than before. 'She seems a bit worn down by his demands and his dependence on her. She told me that she feels guilty because their marriage has caused a rift between him and his children.'

'Well it probably has. But that often happens and then later they come round and return to the fold.'

'That might not happen here.' Lizzie does not choose to enlighten Paul about the blood tie between Malo (whom he once met) and Youenn. Instead she goes on puzzling over her friend's spartan life with her French husband. 'I wonder why Anna has let Youenn imprison her in this corner of Brittany. It's almost as if he has a hold over her. Rather a "Beauty and the Beast" situation.'

'Well, I don't think he's a tormented beast,' protests Paul. 'And nor is Anna a frail beauty.'

'She used to be beautiful. But these days she does seem a

bit frail. I'm going to phone her later this week and have a chat with her.'

'Bit of a surprise – her finally getting someone to publish that academic tome of hers,' says Paul, adroitly changing the subject, because he feels uncomfortable discussing other people's health.

'I don't think it's that astonishing.' Lizzie is irritated by the flippant way he has referred to the book. 'Anna has always been talented and articulate. Admittedly, she took long enough to research and write it. The delay is probably because she's never had the contacts or the drive to get it published before now. I'm pleased for her. She deserves a bit of recognition. And a brief respite from her possessive Frenchman. I hope she enjoys her day of freedom.'

'I expect she's in the executive jet at this moment. Rather exciting for her, I would think,' says Paul patronisingly.

Lizzie does not bother to reply. Her thoughts are with her friend and she hopes the book will be received with the critical acclaim it deserves, because Anna, who has spent too many years writing it, will be acutely disappointed if it is not. She has in the past read some of the work in manuscript form and found it to be a book with ideas in addition to research, and well written. She senses that now it really matters to Anna that it is published. That used not to be so important a goal, but for some time Anna has been obsessed about publication and the idea of her work being printed, read and assessed, a work that has become a part of her life. She pictures Anna sitting in the plane as it wings its way across the Channel, and envisages her staring out of the window at the clouds, wondering whether, after so many rejections and setbacks, the book, finally published, will be a success. She will be worried about its reception, thinks Lizzie, and probably nervous about the flight. 'Stay calm, Anna,' she silently wills the other woman. 'You will get there.'

Paul is driving slowly through a small town and Lizzie notices that there are a number of shops with signs announcing that they sell *Brocantes* and *Antiquités*. Whilst they are momentarily stationary, Lizzie finds herself looking directly into the window of a shop selling furniture and objets d'art. She sees a bronze figure of a man to the left of a large oriental vase, and is immediately reminded of Adam. She thinks of that week many years before when she and Alan, her first husband, had just bought a house in Hampstead, and when Anna wandered around the West Country with her looking for antiques and bric-a-brac with which to furnish it.

At that time Anna had not yet gone away to Paris and was living in a cottage in Wiltshire that belonged to her brother, Gavin. He lent it to his sister from time to time whilst he was working overseas on a contract job. Anna was helping out at a local farm and seemed infused with rural good health and high spirits, in spite of the fact that she had no job, no money and no man. Her precarious situation was probably the reason she had been so carefree and animated. She had infected Lizzie with her sparkling irresponsibility and they had rollicked around the region together spending Lizzie's money, flirting with all the male antique dealers, and doing business with all the female ones.

Anna was a committed feminist and spent a lot of effort trying to boost the confidence and success of other women. Her solidarity with them and her aims to promote sisterhood were constantly undermined by her heterosexuality and her irrepressible inclination for the company of men. Reluctantly, Anna eventually had to admit that she had few close female friends, whilst Lizzie, although as keen on female equality as anyone, had less inclination to promote it publicly, and simply enjoyed the friendship of many women, and in particular that of her dearest Anna. Occasionally the pair pretended to be lesbians, and it amused them to overplay it when faced with a man who regarded gay women as a challenge and who assumed that he would be the one to make them see the error of their ways.

One afternoon during that week together, they found themselves in a small gallery in Devon. Lizzie was talking to the young woman who worked there, whilst Anna was poking around among the various objets d'art that were crowded on every possible surface. Lizzie then wandered over towards her and at the same moment they both spotted the bronze. Standing about 12 inches high, the naked male figure had his back arched, while his arms flexed a sword above his head. The sculptor, who had signed his name 'Fellinge', appeared to be French but was unknown to the gallery owner. The workmanship was exquisite, and the nude male a superb specimen of youth and manhood.

'What an Adonis – physically perfect! I really fancy him,' said Lizzie with a giggle.

'His mind's probably not of matching quality,' said Anna, 'But what the hell. He's lovely to look at!'

They had both wanted to buy the figure and, as they had both seen it at the same time, neither had a prior claim. They therefore bought it together. Though less able to afford it, Anna had insisted on paying her half so that she would have an equal claim to him. Over a bottle of wine in a nearby pub, they admired their acquisition and decided to share not only the ownership but also the actual possession of their treasure.

'We won't fall out over him. We'll have him in turns,' Anna told Lizzie. They both spluttered over their wine.

'No jealousy. He belongs to both of us,' Lizzie told Anna.

They debated whether to call him 'Adonis' on account of his classical good looks or whether to name him 'Adam', representing primal man. They opted for the latter since this name was more normal and would be more likely, when they referred to him in front of others, to arouse jealousy or curiosity. He would be their secret adoration, their private joke.

Lizzie was born in April, whilst Anna's birthday is in October. They made a pact that on each other's birthday, the other would send them the bronze. This way Lizzie would have the fine fellow for the summer months, and Anna for the winter months. It was a witty means of saving them both the trouble and expense of finding appropriate presents for each other, and since it was indestructible, it would not get damaged in the post – or if they were meeting up, one of them could simply hand it to the other in person.

Lizzie smiles as she remembers the bronze arriving in the spring year after year for her birthday, and how she used to pack it up in the autumn to send it back to Anna. One year, Anna had found a very pretty decorated cardboard box, and they used to pack Adam in it from then on. Over the years the box became very dilapidated, but the beautiful man remained forever young and untarnished by time. It was a satisfyingly witty echo of the Dorian Gray phenomenon. Unlike the other men in their lives, Adam never argued back or caused any problems, so they grew very fond of him! In Lizzie's house he had resided on the mantelpiece in her sitting room, whilst in Anna's various homes he stood on her small desk. When he was absent, they both missed him, but knew that he was staying with a loved friend and that he would soon return.

Sadly, however, one year the bronze had been lost in the post, and they never saw him again. It was autumn when Adam failed to arrive at Anna's. A month earlier the two women had fallen out over a false accusation that the other could not forgive, and it was while the anger and acrimony still simmered between them that Adam had gone missing. Anna promptly accused Lizzie of wanting to keep the bronze permanently, and of merely pretending it had been lost. Lizzie was enraged at this allegation by Anna and its implication that she was not being honest. Pigheadedly, neither would back down, and as their earlier quarrel had not been resolved either, they broke off contact and refused to speak to each other for about six months. Though neither of them would admit it, however, the pain of the estrangement was far worse for both friends than the loss of their little bronze.

Lizzie is idly wondering in whose house or on what mantelpiece Adam now resides, and is also speculating as to why Anna has bought a replacement, when they pull up outside a small bar in the main street of a village, and Paul suggests going in for a café cognac. She nods smilingly and they climb out of the car and saunter inside. Paul orders the coffees and chats pleasantly in French to the waitress; he enjoys impressing the locals with his fluency.

The English couple are certainly causing an impression with their vehicle, which sits glowingly alongside the pavement about twenty yards from the entrance to the bar. Two men have paused beside it and are having an animated discussion whilst pointing out to each other the various parts of the magnificent machine.

Paul is used to the admiration his beloved car invokes and still enjoys the feeling it gives him of possessing something special and rare. He knows that he should not feel so proud of a mere car, but he cannot help basking in the adulation it receives. Youenn had been full of praise for it too, and the shared enjoyment of their drive in it is what has made Paul feel cordial towards Anna's husband. He does not really want to listen to Lizzie making quick and probably inaccurate assessments of someone they have only just met. This tendency of hers to delve into others' emotional lives is somewhat irritating – and Anna does it too. He finds it slightly embarrassing and occasionally threatening. He too has strong opinions and sensitive feelings, but does not often feel the need to share them with a friend, male or female. He likes physical proximity to women but knows he cannot handle too much emotional intimacy. And yet last night he had felt excluded when the two women were outside in the dark together, discussing and dissecting. Though they rarely get together now, when they do they are a formidable pair. It is only one at a time that he can cope with them.

Their coffees arrive and Paul watches his wife as she smiles her thanks to the waitress. 'Lizzie, my darling, you are looking very attractive this morning,' he says gallantly. And indeed she does, casually dressed in a pair of dark brown trousers with a soft woollen sweater which moulds itself pleasingly round her breasts and shoulders. She is wearing a small amber necklace that he has recently given her – and he knows that she has worn it to please him.

She smiles her thanks for his compliment whilst stirring her coffee with a spoon. Then, taking a sip, she says deceptively idly, 'Anna was looking very smart this morning ready for her important day – though she's become too thin by half.'

'I think she looks older than she actually is. She's your age, isn't she? I must say she seems much older than her adopted sister.' Paul smiles and looks at his wife, hoping for a response to his flattery. It is not forthcoming, so he continues musingly, 'In fact, I never did really consider her a good-looking woman at all.'

'You didn't always think that!' Lizzie cannot help saying. 'There was a time when you thought her very pretty.'

'What do you mean?' asks Paul, narrowing his eyes and slowly putting his cup down on the small table.

'Nothing,' Lizzie replies airily. 'Something that you once said. I forget when.' She calmly finishes her coffee and places the cup in its saucer. She has decided to retreat from revealing any more of her suspicions. She does not want to spoil the day or the mood, and backs off from the moment of actual confrontation. Perhaps later. Perhaps never.

Paul feels uneasy but decides that her hints do not amount to concrete knowledge and is relieved that she seems to have lost interest in the question of how well he might once have known Anna. He sees that she is now serenely watching the passers-by. He slowly exhales. 'That coffee was delicious,' he says. 'Ready to get back on the road, darling?' He stands up and bends solicitously over her.

'Of course,' his wife responds with a smile. His transparent thought processes and evasions are a source of amusement to her. 'Let's go.' She rises to her feet.

They slowly climb into their aristocratic motor car, soaking up the appreciative glances of the other occupants of the bar peering out of the window. Paul believes they are admiring the beauty of his Bentley, while Lizzie is hoping they are charmed by her English rose elegance; both, however, are fully aware of the effect they are creating as a handsome couple in a handsome motor car.

They drive off slowly and the wide French countryside stretches out in front of them in the May sunshine.

Lizzie is in a good mood. She knows that this is partly as a result of her gaining a tiny psychological advantage over Paul in the conversation they have just had, and partly because she is enjoying the slower pace of life that they have been experiencing over the past week.

'I'm not looking forward to getting back to work and the rat race of London,' she tells Paul. 'I've enjoyed having the time to chill out and unwind. I'm glad you drive this car slowly – it gives us time to look at things as we pass. You drive your other car too fast for us to see anything much. That's like my life, really – I do get tired of always having to rush around to keep appointments.'

'You might feel that now, darling,' says Paul, 'but you know we'd both soon get bored of a life that wasn't fast-paced and varied. I'm rather looking forward to getting back to it all, myself. Quiet backwaters are fine for a short time but they're not for me in the long run. I don't know how Anna can bear to be permanently buried in that tiny village.'

'Well, she's not there today,' says Lizzie. 'At this minute, while we're meandering along the back roads of France, she's dashing to London to keep her various appointments. Which reminds me, we have a ferry to catch. We'd better not meander too much longer.'

'Plenty of time – the port's about an hour away, and the boat won't leave for an hour after that. I've booked us a spacious cabin, so we'll we able to relax and get away from the other passengers.'

Paul is about to add something more, but with a sharp intake of breath he suddenly slams on the brakes, and Lizzie puts out her hand to the walnut dashboard to stop herself lurching forward. A cyclist has just emerged out of a small country lane which crosses the main road ahead of them, but Paul manages to stop before they hit him, because he has been driving fairly slowly and has quick reactions.

'Bloody stupid French idiot!' swears Paul. The cyclist, who

is continuing unperturbed on his way down the small road to the left, has either not seen them or is pretending not to notice that they had to screech to a halt because of him. Too late, Paul realises he has a horn, which he now sounds. Loudly. Angrily.

After the aggressive blare of the horn there is silence.

'It's all right, dear. We've missed him,' he reassures his wife.

Lizzie's rapid breathing gradually returns to normal as the faint echo of the fear and shock which she experienced many years before recedes. She swiftly dismisses from her mind the memory of the biking accident caused by Anna all those years ago, and from her side window she watches the man and his bike disappear down the lane as they move forward on their way to the coast.

# Chapter Four

At the same moment that Lizzie and Paul are climbing back into their golden motor car in north Brittany after their stop for coffee, Anna is descending the narrow aluminium steps from the executive jet which has just carried her across to Farnborough in southern England. She thanks the pilot and then, carrying her small bag and coat, she walks across the tarmac to the building he has pointed out to her. She enters the smart reception area of Anytime Aviation and speaks to a woman behind the desk who says that a car is waiting for her outside. This has been arranged by her literary agent, Moira, and she is grateful that there is to be no further delay. She asks the receptionist to phone her first appointment in London to say that she may be a half hour late. There are no formalities, no one wants to see her passport, so she hurries out to find a sleek Daimler parked close by and chauffeured by a stocky man wearing a uniform and peaked cap, who opens the rear door for her as she approaches. Apologising to him and mentioning that there is now some haste to get to her first appointment on time, she gets in and settles herself on the wide back seat while he climbs into the front and they set off.

The man has not uttered a word, but he drives efficiently and reasonably fast.

She is a little anxious because she is running behind time. The jet had been late arriving in Nantes because of a delayed departure from England caused by one of the businessmen turning up later than scheduled at Farnborough. The flight has taken about an hour, landing at nearly the same time as it took off, since the clocks in the UK are one hour behind the French. Very aware today of the passage of time, she registers that she has gained an hour. She has a curious feeling of acceleration, which is not just because of the speed at which she is now travelling in this comfortable large car; she puts it down to the fact that her days and weeks normally pass slowly and uneventfully, whilst this is a day of rapidity and change. For some reason, her internal clock is transmitting messages of urgency which she finds unsettling. She analyses the expression 'behind time' and decides that it is as illogical as saying 'ahead of time'. There are some turns of phrase that sound all right but are actually absurd. It is simply not possible to step outside time, and she concludes that, if one does not believe in God, there is nothing that is 'timeless'. She has spent hours of her life mulling over such idioms, and wants to steer her thoughts away today from word use and misuse. She tries consciously to relax and slow down the rapid pulse rate of her day on the fast track.

She had enjoyed the flight, though it had seemed a little strange to be all on her own in the cabin, with the pilot and co-pilot up front. At one point the co-pilot had come back to see if she was comfortable and to offer her some refreshments. She had accepted a glass of mineral water and assured him that she was fine. In truth, she had been enjoying being on her own and thinking about the people she would later be talking to. She wanted to prepare herself and decide how she would handle the various meetings and interviews. What did she need to achieve before departing for the Isle of Wight for her brother's party in the evening? She had tried to focus on the London appointments, but the past kept intruding and she knew that it was seeing Lizzie and Paul again that had put her in this reflective frame of mind. She had enjoyed being with them both again, and was pleased and surprised that Youenn had been so amenable. But in another way their visit had saddened her, because it seemed that Lizzie had finally opted for the dependence of marriage in her search for the security she had desperately wanted all her life.

Now, cocooned in the car, it becomes clear to Anna that Lizzie may need her rock-like support and companionship less than she did. She wonders if their friendship is waning but pushes this thought out of her head, and forces herself to think about her appointments and her busy day.

The first meeting will be the easiest. Her publishers specialise in literary criticism and biographies, and having initially been sceptical about *Choices*, they have now become guardedly enthusiastic. Her agent has done all the work, negotiated the contract and dealt with the usual matters. She has met the publishers in person only once before, but has been in contact with them over the months regarding the edit, proofs and final amendments needed before going to press. The book is due out in eleven days' time, and this meeting is to discuss the arrangements that have been made for its modest launch and whether Anna wishes to have a book-signing session in a London bookshop. She does not, and will withstand this suggestion. It is not that kind of book. Press copies will have been sent out, and today she is to see the printed book and receive her own copy for the first time. She is childishly excited at the prospect of holding her first and probably her last published book. She notices that the car has now turned onto the M25. Perhaps she will not be so very late after all and, in any case, it won't matter very much to them.

Lunch with her literary agent, Moira, afterwards will be more tricky. The woman, who is both charming and forceful, has been pressing her to come up with the subject of her next book. Impressed by Anna's critical perception and cogent arguments, expressed in stylish prose, Moira has been trying to persuade her to write a literary biography, which has bigger sales potential. The agent has flattered her by saying she is looking for someone who has the ability to research a subject deeply and sensitively. Anna's decision to firmly resist this not unattractive idea will disappoint Moira, but she feels that she has given enough years of her life already to researching and writing.

She is not much bothered by the third appointment – an interview with a literary magazine. She hopes they will focus on her book and its themes. If they try to pry into her life, she will be more reticent – her personal life has very little relevance, and she knows she can easily withstand any attempts at intrusion into it. She has had a lot of practice. There is only one person whom she will permit to ask about her life, and she is at that very moment in France being driven slowly northwards in an elegant Bentley, in contrast to the Daimler in which Anna herself is travelling with less taste and more haste. She feels amused at the unspoken rhyme. She rather regrets mentioning to the driver that she was in a hurry.

She looks out of the window. There is a fair amount of traffic on the motorway, and it is almost intimidating. She realises that this is because she is unused to hurtling along among so many vehicles – the roads in France are far less crowded. Her chauffeur drives just within the speed limit and has shifted lanes a few times. She speculates about him, and wonders what his voice sounds like – he has not yet uttered a word to her. His impassive face probably masks a lack of patience, or perhaps a dislike of other humans. Either way, she is unaffected by it. Whilst gazing at the traffic around her, Anna visualises Lizzie and Paul smoothly humming along the comparatively empty French roads, Paul purring in self-satis-fied union with his beloved car, and Lizzie sitting next to him with her easy-going smile concealing her alert and feline mind. She wonders if Lizzie is really as happy and content as she makes out. Has she truly succeeded in suppressing her ambi-tion and in overcoming her sense of insecurity? Anna is not sure. What she does know is that she herself has far less influ-ence on Lizzie than before, and that it is now Paul who may help his wife to achieve some sort of equilibrium and peace of mind.

Thirty minutes later the chauffeured Daimler draws up outside the offices where she has her first appointment, and the driver opens her door. As she climbs out, he goes, still without a word, to the boot and hands her the small case that she has brought with her from France. Grateful to him for the silence and for not intruding into her train of thoughts, she thanks him. He nods unsmilingly, which in no way disconcerts her, and she turns and walks up the steps to the entrance door. It is only just a few minutes after eleven in the morning.

The Bentley is making good progress northwards and is now nearing the coast. The soft, rolling terrain of Brittany has given way to the flat, broad fields of Normandy. Lizzie has had a little catnap and Paul is driving with that sense of warm protectiveness which comes with the added responsibility of a passenger who is asleep. The sun filters and flickers through a row of tall trees planted alongside the road. He glances at his watch: it is midday, and he gives a little self-satisfied sigh. Lizzie stirs and is fully awake quickly. It has always been her way – going from sound asleep to alert wakefulness in a few seconds.

'Where are we?' she asks, but does not give Paul time to answer before she switches subject, remarking, 'I expect Anna is with her publishers in London by now. I wonder if they really appreciate her, or whether she is just another dry academic author to them.'

'She's always written, hasn't she?' asks Paul rhetorically. 'You told me she used to be a journalist and I know she's been a teacher too. She's a clever woman.' Paul knows that by praising Anna he will please Lizzie.

'Anna is so gifted that she could have done many things. She just chose to write. I was always less academic and more practical – and I loved drama. That's probably why I ended up on the stage.' Lizzie is habitually self-deprecating about her career, though Paul is well aware of how hard she used to work when she was pursuing it.

'I bet Anna was always top of the form at school.'

'Yes, she was, but she broke so many rules that she was never made a prefect. She was a maverick and didn't care what others thought. I was the righteous goody-goody who achieved the accolades and adulation.'

'You two are so different that I'm surprised you've remained such close friends all these years,' says Paul.

'It hasn't always been harmonious between us – there's been periods of distance and discord. Our quarrels have been intense and over-emotional. But I think there's more that binds us together than occasionally drives us apart.'

This kind of remark makes Paul uncomfortable, so he asks casually about how they kept in touch after they left school.

'Well, as you know, Anna went on to York to study English but I went to drama school in London. I wanted to become an actress, and though my parents had been reluctant they eventually agreed to pay my fees. Possibly they felt guilty about separating me from my best friend and sending me far away to a school which I hated. As students we were free to meet up and Anna used to come down by train to spend a few days with me in my squalid flat in Barons Court that I thought was bohemian freedom. After a few days slumming it with me, Anna would return to her parent's home in the west, and sometimes I'd go down with her and see them too.' Lizzie's voice softens. 'I was really fond of both of her parents – they had been my guardians for some of my school years and they always took a great interest in me and what I was doing. I had always felt that I could tell them anything and they wouldn't judge or criticise me. Her father treated me like a daughter and I thought of her mother as my guardian angel. I was distraught when she died suddenly in my second year at drama school.'

Paul has of course heard all this before, and knows it's the precursor to the subject of her alienation from her parents, which he has no wish to listen to again.

As predicted, though, Lizzie is not to be deflected, 'When my mother died in India a few years later it didn't affect me anything like as much. But Anna and I knew we'd been selfishly preoccupied with ourselves, and felt hugely guilty that we hadn't seen very much of her mother and not realised how ill she'd been. After the funeral, we left her father and brother to console and support each other, and the two of us took off to the Brecon Beacons for a few days walking and talking.

Rambling had taken over from biking for us after that accident we had.'

'I didn't know you used to go hill walking,' says Paul, surprised. 'I wouldn't have thought it was your thing.'

'Well, it isn't now,' Lizzie says with a smile. 'But it once was. A couple of days of country air was a blissful contrast to intense weeks of fetid city life with nerve-wracking auditions and tiring rehearsals. Anna and I occasionally met up for a day or two to stride across the countryside together. We'd talk all day, putting the world to rights and things in perspective.'

Paul remains silent. The topic of Anna comes up too often, and his silence might put a temporary stop to it. But Lizzie continues thinking about the past, and recalls how the two girls had returned from Wales exhausted but drained of the sharp pain of their joint bereavement. She tries to work out how long after that it was that Anna began to take on her late mother's role of guardian angel.

Anna is also thinking about her mother. She is in Simmons Restaurant in the West End, having lunch with her literary agent, a woman who is younger than her, but who has an air of authority that gives the impression she is older. Moira is, as ever, urbane and charming, with her usual blend of vivacious enthusiasm and lurking persuasion. Her agent has a mannerism which is very familiar – she has a habit of tilting her head to the right and looking over her glasses while she is listening to others. This is something that Anna's mother used to do too; but whereas her mother's face was suffused with warmth and genuine affection, Moira's wears a slightly superior smile which combines tolerance of the waywardness of her authors with professional encouragement for them to perform at their best.

'So how did this morning's meeting go?' asks Moira, who knows the answer already as she has talked on the telephone to her contact at the publishers.

'It was fine. They were very kind, as ever. They gave me a copy of my book – I'm pleased with it.'

Anna is typically succinct and does not wish to tell Moira about the delighted surge of achievement she felt when she was handed the heavy book in its pristine dark red jacket, across which the title appears: *Choices: A Study of Shakespearean Themes*. And below, in smaller type, her name. She knows very well that in order to have your name in larger type than the title you have to be an established author. This is her first published work. All those years of unmethodical research and intermittent writing have finally resulted in this one book. There was a time when she thought she would never finish it. She is passionate about Shakespeare, but there were occasions when she felt stale and devoid of enthusiasm for her project and the plays on which she was focusing. She knows the simple truth is that she wasted vast amounts of time assembling too much material from which she then had to select and discard. The irony was that she had, indeed, given herself too many choices! Only Lizzie knows how initially excited she was about her project, and how weary and disillusioned she became with it towards the end, by which time she had worked sporadically on it for nearly seven years.

'Well, I'm glad you like it. There is a certain academic weightiness to it.' Moira has not actually read the entire work. 'You should get five author's copies altogether. That's the usual number.'

'They told me that but I didn't want to carry them with me, so I've asked them to send the others to the home of a friend of mine in London.' Anna knows that Lizzie will want to have a copy, and she is one of the few people whose good opinion matters. She will ask Lizzie to send one on to Gavin, and perhaps one might go to her old English teacher who has long since retired and would, she knows, love to have a published work of literary criticism by a former pupil. They have kept in touch irregularly over the intervening years, and Anna always attributes her love of literature to this woman who was more inspiring than any of her university lecturers.

'Did they mention if they want you to do anything to promote the book?' asks Moira.

'I don't think a book-signing session would be appropriate, so I said no to that suggestion,' says Anna.

'A pity,' says her agent. 'But perhaps you're right.' She looks at Anna critically, thinking that she looks rather anxious and seems to lack confidence in herself and in her book. Perhaps a personal appearance would not, after all, be a good idea. Anna does not have an authoritative bearing or inviting features, though the photograph on the inside cover of the jacket shows her with a thoughtful, serious expression which sets the right tone.

Moira then smoothly changes the topic to talk about royalties. 'You must expect sales to be modest and slow but, hopefully, steady. We're hoping for a few reviews and have sent out a number of copies to possible reviewers.' She already knows that Anna will not be in the country for publication day.

'Moira,' says Anna earnestly, 'I want to thank you so much for persevering with me. I used to be a quicker decision-maker than I am now, and I'm grateful for your help and advice.'

'We got it right in the end,' says Moira. 'I'm hopeful of a quiet success.'

Anna smiles. 'Avoidance of total flop would be good, and a limited success much more than I expect.'

'Don't underestimate yourself, my dear. It's a well-written work and you can be proud of it.'

Anna knows that this soothing and encouraging flattery on Moira's part will soon evolve into assault mode. She is mentally gearing herself up to withstand her agent's potent persuasiveness and convincing arguments. I can be forceful too, thinks Anna, and I've always been able to say no. Unlike Lizzie! Anna smiles outwardly at her inner reflections, and her agent mistakenly takes this as a cue to switch from the praise of the completed book to discussion of the next one, and what project Anna might like to undertake.

'Let's think of the future. We need to discuss possibilities and make some plans.' Moira then elaborates on the ideas she has already formulated for Anna, which involve a biography for which she thinks Anna's style and approach will be suited. Flattery is part of her attack aimed at battering down Anna's resolve to keep her options and ideas open. But she meets unexpected resistance: no matter what she suggests, Anna will not be drawn into making decisions or agreeing to anything definite.

By two o'clock the lunch is over and the two women are getting ready to part. Anna knows that Moira is concealing her disappointment beneath her habitual good manners and thinks that by biding her time, she will in the end persuade Anna to undertake the biography that she has been asked to commission. Anna knows, however, that she has absolutely no intention of 'coming round' in time. Moira gives her a few words of advice about the interview that is next on the agenda that afternoon, wishes her luck and says that she hopes the book will do well. She will contact her in France after publication day to let her know how it has been received, and she will send her author copies of any critical reviews.

Outside the restaurant they say goodbye to each other with every appearance of goodwill, and walk off in opposite directions, Moira back to her office near Russell Square, and Anna to her appointment at the magazine offices in Holborn.

The spring day is dry with some warmth from the sun, and Anna notes that, curiously, the urban scene does not depress her spirits as it has done in the past. She can handle it for one day. Her bag feels slightly heavier with the solid weight of the book in it. Her book. She feels as if a significant chapter in her life has come to an end, and is oddly relieved and light-headed. She can now let her work become an entity in its own right; it will either sink or swim. She is not sure if she really cares whether it sells well or not. It is done. She has passed it on to others who will read and judge. She can move on. The sense of release is also because she feels she has just, in some way, divested herself of her agent, who is not on her wavelength and is anyway too controlling. Yes, there is a sense of liberation here. She is content.

Moira may have been less than satisfied with how their lunch meeting went, but Anna is quietly pleased to have come away from it unscathed and without having given in to any further commitment. Her meeting with the publishers went well for her too. Anna is under no illusion that she is going to make money out of her book – the distillation of a multitude of ideas and many years' work – but she is quietly pleased that it is at last going to be in print, available to other Shakespearean scholars and discerning enthusiasts. She is quite happy to co-operate by taking part in this short magazine interview if it will help to demonstrate to her publishers that she is prepared to help them in marketing her book. After all, they have so far made few demands on her.

She realises that very few people make demands on her,

with the exception of Youenn, who does so wordlessly, but he is in France and today she is in England. Perhaps the fact that he is so far away accounts for her sense of freedom. Will his magnetism be enough to pull her back tomorrow? She is unsure, because at this moment everything seems possible, even breaking the bonds and leaving – for a day or for a week or for ever. Just as she has left other lovers in the past. She stops at the corner of a street and looks not at the traffic but up at the sky, where she sees the sun at its zenith. Its yellow warmth filters down through the London atmosphere. Shivering suddenly and unaccountably, she lowers her eyes and registers a red light and waiting cars. She crosses the road.

Years before, she had once driven through a red traffic light in a car in which Lizzie was a passenger on their way back from an evening at the theatre. The young women had been talking about plays and Lizzie had been describing her reaction to the performance of Romeo and Juliet and explaining why she found it a compelling and beautiful play. Anna had agreed it had sublime poetry but had insisted that the play was basically flawed. She had always felt irritated by the plot – the tragedy being one of circumstance and bad timing. If Juliet had woken up two minutes earlier, all would have been well. Shakespeare's more powerful tragedies relied on noble but flawed characters who make the wrong choice. She had said then that one day she would write a book about this. Bad luck in a play did not have the same tragic impact as bad decisions. Carried away by the force of her own arguments, and with very few other vehicles at that time of night to impinge on her attention, she had lost concentration.

'You've just driven through a red light,' Lizzie said, interrupting her friend's enthusiastic assertions.

'So I have.' Anna did not sound at all bothered. 'But there

are no other cars around. And anyway, I've been given permission.'

'Don't be silly. It's against the law.'

Anna said firmly, 'I've given myself permission. "I am the master of my fate. I am the captain of my soul."'

'And now you're going to tell me who said that, I suppose.'

'It's from "Invictus" by W. E. Henley, a minor mid-nineteenth-century figure – the same chap who said that his head was "bloody but unbowed". Mum was mad about Victorian poets and was always quoting that line. Its sentiment's been impressed into me – that I have choices and can alter the course of my life. Nothing's laid down.'

'I'm not sure I agree with you,' said Lizzie. 'We can't control everything in our lives. So much is due to luck and chance. I'm not a complete fatalist, but I do think that some things are destined to happen.'

'Come in number five, your time is up,' Anna called out jeeringly, knowing that five was Lizzie's lucky number. 'You'll turn to God one of these days, which I consider is the ultimate way of avoiding responsibility for your own life.'

'That's not fair, Anna. I find life works better within a framework of rules. And whether you believe in Jesus or not, Christian behaviour is a good pattern to follow. I'm conventional and don't approve of having no parameters. Tolerance, kindness and compassion can help make this difficult life a little easier to cope with.'

Anna actually admired her friend's earnestness but pretended to mock it. 'You're such a law-abiding citizen, Lizzie. The truth is, you never wanted to break free of restrictions. That's why you liked school and I didn't.'

'That's why you never fitted in and I did,' said Lizzie, remembering how much of an outsider Anna had been during that first term when they had met for the first time. 'Don't get me wrong – I envy you your carefree attitude to conventions, your nerve and self-sufficiency – but I can't emulate them.'

'And *I*,' said Anna emphatically, 'don't waste time with envy. I hate rules. You've always been happy to fit in and keep the peace. The perfect prefect!'

'I got made a prefect at school because I was nice and helpful to people, and you were tactless and uncooperative. No wonder my parents thought you were a bad influence on me! I toed the line because I needed to fit in, because I felt insecure with my parents far away in India, but you had the huge advantage of a family who were lovingly tolerant of your outrageous comments and your professed waywardness. Your views have always been so unorthodox. And now you're even more unconventional, never having a proper home and never staying with one man for long. It must take courage to choose be to so rootless and solitary.' Lizzie genuinely admired Anna for being true to herself.

'Whereas your ability to compromise and your adherence to conventions has meant you've never lacked for friends and suitors,' Anna interjected, pretending to condemn Lizzie whereas, in reality, she was envious of her social poise. 'I've been more unpredictable and capricious, and that's only ever brought me disapproval and distrust,' she concluded with a note of pride, pulling the car into the side of the road outside their destination – Lizzie's flat.

Many years on and with the benefit of hindsight, Anna continues walking along the London street bathed in afternoon sunlight, inventing the end of the conversation as it would be if they had it now.

'That's why you had lovers and I had husbands,' Lizzie might say with a smile.

'Well, I've finally got a husband myself now. And much good it does me!' There would be a brittle edge to Anna's voice.

'It was never worth sacrificing my freedom for marriage,' she murmurs aloud as she refocuses on the unfamiliar street that she now finds herself in.

Anna realises she has taken a wrong turning, and stops so sharply that a man walking close behind nearly collides with her. With an exaggerated swerve round her, and directing a look of annoyance and pity at the silly woman who, without warning, stopped dead in front of him, he strides off. Muttering an irritated apology to his back and mentally swearing at his witless assumption of her imbecility, Anna retraces her steps and finds herself in the parallel street to the one she wants to be in – as it happens, not far from her next appointment. She tells herself she really must stop daydreaming about the past and concentrate on the present. Why is she unable to banish Lizzie from her thoughts? Their conversations in earlier decades flood her mind. She shakes her head as if to clear the images and the words away. For now she must centre her attention on today and make it through to the end of it.

# Chapter Five

Lizzie and Paul are now entering the outskirts of the ferry port, the sun glinting on the sheen of their car's long bonnet. They have made good time and are not feeling pressurised in any way, though now there is a fair amount of traffic on the roads. They have been travelling in comfortable silence for about half an hour, and are waiting in a queue at traffic lights. The tall French houses in this suburb rear up along the road behind a row of pollarded trees that are now coming into bright green leaf. As they wait for the lights to change, Lizzie notices a man in front of the house adjacent to their car. He is standing beside one of the trees looking up at the first floor of the building on the opposite side of the road. He is a dark-haired man in a short grey coat and he appears to be staring at a shuttered window. There is something about his stillness and intensity that gives Lizzie a flash of remembered apprehension and fear. The cars in front of them are now moving and Paul puts the car into gear and moves smoothly forward. Lizzie turns her head to look over her shoulder at the watcher – she sees him step back out of her sight behind the tree, whilst still gazing upwards.

A flood of nasty recollections invade her mind and she is

taken back to that sinister summer in her twenties when she had been harassed by a stalker.

The year had begun well. Her agent had sent her to audition for a TV commercial for a new car coming on the market. Along with about twenty others on a cold January morning, she had turned up at the audition, and four of them had been selected and videotaped. The producer for the advertising agency would then recommend to the clients the girl he thought was most suitable for the shoot, and it would then be up to them. She remembers the elation she had felt when about ten days after the audition she was told that she had been chosen. A month passed before the shoot began, and over the course of a day they shot a 10-second and a 45-second version, both of which were shown on television a number of times during the spring.

There had been a hint of mystery, glamour and allure in the advertisement – and over the following months friends teased Lizzie about being a sexy lady. She had just split up with her boyfriend Steve, who had been one of the camera crew involved in the two-day shoot for a commercial she had done in September for the Highlands and Islands Tourist Board. They had been going out together for over six months, but it was not really serious on either side. So Lizzie was not too upset when, having gone over to Canada for an assignment, Steve then decided to stay there. She wanted to move out of a flat she had been sharing with two other hopeful, but as yet unsuccessful, actresses to rent a place on her own.

Through the *Evening Standard*, Lizzie had managed to find a small one-bedroom first-floor flat in a terraced house on a quiet road near Hammersmith in West London. She had taken some trouble with redecoration – funded by the earnings from her commercials – and had tried to create an atmosphere of arty exotic chic in her sitting room, painting the walls a deep golden yellow and having two low sofas covered in multicoloured printed Indian fabric. She had bought at auction some low wooden tables, a battered wooden chest and a pair of brass candlesticks. She filled bowls with pot pourri, and framed a couple of theatrical posters to hang on the walls. She had unconsciously tried to emulate the unconventional and care-less eccentricity of the rooms which Anna inhabited, but somehow her domain was always too carefully arranged to be able to achieve the desired bohemian look and casual atmos-phere.

It was around June when Lizzie became aware that a man was hanging about in the road outside the house. She had noticed him a few times, and thought that he was just someone living in the area who was out of work and had nothing better to do than wander around and stare at people. The night she became alarmed was when she looked out of her first-floor sitting-room window and saw him standing on the other side of the street staring up at her. She had quickly backed away so he wouldn't know she had noticed him there. Half an hour later he was gone. After that she kept her curtains drawn after dark, but was worried that he could see in during the day, so she bought some opaque nylon fabric and went round to Anna's flat nearby to borrow her sewing machine.

Anna laughed when she told her she wanted to make some net curtains for her flat. 'Oh Lizzie, I'd never have believed it of you. Is your exhibitionist bohemianism now reduced to bourgeois decorum?'

'You always did use words that were too long!' responded Lizzie with a sour look. 'If you'd given me time to explain, you'd know I'm only doing this out of dire necessity.'

'Surely even you can't be that hard up. I mean, I know

actors are always "resting", but to put up nets instead of proper curtains – well, how are the mighty fallen!' Anna went on teasingly.

'Oh do shut up,' said Lizzie in exasperation. 'I'm being serious. I have a problem. With a voyeur. He lurks outside the house and keeps staring in through my windows. If I'm not going to live in semi-darkness behind drawn curtains, then I need something so that I can see out but he can't see in.'

'Oh how horrid,' said Anna in a contrite voice, 'I'm so sorry. How awful for you. Tell me what's been going on.'

So Lizzie told her about it all, and the mere fact of sharing her uneasiness was enough to make it feel less threatening and more bearable. Anna listened carefully and then advised her friend to go to the police if the watcher became more persistent.

'You must also tell me if you spot him prowling around again,' she insisted. 'I'll come round and stare back at the creep in my menacingly intimidating way. If I'm out, my flatmates will be only too happy to come round instead if you want some moral support. Just ring us and we'll be there.'

'It's just very unnerving,' Lizzie told her. 'Thankfully, he keeps his distance at the moment. I don't think he's going to approach me or attack me, but I can't be sure. I do wish Steve hadn't gone abroad – his presence might have put the bloke off.'

Anna patted her arm. 'Don't worry, kid. The nasty man'll probably get fed up soon, disappear from your area, and go and bother someone else instead.'

For a few days there was no sign of the man. Then Lizzie saw him again in the street, twice. She was perturbed, but this time he didn't linger any more like a black shadow below her window.

She'd recently landed a small part in a comedy at the Lyric, and was pleased to have some regular work, first in the form of rehearsals held in a chilly hall near Holborn and then, when the play opened, at the theatre itself. Her part amounted to a mere ten minutes on stage, but with a two-month contract she settled down, hoping audience numbers would remain high enough to keep the play running longer.

During the third week of the run, she noticed a man standing twenty yards from the stage door when she left the theatre, and the next night she recognised him as the same person who had been loitering in her road. That he had followed her to work was seriously worrying. He was there again the next night, so she asked another member of the cast who took a taxi home to drop her at an underground station. As they drove off, she turned and managed to get a good look at him in the light from a streetlamp. He had a strangely round, smooth face and short cropped fair hair. He was not tall, but with his arms folded he appeared to be quite stocky and he had an air of slight menace about him. He always wore dark glasses and a denim jacket.

For a few nights he wasn't there, and then he reappeared. Lizzie became angry and asked one of the men who worked back-stage to tell him to clear off, but when asked to move along, the stalker just shook his head and remained outside the office building opposite. He did not seem threatening, but his presence made her feel insecure. After that, she arranged for a taxi to meet her at the stage door every night to take her home, but one evening he pulled up alongside her taxi in a battered Range Rover at traffic lights near her home, turned his head slowly and grimaced at her in an intimidating way.

On another occasion he was waiting in the street outside her flat in a car – a buff-coloured Ford Escort – when she arrived home. She explained the situation to the taxi driver, who walked with her to the front door and waited until she had closed and locked it. After that she always asked her taxi driver to wait until she had gone in before driving off, and they were always happy to oblige the pretty actress.

The stalker seemed to be harmless enough, but things took a new and nasty turn when he approached Lizzie and attempted to touch her arm. This happened when the play had closed after three months and Lizzie was without work. She had been to an afternoon audition and had been told she was too young for the part; she was returning home at around six o'clock, just as it was getting dark. She had taken the Tube and was walking back to her flat, carrying some food she'd just bought at the corner shop. There were a lot of people around so she was not on her guard, and did not see the man until he was a yard from her on the pavement outside her flat. She stopped dead and stared at him in horror – he had never got that close to her before. He made a sudden lunge towards her with an outstretched arm. She shrieked at him, pushing him away, then sprang up the steps to her door. Her plastic bag caught on the railings, ripping open and spilling its contents, which clattered onto the steps. Her heart was thudding and her hands shaking as she frantically tried to get her key into the door, expecting every second that he would rush over and bar her way. As the key finally meshed and turned, the door swung open under the pressure of her weight and she almost fell into the hall. Slamming it shut, she caught another brief glimpse of her stalker standing immobile at the bottom of the steps, his face impassive.

For a minute she leant against the closed door whilst the feeling of terror subsided. Her next emotion was anger. How dare he subject her to this? She ran up the stairs to her flat, let herself in, and charged across the sitting room to the window. He hadn't moved, and was still leaning jauntily against the rails with his hands in his pockets and looking up at her with an enigmatic smile. The carton of orange juice which had fallen out of her ripped bag had exploded on impact and she could see the sticky liquid trickling over one of the steps. She was about to open the window and shout at him when she thought better of it and instead strode decisively across the room to the telephone. Though Anna had advised her to do so some weeks back, she had delayed involving the police because she had hoped that perhaps he was just a snoop who posed no threat. She knew now that she had been wrong.

The police were polite and cautiously sympathetic, telling her to stay inside until they arrived. Two of them came round within the hour, by which time the stalker had disappeared. Lizzie was upset and talked wildly about the need to catch him, prosecute him and get an injunction served on him, forbidding him to harass her. The problem, the police quietly explained, was that they did not know who he was. They gave her some advice about personal protection and for a few weeks tried to monitor the situation, but they could do little else as the time they were able to give to this type of situation was limited. The stalker seemed to have realised that there was now an occasional police watch on the flat, as Lizzie did not see him for three weeks. She started to relax a bit, hoping that the fact that the police were involved had driven him away and that his interest in her had diminished. But she was too optimistic.

Still 'resting' from acting work, she managed to get a temporary job for a fortnight answering the telephone in a photographer's studio while his assistant was away on holiday. The photographer was easy-going and mildly chaotic. When he was in the studio, she was able to slip out for half an hour over lunch to a sandwich bar a couple of streets away.

During the second week when Lizzie was on her way back from the sandwich shop, she glimpsed the stalker leaning against the brick wall about fifty yards from the studio. Her heart sank and her pulse raced. She darted into the studio feeling distressed and unable to understand how he knew where she was working. She phoned Anna and told her what had happened. Anna had tried to calm her and reminded her that there had been no indication that he wanted to harm her, so she should just try to ignore him.

This advice was impossible to follow. Lizzie began to worry that he was shadowing her every movement and became convinced that he was out there even when she couldn't see him. Even though he now kept his distance and made no further attempt to approach or confront her, Lizzie knew he was there because he also started turning up in places she had gone to for the day or the weekend, and she would suddenly catch sight of him in the lane outside a house in which she was staying, or in the next train carriage. He followed her, he watched her, he frightened her.

Then the phone calls started. Her number was ex-directory and she didn't know how he had got hold of it. At first there were no words, just the feeling that someone was there when she picked up the receiver. She stopped answering with her habitual friendly greeting of 'Hello, Lizzie speaking' and took to saying a tentative hello and waiting for a response. If there was no reply she hung up. But she knew with absolute certainty that the silent caller was the same man who had been stalking her. Then one day for the first time he uttered, 'Hello Lizzie.' She realised that she had never heard him speak before and was disgusted by the tone of intimacy in his voice. She slammed the receiver down. But he did not give up, and rang at random times, often saying her name and laughing before disconnecting.

Occasionally he varied his assault on her privacy with such remarks as, 'It's me again. I'm not giving up, you know,' and if she lost control and shouted at him, he would say derisively, 'Getting a bit upset, are we?' She became really frightened when he seemed to know what she was doing – 'Off to bed now, are you? Sleep well' – or what she was wearing – 'I like you in that yellow dress.' His voice was soft but insistent and there was an underlying sneer and occasionally a hint of elation to it.

She went back to the police and told them that he was wrecking her life. The police tried to track the calls and lay traps for him, but this was difficult because he phoned from call boxes spread across a wide area, made his connection brief, and seemed able to evade all attempts to identify and apprehend him. She changed her phone number but, although she gave her new one only to a few chosen friends and her agent, somehow her tormentor managed to find it out. Lizzie started sleeping badly and was nervous when she went out. Good-looking and self-assured, she usually attracted men easily, but now her worried demeanour and air of insecurity kept them away. She lost her habitual *joie de vivre* and found she was unable to concentrate when auditions came up, so she didn't get chosen for a couple of small parts that she thought she might have got. As a struggling actress she needed the work and she found herself unable to prevent her career from slipping into free fall.

Over the months he had been bothering her, Lizzie had had many conversations with Anna about the stalker and how to avoid him or cope with his incessant intrusions into her life. From time to time, she went round to her friend's Fulham flat and sometimes Anna came round and slept at hers. Lizzie found Anna's practical common sense very calming and beneficial, as she badly needed to relax and unwind. Even though the stalker never appeared when Anna was around, Lizzie convinced her that he was a constant and real worry. Anna never doubted her word. However irrational her friend seemed, Anna always believed her and gave her her total support.

If she was going out, Lizzie would phone Anna and tell her where she was going, so that someone would know where she was, in case anything happened. Sometimes, the stalker would ring just as she was going out and say that he hoped she would enjoy the party or film or restaurant. His accuracy was uncanny. She had become so paranoid about his knowledge of her life that she felt he must somehow be able to overhear her conversations. If she was away for the weekend, she would let Anna know the address in a written note – she didn't dare give the details over the phone in case he was somehow listening.

She even abandoned her newly decorated flat and moved in secret to another part of London, where she rented a flat in a large mansion block. Somehow he found out where she was, and continued shadowing and taunting her. To make matters worse, at that time Anna had decided to leave town for a couple of months. She had gone down to a cottage in Wiltshire to get away from the distractions of London and try and write a series of commissioned articles. The cottage belonged to her brother, Gavin, who lent it out when he was working abroad, which was fairly often. Anna felt it was all right for her to go away because she was convinced by this time that Lizzie's stalker would do her no harm. The police were of a similar opinion, and thought that he was probably just trying to upset her. But for Lizzie, Anna's physical defection only increased her sense of insecurity. Anna had told her that the police would keep an eye on her and that, if she wanted, she could come down any time and stay with her at Gavin's cottage. All she had to do was phone and say 'I'm coming.'

One Friday afternoon in early summer, nearly a year after the stalker had started making her life miserable, Lizzie, exhausted by her constant vigilance and her strategies to avoid him, suddenly encountered him inside the building in which her new flat was situated. He was on the stairs, coming up as she was about to descend. She let out a horrified scream and fled back upstairs to her flat, with the sound of his mocking voice pursuing her. Luckily one of the other tenants in the block opened his door on her landing to see what the noise was about, and the stalker turned on his heel and quickly ran down the steps, letting himself out through the front door, but not before shouting that he would be back.

For Lizzie this was the final straw. How had he managed to gain entrance to the building? Even more frightening, did he have a key to her flat? She phoned the local police and reported what had happened, ending by telling them she was going away to the country as she was now too frightened to stay there. Frantic to leave without delay, she wouldn't even agree to wait until they came round but, throwing some clothes in a case, she phoned for a minicab and asked the driver to take her to Paddington Station. While she waited on the platform, nervously looking around to see if he was on her trail, she called Anna to tell her she was coming and ask her to meet the train at Great Bedwyn station. Anna's familiar voice had the instant effect of steadying Lizzie, and she climbed onto the train with a huge sense of relief that soon she would be safe.

The train was fairly full and Lizzie felt reassured to be amongst a crowd. Even so, she had an irrational feeling that he was probably there – just out of her vision. After about an hour and a half the train stopped at Great Bedwyn and, as she got off, she was relieved to note that he was not among the other passengers alighting. Then she saw Anna waiting for her by the barrier.

Anna silently put her arms round her friend, kissed her on the cheek and, taking the small bag from her with one hand, she guided her down the platform towards the exit gate. In a mood of nervous euphoria, Lizzie thanked Anna three times for coming to meet her and for being such a support, and began to chatter about a number of trivial incidents that had occurred during the train journey. She registered that Anna was in one of her quiet moods, but knowing her friend well and confident in their regard for each other, this did not bother her. She talked on while her companion drove Gavin's rusty old car with more care and less reckless speed than was usual. Lizzie was distantly aware of this uncharacteristic restraint being a mark of consideration and affection.

After about twenty minutes, they turned off down a track and parked outside a small red-brick cottage with a sagging fence and an overgrown path to the porch. As Anna switched off the engine, Lizzie finally stopped talking, and they got out of the car

'I love the summer,' Anna said softly, looking around her at the velvet green shadows under the trees and the blue patches of sky which quivered in the spaces between the leaves. Lizzie took a deep breath and she too became aware of the calmness and beauty of the unspoilt scenery to which she had been transported. Anna had just said that it was summer but it was only now that Lizzie registered this fact in its completeness. As they stood there in the small unkempt garden, Lizzie found that she was no longer anxious to scuttle inside, and was content to linger in the fresh air and enjoy the feeling of safety to which both the country and Anna's presence contributed. Now she could hear some distant birdsong and there was the rustle of a light wind in the trees and bushes. She could also detect the faint noise of some farm machinery further off and a small buzz from an insect close by. It was as if her senses had suddenly come alive with the shedding of her fear.

'Do you know, Anna,' she said, 'until now I had even forgotten what season it was. I've been so eaten up with this awful problem that . . .'

'You've "had no time to stand and stare",' Anna finished for her with a smile. 'The trouble with living in London is that the passing of the seasons is less obvious than here and it's possible to remain unaware of their progression. It's only the weather and the temperature that we register. When I came down to Wiltshire I found the change from the city both invigorating and calming. Here in the countryside the changing seasons are always conspicuously flamboyant – as plain as the nose on your face.' She paused with a laugh. 'Well, as plain as the nose on *my* face – no one could ever call *you* plain, Lizzie! Although right now you do look a bit pale and pinched.'

'I look haggard, I'm sure. I've been hibernating in my nightmare. I need some air and sun.'

'You certainly do need some sunshine in your life. And a break from all the worry that's been eating you up. You need to relax and unwind. We're both in the summer of our lives and we should be blooming! A spell of rural life will do you the world of good. I think you should borrow my Andrew Marvell whilst you're here. One of his best poems is called "The Garden", and in it he describes the luscious scene around him, and then goes into the mind, which "Withdraws into its happiness.../ Annihilating all that's made / To a green thought in a green shade". The poem always makes me feel cool and untroubled. Come on, let's go in and I'll show you the simple delights of my rustic paradise.'

Lizzie followed her up the path to the door, reflecting that Anna often became disenchanted with the noise and pace of London and needed to get away into a less populated and rural environment, whereas she, herself, loved living in the metropolis with the occasional foray into the country by way of weekend contrast. Anna had been staying in the cottage for about a month, and Lizzie saw that inside it was small but adequate and comfortable in a slightly sparse, masculine way. It was also very untidy.

'It's not very luxurious, and I don't keep it too pristine,' said Anna on entering, frowning at the sight of the mess. 'I just don't seem to see disorder around me, but luckily it doesn't affect my work – I still manage to create order out of chaos!'

Lizzie laughed and bent down to pick up a cushion from the floor. All was well. She was with Anna, strong, loving Anna. 'How long has Gavin owned the place?' she asked, looking round the open-plan ground floor, with a small kitchen opening off it to the rear.

'I think he bought it a couple of years back. He rents somewhere in London and is often abroad with his job. He wanted to have a toehold in the property market, but could only afford a modest cottage here in Wiltshire. It's not ravishingly pretty, but it's quiet and secluded and I rather like it. Though he doesn't come here often, thankfully he refuses to rent it out because he likes it to be available.'

'Good of Gavin to lend it to you. How is he, by the way?' Lizzie blushed a little as she asked this.

'He's fine, as far as I know. He's a bit of a rolling stone – rather like me. I think he may have a girlfriend in Budapest, where he's working now. What about you, Lizzie? Any man in your life at the moment?'

Lizzie shook her head. 'No one since Steve left. I've been rather unsettled on account of this bloody stalker. But from time to time I go out with a couple of friends who work in the theatre. What about you?'

Anna looked a bit rueful. 'I seem to attract men younger than me – though I must admit I find their innocence and raw enthusiasm quite appealing – youth unpolluted by cynicism! Recently I've been seeing a colleague of Gavin's – Martin – he's nice enough – a bit reticent and not too stiflingly attentive. In fact, I ought to warn you that he's probably going to drive down from London later this evening.' Lizzie looked up and Anna responded to the unasked question firmly: 'No, I'm not having an affair with him – and because there are only two bedrooms, you and I will have to share one of them, and let him have the other. I'm afraid I can't put him off now, but he won't be here for a couple of hours, so let's get something to eat.' Lizzie was unable to conceal her slight disappointment that her cosy evening with Anna would be interrupted.

After a simple meal of soup, salad and bread, they sat round a small wood-burning stove, alight to heat the hot water, and Anna had decided to open the front, so it radiated an atmosphere of comfort. Lizzie was sitting in a lopsided old armchair with a shawl over her, and Anna was sprawling on a battered chintz sofa. They shared a bottle of red wine, whilst talking together in their usual uninhibited open way, Anna expertly mimicking some of her neighbours in an effort to make Lizzie laugh and cheer up.

'I'm sure they can't really be like that, Anna! How do you get on with them?' Lizzie asked.

'Quite well really, because I can be whoever they want me

to be – a mysterious solitary female, an absent-minded writer if that's the impression I want another person to have, even a country bumpkin, if I try!'

Lizzie laughed and said, 'We both of us act, it seems – me on stage and you off it. I like acting, but only when I'm working. You do it all the time – how tiring that must be!'

Anna replied, 'Yes it can be – it can get confusing, and sometimes I don't really know who I am.' She tapped her heart with one hand and shrugged her shoulders. 'But my loss of identity doesn't seem to put me off my work. I scribble away most of the day, with just the occasional break when I wander outside and pull up a few weeds.'

Lizzie then said wistfully, 'I can't seem to find any acting work at the moment – I'm too tense, I suppose. There seems to be more drama in your life than mine.'

'Not really. Anyway, what are you on about? Dashing down here to escape from your nasty stalker – now *that* is dramatic.' Anna watched her friend's face break into a smile and realised that if Lizzie could take a joke about it, it must mean she was feeling safer.

Anna wisely changed the subject to say that that she might, one day, become interested in gardening – if ever she had time. They also moved on to a bottle of white wine that had come out of Gavin's modest store cupboard.

'Here's to Gavin,' Anna said, raising her glass, and Lizzie did the same. After they had taken a few sips, Anna said reflectively, 'Remember how mad about you he was when we were all at school?'

'Mmm, I do,' Lizzie remembered very well. Since he was three years younger than her, the boy had been beneath her interest but she had been well aware of his adoration for her. Awkward and embarrassed, he used to hang about in the hall, waiting to catch a word with her. She had laughed at his inane comments and was cruel enough to tease him about his obsession with her. 'I feel rather ashamed about how I treated him,' she now confessed to Anna. 'I was horribly superior and selfish. Were you annoyed with me for teasing your little brother?'

'No. In fact I probably connived with you in making him feel excluded and rejected. We were both unkind and unsympathetic towards him.' Anna looked across at her friend. 'You were rather pretty and flirty, after all, and I think he was fascinated by you.'

'I know now Gavin was in love with me.' Lizzie said in a serious tone. 'I feel ashamed for laughing at him for what we thought was just an embarrassing teenage infatuation. After that he avoided me for a while because he couldn't hide how he felt. And then I went and seduced him at my twenty-first. He wasn't even eighteen and was a virgin – I'm still amazed that you weren't angry with me. You even said you were pleased he'd had his first sexual experience with someone you knew would be kind to him. And you were right, you know – I was kind to him, then and afterwards.'

'Afterwards?' Anna had always thought that the escapade at her party had been a one-off.

'I never told you – I suppose I felt bad about it. While Gavin was still doing his A levels, I used to see him when we went down to your parents for occasional weekends. We'd jump into bed when we got the chance. It was all a bit frenetic and immature, but he got better at it and was rather sexy at times. The trouble was that when he went to college the following autumn, he still wanted to continue seeing me. I was gadding about at drama school and had had a couple of affairs under my belt by that time and I wasn't into commitment. For me it was nothing more than a fling, but I think for him it was a bit more serious. He used to write and telephone me quite a lot, even after I'd started seeing someone else. I tried to let him down gently but I think he had a bit of a hard time over it. He may have suffered but I'm certain he wasn't left with a permanent scar over what happened. He did write a few heart-rending letters when I finally broke it off for good during his first term at Leeds, but I thought that was for the best – he needed to gallop into college life feeling free.' Lizzie put her empty glass on the table.

Anna was surprised that the normally restrained Lizzie should talk so freely about her up-until-now secret affair with Gavin, which she had evidently felt too embarrassed and guilty about to reveal at the time. But they had drunk quite a bit of wine and she was no doubt by now feeling sleepy and secure, and all of this had probably loosened her tongue.

As if echoing Anna's thoughts, Lizzie said, 'I can't tell you how relieved I am to be here, Anna, after everything that's happened recently – not getting the acting jobs I've gone for and feeling so stressed about that beastly stalker. I know I'll sleep better here than I would in London, too. I felt so vulnerable there.'

'Well, you're quite safe here. How about finishing off the wine we filched from my brother?' Anna waved her empty glass at the bottle.

Lizzie leant across to pick it up but in doing so, knocked her own glass off the table; it crashed to the wooden floor and broke. 'I'm so sorry – how clumsy of me.' Lizzie remained seated with a look of dismay on her pallid features, but Anna was already bending down and picking up the pieces of glass.

'Don't worry,' she murmured soothingly. 'Cheap glass – easy to replace. I'll just get a cloth to mop up the wine.' She walked into the kitchen and Lizzie heard a muffled crash as she threw the broken glass into a bin. At the same moment, she heard a knock on the front door.

'I'm just washing my hands, Lizzie. That'll be Martin,' Anna called from the kitchen. 'Can you let him in?'

Lizzie stood up and went to the door, walking somewhat unsteadily due to extreme fatigue and the amount of wine she had consumed. As she opened the door and the night air flowed in, she felt faint and then overwhelmed with alarm. In front of her stood the embodiment of her worst nightmare. As she recognised the stalker and registered that by some uncanny means he had managed to find out her whereabouts, she was flooded with panic and fear. She reeled back, crying out Anna's name in a choking voice. Her knees crumpled and she blacked out before she had time to see the startled look of surprise on the man's face, an expression which echoed her own shock and bewilderment.

Lizzie is suddenly jerked back to the present by Paul saying, 'Well, here we are,' as he pulls the large car up at the ferry terminal area and stops the engine. She emits a slight gasp as awareness of her present surroundings supplants the image of that grotesque night.

'You all right, my dear?' he asks looking at her. 'You've been very quiet for a long while, and you're a bit pale.'

The sunlight is glancing through the wide windscreen and Lizzie blinks to try and dispel the memory of that dark encounter so many years ago.

'I've been thinking about Anna, and how she helped me in that dreadful period when I had to cope with a stalker.'

'I remember you telling me about that incident,' says Paul. 'It must have been awful for you.'

'It wasn't just one incident. It went on for over a year, and it really made me very distraught and neurotic.'

'When was it again?'

Lizzie screws up her face in an effort to remember. 'I suppose it happened about a year or two before I met Alan. I sometimes think that was one of the reasons I married him so quickly – I needed a safe haven and I thought a husband would provide it. Big mistake. He only increased my feelings of insecurity. It was Anna who calmed me down and helped me overcome my fear of that horrible man. In fact she finally got rid of him. I mean the stalker, of course, not Alan. Though, come to think of it,' Lizzie continues thoughtfully, 'she was also instrumental in the disintegration of my first marriage. In an indirect sort of way. But she did drive the stalker off in a very forceful way.' She stops, realising that Paul is not listening because he is looking in his briefcase for the travel documents.

They are waiting in a queue of cars to check in for the ferry. Paul locates the passports and ticket and places them on the dashboard, ready for inspection. He is a practical man and is always well organised on their frequent trips abroad. But although they are well adjusted to each other's habits and share much in common, this does not always include what each other is thinking. What Lizzie has decided not to tell Paul on this occasion is the bizarre end of the stalker nightmare. She, however, remembers it vividly.

When Lizzie regained consciousness, she was lying on the cottage's living-room floor. Anna was kneeling beside her saying, 'It's all right. It's all OK. It's only Martin.'

Lizzie reached up and clutched in terror at Anna's shoulder. 'But it's him. I know him.' She was whispering in her agitation and fear. 'I recognise him – it's the stalker.' Until now,

Anna had thought that Lizzie's overtired and distracted brain had somehow mistaken Martin for her persecutor. But now, knowing Lizzie almost as well as she knew herself, a germ of doubt entered her head. She raised her head slowly and there was a look of puzzled interrogation on her face as her eyes met with those of the young man standing silently on the other side of the room out of Lizzie's line of vision. His face had a look of trapped guilt, and the awful truth dawned on her that Lizzie wasn't mistaken – he was indeed the stalker.

She looked down at Lizzie, who was now trying to sit up. Putting a calming hand on her shoulder, she said quietly, 'Don't move, Lizzie. Don't be frightened. I will deal with this.' And with that she stood up.

Looking wildly round, Lizzie caught sight once again of the man who had caused her such anguish over the past year and who was now in the same room as her. Whimpering in fear and unable to stand up, she crawled wretchedly on her hands and knees away from the familiar hateful figure, collapsing behind the sofa, where she lay in sick terror.

'You unbelievable shit. How could you do this to my best friend? How could you use me to help you to terrify the person I love most in the world – someone closer to me than a sister?' Anna yelled.

The soft voice Lizzie recognised from so many telephone calls replied: 'I'd never have come tonight if I'd known she was going to be down here. You weren't meant to know about this. I just wanted to get some revenge on her for what she did to my best friend Gavin – your brother. She fucked up his life and she deserves to suffer for it.'

'Don't even attempt to make excuses.' Anna spat out these words. 'Nothing can possibly excuse what you've done to her – the acute distress you've caused her. Get out. Now.' She shouted these last three words and Lizzie heard some heavy, rapid footsteps cross the room, and then the sound of the front door opening.

'Don't ever, ever come back – I never want to see you again,' Anna was screaming in incandescent rage. 'And don't you ever, ever stalk Lizzie again. Tomorrow I'm going to tell the police who you are, so you'd better disappear. If they find you, they'll arrest you and you'll end up in prison. You'd probably better leave the country, in fact, because when I tell Gavin what you've done, he might just try to just kill you, too. If I don't first.'

'Bloody hell, woman, stop screeching like a banshee. I'm going. And don't worry – I won't come near either of you again. I'm sick of you both anyway. And I'm not sorry for what I've done to your actressy friend. I quite enjoyed the months I've spent making her shit scared.'

'Get out!' A rebounding crash followed this shriek, and then the door was slammed so savagely that the room shook. In the stunned silence that followed, Lizzie shakily sat up and peered over the top of the sofa, not knowing what to expect. What she saw was Anna standing in the middle of the room, breathing heavily. Scattered across the tiled floor were jagged pieces of the heavy glass bowl which had contained the salad they had eaten. Evidently Anna had hurled it at Martin as he backed out of the door. Then the two women heard a car door slamming and an engine starting. They looked at each other as the sound of the car receded and the electric atmosphere of the violent exchange gradually dissipated. Lizzie looked at the door and the shattered shards of the bowl. 'I'm sorry you missed him,' she whispered.

'So am I. He deserved to have his head smashed in and he certainly needs to have it examined – he must be mad.' Anna had a savage expression on her face.

'There seems to be a lot of broken glass round here this

evening,' murmured Lizzie, with a nervous giggle. 'He won't come back, will he?'

'He'd bloody well better not,' said Anna grimly. Then her expression softened and she knelt down by Lizzie, giving her a hug. 'Don't worry. He wouldn't dare. He's not a violent man – merely a vile, nasty, sneaking bastard, as I've just discovered. He's a coward too, and he knows I'm going to the police about him. I am *so* sorry, Lizzie. Come and sit on the sofa and let's have a glass of wine – or perhaps a brandy, if Gavin's got any stashed away around here.'

When Lizzie was installed on the sofa rather than behind it, Anna swept up the broken pieces of glass and poured them both a tot of whisky, which was all she could find. Then she sat beside her friend and together they conducted a post-mortem. Anna felt bad because she realised that over the past months she must have unwittingly given Martin information that had enabled him to stalk and frighten her closest and dearest friend. Lizzie had been shocked by the unexpected appearance of the man who had tormented her so deeply and haunted her for so long. But she was also relieved that the unknown stalker had now been identified and that, as a result, the nightmare might at last have come to an end.

'I can't believe that I ever liked him,' said Anna 'I thought he quite liked me too. But perhaps all along he was just using me to get at you. I don't know why he seems to think that you messed up Gavin's life. Clearly my brother has told him about his teenage infatuation with you, and for some reason Martin thinks he's been permanently damaged by it. I know Gavin was potty about you for a while but I never felt he was really injured by the experience. Perhaps I'm wrong. What do you think, Lizzie?'

'I wasn't aware that I'd caused him any real pain until about five years later when we met up in London at one of my first-night parties,' Lizzie answered slowly. 'He told me then that he'd never stopped loving me, and that I'd hurt him very much when I dumped him. He was a bit drunk at the time, so I took it all with a pinch of salt. Since then he's never mentioned it again, and I assumed it was all OK. He seems a pretty successful chap and I've never picked up any signs of him blaming me for destroying his peace of mind. But maybe when Gavin told your nasty friend about the affair, he over-exaggerated his suffering and feeling of injury.'

'Let me make it quite clear, Lizzie,' Anna said indignantly, 'Martin is no longer a friend of mine. I completely agree with you that he's a nasty piece of work, and I feel mortified that I was taken in. I must be losing my judgement, and *that* is worrying!' She smiled to soften this last remark, and looked across at Lizzie who, though pale and weary, had a delicate beauty which attracted men. 'Perhaps while trying to frighten you on Gavin's account, Martin became obsessed with you too. I think that's quite possible.'

Lizzie sighed.

'Sad that our lovely lazy holiday is over?' Paul leans across to his wife and kisses her affectionately just below her ear. Lizzie realises that her sigh was in the audible present and not in the silent past. She nods and gives him a grateful smile – not for his understanding, but for his love.

The car is now in a queue waiting to board the ferry. Paul is looking forward to an excellent meal in the ship's restaurant later on before they dock in Portsmouth. They might even have a sleep during the afternoon and, who knows, if Lizzie feels like it, they might make love. Echoing his wife, he sighs, but for a different reason – in anticipation rather than in guilt.

Fifteen minutes later, they drive sedately onto the lower deck of the ferry, and the crew duly accord their respect and admiration for his handsome motor vehicle as they indicate where he should park it. The couple climb out of the Bentley armed with a day bag containing a few things they might need for the crossing, lock their car carefully and ascend to the information desk to collect the keys to their deluxe cabin. Once they are settled in, they then go on deck for some fresh sea air and to watch the departure. There are some wisps of clouds now across the clear midday blue of the May sky, and a light breeze ruffles the dark green harbour water.

Lizzie gazes upwards to the noisy swirling seagulls and takes a deep breath. She feels it is destined that a sea voyage should be taking her back to England and to where Anna is. She feels that it is some appropriate reversal of the many times Anna used to return by boat from the Continent, and come to stay with her and Alan on her arrival in London by train from the coast.

The friends used to sit up late on those evenings and regale each other with what they had done and seen, and how they felt about the people they had met along the way. Alan, feeling slightly superfluous and irritated, used to watch them eagerly swapping news and views much as couples do after they have been apart. He usually left them to it and went to bed, knowing that later on he would make Lizzie suffer for her lack of consideration and attention to him, her husband. Lizzie was well aware of Alan's and Anna's mutual dislike. Alan felt that Anna was demonstrating her power to deflect his wife's attention away from him. This made him feel hot and jealous and also savagely keen to break up their friendship, which he viewed as almost unnaturally obsessive. Lizzie remembers the rows that she and Alan had over Anna. It was a major cause of the eventual breakdown of their marriage.

## Chapter Six

Anna does not like tape recorders but cannot think of a good reason why she might object to the use of one now, except that she feels if she makes an error or an ill-judged remark she will not have the opportunity of retracting it. Her interviewer is a young journalist who works on the book review section of the magazine. Her name is Miranda, and she has already admitted with an apologetic smile that she has not read all of Anna's lengthy work, but has 'looked through it'. This means, as Anna knows, that she has given the pre-publication review copy barely half an hour of her attention this morning in hurried preparation for her interview with its author. The questions will not be very demanding, and Anna knows she will be expected to set the pace and support the interviewer by guiding her to the salient points. She is not sure whether she can be bothered.

The tape recorder is switched on. Miranda makes a few introductory remarks and then asks the obvious question about why the themes of Choice and Fate were chosen in this study of Shakespeare's tragedies. Anna repeats what she has said so many times to various prospective publishers. The younger woman then asks the new author to say what the basic message of the book is.

'If I could sum it up in a couple of sentences, I wouldn't have taken the trouble to research and write a long book on the subject,' Anna responds rather crisply. A look of reproachful embarrassment crosses the interviewer's face, and Anna relents and tries to encapsulate the ideas and theories she has put forward in her work. This takes a few minutes and her interviewer does not interrupt. Indeed, she listens, having composed an earnest look of keen interest on her pretty features. She then focuses on *Macbeth*, which is maybe the chapter she has glanced through, and which, Anna guesses, is probably the play that Miranda had done for A level at school. Does the author think that Macbeth is in control of his own destiny? Do the witches undermine his ability to make decisions? Anna answers these questions with the brevity they deserve. There follows a brief and superficial discussion on the protagonist's surrender to fate at the end of the play.

After a few more isolated comments, Anna is asked why she lives in France, and she responds with some reluctance, since this question seems to have little reference to the subject of the book. She is then asked about the popularity of Shakespeare in France, whereupon she replies briefly that Shakespeare has been dead for nearly four hundred years; and that his plays are universally acclaimed but not always popular. When asked how long she has worked on her book, Anna is vague because she does not wish anyone to know how long it has been festering unpublished. Miranda has by this time decided that she will not manage to get any personal angle and suspects that the author is unlikely to answer simple questions about which plays she likes best or least, so she brings the interview to an end. It has not been wholly satisfactory for either of them. When

116

the tape machine has been switched off, Miranda thanks Anna politely and warmly for her time, and says she will be including the interview in next month's issue together with a review of the book. Anna resigns herself to a short piece, which will do nothing for the sales of the book. She mentally shrugs as she has already admitted to herself that she knows the book's sales and monetary return will be modest. At least it can now be cast adrift to make its own way, and she can move on.

By 3 p.m. Anna has already made her exit and Act IV is about to begin. Her day is unfolding like a series of scenes in all of which she appears, but remains uninvolved before passing on to the next one. There is a kind of detachment from the other characters. It is almost like a dream in which she cannot change the outcome of each confrontation but has to be present as a witness, watching but ineffectual. All morning she has felt that if she were to stretch out her hand to someone, it would not really touch the other person. She thinks, perhaps, it is her own self-absorption that is repelling any genuine communication or sympathetic human interaction.

The business meetings have now concluded, and she feels strangely light-headed. She is still tired with the habitual physical weariness which has affected her for many months, but her mind is alert. She must make the most of it. Next on her busy agenda, she is going to see a doctor. She has seen him before but not for over a year, as she generally uses the excellent French health service. She has already sought and received advice from French specialists on her condition, but has decided to consult a doctor privately in England for a second opinion. The appointment has been arranged for 4 p.m., so she decides to have a cup of tea before she takes a taxi to Devonshire Place, where the doctor has his consulting rooms.

She goes into one of the ubiquitous coffee shops, earns a

look of contempt when ordering Indian rather than herbal tea, and sits quietly on a stool at the rear of the cramped customer area. She has never been the type of woman to locate a comfortable hotel, install herself in the lounge and order proper tea with all the trimmings. It would be more relaxing, she thinks, but it just isn't her scene. She has always been in too much of a hurry, and today seems to be no exception. This is merely a brief intermission, and she forces herself to relax. Staring into the brown tea, which is too hot to drink yet, she once again sets her mind free to roam.

The young woman on the next stool is reading *Hello* magazine and Anna notices that there is a picture of some celebrity's wedding on the front cover. The association conjures up in sharp detail a picture of Lizzie's first marriage.

Alan was an actor, and though heart-breakingly good looking, he was conceited and self-centred. Anna had never been able to understand what Lizzie found in him that endeared him to her, but clearly there was a huge attraction on her part. This adoration fed the vanity of the love object himself, and Anna had found no difficulty in identifying why Alan was attracted to Lizzie – she was intelligent, amusing, full of loving kindness and beautiful as well. His taste and discernment in selecting her as his wife would be applauded. She would be a useful adjunct to his life and career. He could do no better. Anna did not like Alan but she was not jealous of him, as being with him had not caused Lizzie to neglect her or see her less. Far from it, she actively sought out her closest female friend and wanted her approval of Alan. Unfortunately, on that score, Anna could not oblige – she found him shallow and selfish.

On the morning of the wedding, Anna – who was to be an

unofficial bridesmaid – was helping Lizzie dress. The latter had the usual 'big day' nervousness but not for the usual reasons; she was not worried about her appearance or that she might stumble over her words. Even if she had not been beautiful and word perfect she could have acted her way through. Lizzie was actually questioning whether she was doing the right thing in marrying Alan.

'Does he love me enough?' (No, thought Anna. He only loves himself. But she kept quiet.)

'Has love blinded me to his real character?' (Yes, Anna had to prevent herself from shouting out. He's a bastard and you don't know it. Yet.)

'Do you think we'll be happy?' (No, categorically not, Anna smiled as she reassured Lizzie by saying Yes – which is what the bride wanted to hear.)

'Should I call the whole thing off?' (Yes, Anna wanted to say. Call it off! But she knew that Lizzie would not have the courage to do that – it would be a ghastly nightmare to cancel the whole circus at the last minute.)

Anna recalls that on that morning both of them knew very well that marriage to Alan would be no bed of roses. But Lizzie did not intend to back out, and her questions were just an expression of her private unease. Even if she blurted out the truth, Anna knew it would not stop the inevitable, nor would Lizzie really want to hear it. It was a game of bluffs and lies – quite the opposite of their usual openness with each other.

Finally the bride, when she was ready to go downstairs and set off for the church with her father, turned to her best friend and said in a low voice, 'Am I doing the right thing?'

Anna's patience snapped, and she said in exasperation, 'What do you want me to say? Tell you what you know already? Lizzie, you don't want to face up to reality. I've had enough.

119

I'm not going to stay to witness what we both know is a huge mistake.' She walked to the door.

Lizzie wailed, 'Don't leave. Please. Anna, I need you here. Today. You're my rock.' She gave a mock desperate smile in the manner of a tragedienne, and they both dissolved into emotional giggles.

Looking back, Anna realises that she was flattered, secretly pleased. She agreed to stay though she was at the same time irritated with Lizzie for subduing her better judgement. In fact the wedding was lovely, and she enjoyed every minute of it. For once, Alan was very cordial and charming to her. And she had to admit that both of them had been wrong – Alan did love and treasure Lizzie, almost as much as he loved and cherished himself, and the marriage was initially a happy one. It lasted much longer than anyone expected, and when it fell apart, it was not only Alan's fault but Lizzie's too. And, Anna accepts, hers as well.

Anna had spent most of her twenties wandering around Europe living on a shoestring, getting occasional work writing articles, teaching English or working as a waitress. Before her marriage, Lizzie had been doing small parts in the theatre and had made a few commercials. Anna had occasionally tried to entice her to go roaming with her for a few months, but Lizzie had always said: 'I need to stay here to get my career established,' or 'I'm not going to rush off abroad until I can do it in style.' The impoverished journalist and the struggling actress remained good friends even when Anna returned to London and managed to get involved in a trendy new arts magazine as its theatre reviewer. This could have caused friction because Anna, who was a passionate theatre-goer and had a degree in literature, felt slightly superior to Lizzie in taste and discernment. Lizzie knew that her friend regarded the type of plays in which she performed as slightly lowbrow, and she was therefore defensive when discussing them. It was true, however – Anna did regard them as inferior, and she therefore took care not to review anything in which Lizzie had been lucky enough to land a part, even though she might appreciate Lizzie's competent ability in a modest role.

When Anna lost her job with the magazine, having had a row with the managing editor over the merits of truth versus flattery, she turned to supply teaching in various secondary schools in south London. By then in her early thirties, Anna was living in a dilapidated house in Stockwell with a gay man who also shared her love of theatre. She was as argumentative and contentious as ever, but now her wrath was directed against the powers that devised school curricula and in particular against those who expunged Shakespeare from English courses, so that students were never given the chance to study the greatest of all dramatists. She became very disillusioned, too, with the lack of discipline in some of the schools where she was allocated some of the worst classes. She had always nurtured the illusion that she had the ability to be an inspirational teacher who could arouse enthusiasm and dispense enlightenment. The harsh reality was that she had not taken into account the aggression and apathy she often had to face in class, and had less tolerance than was required for the social problems that had led to this hostile atmosphere. There were times when she felt it was impossible to teach the pupils anything at all. She battled on but gradually grew despondent. She worried that she did not have the strength and dedication she saw in some of the more pragmatic teachers. She stuck it out for a few months before, thoroughly exhausted and disenchanted, she gave it up. She consoled herself that she had been rewarded with new insights into the minds of children.

Lizzie, newly married, was living with Alan in a rented flat on the third floor of a house on Baker Street. He was landing small roles in films, whilst she was working for a production company with a contract to make brochures in Europe for a UK-based travel and tour operator. This meant that she was the one now doing the travelling while Anna was stuck in the quagmire of her short-lived career in secondary education. On location, she tried to copy Anna's habit of smoking exotic but evil-smelling French cigarettes, but soon gave them up as they made her feel unwell. The two young women still met up from time to time when work allowed them some space in their busy schedules, and now it was Lizzie's turn to dispense comfort, offering the bruised Anna some much-needed support, teasing and encouragement. Both had always been keenly aware of each other's situation and they had evolved into a mutual balancing act, so that the one who was up would lovingly try and bring the other up to her level. They were able to joke about whose turn it was to take on the morale supporting role whenever they met up.

Before their marriage, both Lizzie and Alan had made their living by acting on the stage, but afterwards, Lizzie had started doing commercials and Alan made the move into films. This meant that now he was away more often than her, but this did not bother Lizzie too much as she had discovered the delights of home-making. When they found they could no longer tolerate the run-down and noisy Baker Street flat, the couple had rented a cramped rented Pimlico maisonette, where Lizzie had created a love nest. When finances improved, they moved again just before the birth of their first child to a small but pretty terraced house in Hampstead, which gave Lizzie more scope to indulge in her love of renovation and redecoration. During the six years of this, her first marriage, Lizzie had two children and

Alan unexpectedly evolved into a good father. In fact, he became so besotted with the children that he neglected his wife. Or it may have been because he was having an affair with his co-star in a film he had shot in Italy. Lizzie was taking a break from her acting career to embrace motherhood, and Alan's talent as a perfect parent blinded her to his lapses as a husband.

Anna, fed up with supply teaching and with recurrent itchy feet, took herself off to Paris for a few months. Lizzie was very preoccupied with her baby daughter, Katrina, and, with the inwardness of new mothers, had little time for anything outside the warm confines of her home, her baby and her new role. Anna had thought that she might be happy to play the part of supportive aunt to a small child, but she was aware of having a slight feeling of jealousy towards Lizzie, who seemed to have everything sewn up, whilst her own life seemed to be full of loose and fraying ends. She felt tainted by this envy and despised herself for it. When Lizzie became pregnant again, Anna found herself a job for six months in Prague teaching English, and this was followed by a couple of months back in Paris tutoring the spoilt child of an affluent American couple.

She returned to London briefly to buy some books and see some friends – in particular Lizzie, who had recently given birth to her second child, a boy. When she phoned to announce her arrival and beg a bed for a couple of nights and an intro-duction to her new 'nephew', Lizzie had been delighted to hear from her and said that her son, who was named Ralph, was to be baptised that week, and would she come to the cere-mony in their local Catholic church? Deeply suspicious of Lizzie's recent conversion to Catholicism, Anna was uncom-fortable during the ceremony, and felt very much on the periphery at the family party afterwards. She did not know any of the godparents and friends, and only barely knew Alan's parents and other relatives, whom she had met only once before, at the wedding. But she was happy to see her own father, who had come up to London for the christening, and who was still very fond of Lizzie. She had continued to keep in touch with him, and Anna had to admit that now their bond was closer than her own to him, since she had almost severed it by her selfish behaviour after her mother's sudden death.

She had rarely gone home after the loss of her mother, because she could not bear to be there, wandering aimlessly in the empty desert of her mother's absence and witnessing her father's pain. She knew that Gavin had been very supportive and felt guilty for escaping and leaving the two of them to work out their grief without her. Like a wounded animal she had preferred to slink away and find her own way of coping with the death of her favourite parent. Gradually, not visiting home became a habit.

But at the christening her father, with no hint of any resentment at her neglect of him, had clearly been delighted to see her, and they had enjoyed a precious hour chatting together.

Later on that day, after the guests had gone and Ralph was asleep in his cot, Alan had taken Katrina out for a walk to calm down the over-excited child who was also jealous of the attention paid to her tiny brother by all the guests. The two women were together on a sofa in the sitting room, Lizzie leaning back with her eyes closed, happy that the day had gone well, and feeling relaxed with her oldest friend beside her.

Anna was feeling moody and resentful and, though she knew this was entirely unreasonable, she was unable to snap out of it. Was it jealousy? Surely she did not hanker after conventional marital bliss or the more prevalent marital disharmony? She didn't want to have her own children – they would chain up her emotions and restrict her choices. Why, then, did she feel restless and alienated? It was, she realised, partly because the freedom from commitment she had once advocated now seemed a little hollow and she needed to reassure herself that she was not on the wrong path. She looked at her friend's contented face. Was there a hint of smugness there? Why did she sense that Lizzie disapproved of her?

Anna broke the silence by asking, 'Why did you never ask me to be godmother to either of your children?' She could not quite conceal the note of grievance.

Lizzie opened her eyes and regarded her prickly friend with her usual warm smile. 'Because you are *my* self-appointed godmother already, and that would have made you 'godgranny' to Ralph – a role for which you are too young. Anyhow, you don't believe in God.'

'I came to your father's funeral in the chapel at that ghastly crematorium,' Anna protested. Lizzie's father had died a couple of years earlier, a lonely widower bored by his retirement taken early due to ill health, and resentful of the necessity of living in England after his years in the East. He missed his luxurious expatriate lifestyle and refused to become reconciled to a lesser existence in the UK. After his wife's death he had become increasingly embittered and solitary, and had taken little interest in his daughter's marriage and his first grandchild.

'Going to weddings or funerals does not require a belief in the Deity any more than going to church at Christmas and Easter qualifies you as a Christian,' said Lizzie. 'Take your father – he never goes to church, but I think of him always as having a devout and firm belief in God.'

'That's because he needs comfort and hope, and has since Mum died. When they were together, neither of them was particularly interested in religion, as I recollect.'

'Religion is not the same thing as God. There are many

paths – or religions, if you like. I suspect that your parents have always had a relationship with God, though it may not have involved going to church.'

'I'm surprised Mum's death didn't dent his faith rather than increase it. He didn't deserve to lose her so soon. None of us did.'

'Perhaps your father was angry with God for allowing your mother to die, and then turned to God's word to try and find a reason. There perhaps he found guidance and the strength to carry on. He has certainly found a new lease of life. It was so good to see him here today, and I'm only sorry he didn't stay on.'

'He wanted to catch the train back home – he doesn't care for London. Gavin's the same. They're both country boys at heart. But I was very pleased to see Dad.' Anna didn't add that she felt guilty that she rarely visited him, but they both knew it.

Anna's father still lived in Somerset and he had become very involved in village affairs, having decided not to become the eternally grieving widower but to fill his retirement days with activities which he had never had time for before. He had become active in the local Gardeners' Club, to his daughter's amazement, since it had been her mother who had always done the gardening; he was also involved in various charitable projects, and had joined the Parish Council. Anna admired him and was relieved that he was not sad and solitary. She was aware that Lizzie kept in touch by letter and occasionally by telephone. Though he never said so, Anna felt sure that he was disappointed his own daughter kept her distance. How selfish she was!

'I'm going to make a cup of tea for us both.' Anna abruptly got to her feet and left the room. Lizzie sighed and closed her eyes again. Her friend was undemanding but not uncomplicated.

Whilst she was in the large kitchen waiting for the kettle to boil, Anna wandered around the room and the adjoining dining area in some sort of desultory search for abstract clues as to why her friend was so serene. Was it because of motherhood, her faith or her husband? Surely it wasn't Alan – he couldn't be the source of her tranquillity. And as for her children, they were tiring, absorbing her time, energy and love. No, the secret of Lizzie's peace of mind must be her religion, and this, of course, was puzzling.

Anna, who often changed her allegiances and opinions, had always respected those with a passionate commitment to any place, culture or point of view – in the same way that she used to admire in others the single-minded pursuit of a goal, such as walking to the North Pole or sailing round the world, or development of a talent such as the demanding training required by classical ballet dancers or olympic gymnasts. Looking back after two decades, she still feels that she lacks the vital and special ingredient required for these wonderful obsessions. Even now she admires absolute convictions but is incapable of embracing them herself. There is no proof for the existence of God and she doubts whether she could ever make a leap into the unknown and find the faith that Lizzie so clearly still clings to. Anna regards her scepticism as a necessary flaw which makes her a lesser, though more rounded, human being.

Lizzie has been unable to inflict her beliefs on her best friend or to instil them in her children, and Anna thinks this must be a disappointment though Lizzie does not show it. On that day of Ralph's baptism all those years ago, she would have been full of hope that she could bring up her children as Christians.

Anna remembers that, when coming out of the kitchen bearing the mugs of tea, she passed Lizzie on her way upstairs to pick up and comfort her son, who had woken up and was whimpering in his cot. Whilst waiting for her to come back down, Anna returned to the sitting room and began looking at the many family photographs that littered all the surfaces and hung on some of the walls. She had always preferred words to pictures; and though she loved paintings and art, she had little time for blurry family snapshots. Who, she asked herself, would want to live with such grinning or grimacing images of themselves and to inflict them on their friends? She did not need such devices to remind her of people she loved. But she had to acknowledge that the photographs of Alan's family showed them as quite good-looking, and, of course, the pictures of Lizzie were also the exception – she always looked wonderful in films and photographs. Katrina, though obviously adored and idolised as the daughter of the house, was, in her view, a very ordinary-looking child and the gilt-framed photograph on the mantelpiece depicted her with a look of wary suspicion on her small two-year-old face. The baby, though adorable in the flesh, had squashed features and tiny eyes in the few framed snapshots of him taken shortly after his birth. Though she would not, of course, ever have wished her features to be inserted into a frame, Anna was wistfully aware that Lizzie had no photograph of her on display – her closest friend whom she thought of as a sister. Perhaps she was not handsome enough to grace Alan's elegant front room.

'There isn't much definition in those photographs of Ralph,' Lizzie remarked as she re-entered the room carrying her baby on her chest with his tiny head flopping on her shoulder, and saw Anna looking at them. 'I've got some better ones, but haven't got round to putting them in a frame yet.'

'"To define is to limit,"' Anna said, quoting Oscar Wilde. 'Most photographs hinder the imagination. You've far too many,' she said in her candid way.

'Alan likes having them around to look at – he adores his children.'

On the subject of Alan, Anna remained silent. There were occasions when she could restrain her outspokenness. She simply walked back to the sofa and sat down again beside Lizzie. They finished their tea in contemplative companionship.

Anna finds herself staring at the cold dregs in the cup on the plastic shelf in front of her, stands up and leaves the cafe. She walks down to a busier street, where she is lucky enough to get a taxi immediately. She leans back with her eyes closed and her small bag beside her, glad to have decided that today she would allow herself the extravagance of a taxi. She recalls the many taxi rides she had with Fynn, who did not drive and who took taxis everywhere even when he couldn't afford to. He once leant across her in the back of a London cab, laughing, to rifle through her bag for the money to pay the cabbie, and after he had plucked a fiver from her purse, he had kissed her passionately. She remembers hearing the note in his fingers crackling by her ear as he held her head.

She had met him at a party in Brixton, to which she had been reluctant to go, feeling pressurized by an imminent deadline for an article. But her gay friend Roland, with whom she had once shared a flat, persuaded her to take a night off and go with him to the party at a friend's house. There they saw a beautiful young man who was behaving outrageously – probably drunk, she had thought, and almost certainly gay. But when, having fended off advances from Roland, he cornered her at a later stage in the evening and said he wanted to get to know her, she realised how wrong she had been.

He was called Fynn, and he was almost immoderately heterosexual – and also, conveniently for him, attractive to women. He told her that he had resisted the advances of two rapacious women and one randy homosexual in order to throw himself at her dainty feet. Definitely he was drunk: dainty she was not.

The next day he contacted her and suggested they have an affair, so they went out to dinner to discuss his proposition. She delayed for three weeks before accepting, and he waited impatiently, spending money extravagantly on flowers that he couldn't afford. She soon realised that he was as impoverished as she was, and after that, whichever of them was in funds paid for the film, meal or drinks. Fynn was entertaining, intelligent and affectionate. But he was reticent on how he coped with the practicalities of life – such as work, of which he seemed to do little. He told her he was an artist. He had been to art school in Camberwell, and had then gone to Spain to paint. There, he admitted, he had done more travelling than painting, more revelling than creating, more spending than earning. He was seductively, provokingly irresponsible – and he said he loved her.

Fynn confessed that he was following in the footsteps of his grandfather, who was a dissolute with a ditty, which ran:

> I burn my candle at both ends.
> It will not last the night.
> But O my foes and O my friends,
> It gives a lovely light.

Fynn used to announce that he had a premonition that he would not live to old age, but Anna suspected that he did this to make himself sound more pale and interesting. He was too busy cramming all sorts of experiences, over-indulgences and lovers into his young life to worry deeply what the consequences might be. He said he adored Anna and her Bohemian way of life, and they had rollicked about the city in taxis or in one of the many battered cars she drove which were borrowed from friends. Sitting in another London taxi in another part of her life, Anna reflects that it is often the most vital and energetic people who are struck down by malignant diseases, which consume them at the same fast pace as they have led their lives. Fynn has been dead for ten years.

The young man suffered so dreadfully with cancer; a patch on his skin had been diagnosed as a melanoma and second-aries had rapidly spread throughout his body. She had been appalled at how quickly he had succumbed, he who had once seemed to her the embodiment of health and youthful vitality, with his keen intellect, inspired decisions and joyful sense of humour. How she had loved him! And wanted him. He had without doubt desired her and perhaps for a time he had loved her too. Until he met Lizzie.

As she recollects her lover with her eyes closed, she can almost visualise him – with his wide, generous smile, his long eyelashes, and the soft blond hair at the back of his neck. She remembers his thin hands (almost as bony as hers are now), and his grubby feet. She can't quite evoke a picture of the young man in his entirety, but she can almost remember the way he used to smell – and the sensual magnetism he emanated. Having often maintained that a man is attractive to her only for the fineness of his mind and not for the lesser merits of his body, she now admits that the physical electricity she felt with her various lovers was important. She wonders sadly whether she will ever again experience that hedonistic sexual frisson. Is she capable of feeling it or inspiring it in others any more? Is life worth living without that spark?

Why is she thinking of Fynn now? Is it because her malady is possibly the same as his? Can she bring herself to face up to the frightening fact that she probably has cancer? What will that mean? Not knowing is almost as distressing as any certainty would be. Fynn did not survive, but many do.

Anna jerks herself out of what could become a mire of wallowing self-pity. She won't allow herself to go down that road. Not even after what she expects to hear from the doctor during her consultation. She looks out of the window to force a change of mood and thought, but as the taxi is just arriving in Devonshire Place, she cannot avoid the coming confrontation with the fears and worries she has pushed to the recesses of her mind over the past year. Aware of how much her energy has declined in recent months, and how her symptoms have become exacerbated, she dreads a confirmation of what she suspects.

The taxi driver stops at her destination and she climbs out and pays him off. With her bag on her shoulder, she walks across the pavement and stops in front of a tall, elegant Georgian house. Before stepping up to ring the bell, she lingers for a few minutes in the afternoon sunshine outside the large blue door, which, like so many others in this and the surrounding streets, give access to medical expertise.

She tries to savour what may be the last few minutes of her carefree ignorance concerning the length of the rest of her life. Will it be another couple of decades or prompt curtailment? She suspects the latter, but nothing is yet certain – she does not yet know how much time she has. Very few people do, and most prefer not to know. It seems to Anna that there are two futures: the one she will be a part of, and the long, endless one of which she will know nothing. She has had many discussions over a number of years about dying, but always with the comfortable conviction that it was a long way off – that it wasn't just yet. And along with it there was the assumption that achieving old age would happen as a prerequisite step. That she wouldn't be one of the unlucky ones to be cut short in her prime. That she would be allowed, as it were, to become old.

The act of dying is another insoluble enigma. She has always firmly announced that she is not frightened of dying, and she has almost convinced herself that this is true. She has taken risks and lived life on the edge in order to demonstrate her courage. Unlike Lizzie, who does not like leaving things to chance or exposing herself to danger or feeling vulnerable, Anna knows it is things precarious and random that give her life its zest.

Anna has always stated with conviction that she hates the distant prospect of ageing, with the probability that goes with it of mental faculties failing and having to cope with demeaning physical malfunctions, but she has said this from the viewpoint of a healthy young person who cannot quite envisage that this may actually one day come to pass. She has declared that she would rather die than 'lose the plot'. Lizzie, though admiring Anna's bold views, has said that as she grew old she would be prepared to accept the inevitable diminution in her health and would try to accept and become comfortable with her disabilities and those of others. She has always claimed to be a coward and frightened of dying, and is sure she could never face the ultimate act of self-destruction which would, any case, be contrary to her beliefs.

Anna has always pretended to despise this view, and has

condemned acceptance and compromise, but in fact she admires and envies her friend's more adaptable and more honest approach to life. Now she needs the uncompromising courage she has always professed to have in order to ring the doorbell and gain access to whatever is in store for her. She steps forward and presses the bell.

The door is opened by a bland-faced receptionist who, after noting her name and her appointment time, conducts her to a large room to the left of the entrance hall.

As she sits in the waiting room with its solid dark furniture, its thick curtains and its even heavier atmosphere, Anna speculates on how much one's frame of mind is affected by one's surroundings. She picks up a magazine to divert her mind, but soon realises that she is not taking in what she is looking at, and replaces it on the table with all the other outdated issues. When, after ten minutes, the receptionist comes in to conduct her upstairs to the consulting room, it is as if her feet have become weighted down and reluctant to move. She forces herself to rise and follow the woman, and gives herself a mental shake to try and snap out of the feeling of suffocation which has descended on her. As she enters the consultant's room, she raises her head and places a look of calm detachment on her features to confuse her adversary and confront her fate.

puts up with her foibles and fears. He gives her a smile as he hands her the tea and he registers the fact that her look of gratitude is disproportionately warm.

As they drink their tea together they both look out of the window and watch the waves as the ferry pushes its way through them. They stare at the external panorama — separate individuals with their own distinct thoughts. Actions bind us together but thoughts keep us apart, thinks Lizzie, while Paul is gently musing on the enduring fascination of moving water. She thanks her God for her blessings; he thanks his good fortune.

Across the other side of the wide lounge is another couple similarly engaged in staring at the sea, and Lizzie now turns to look at her surroundings and sees them. There is something familiar in the tall man's back, his slender neck and his averted profile. She has an immediate flash of recognition and she feels certain that the man is Fynn. An older Fynn. It is the shape of his head and the slight hunch of his shoulders, and even though he has lost his superb blond head of hair, she is convinced that it is him. She almost gets to her feet to claim recognition, when a flash of disappointment with her total stupidity comes over her. She must be having a hallucination because Fynn is dead — he has been dead for years. Almost as if to confirm this unpalatable truth, the couple across the lounge start to talk, and Lizzie can at once see that she has been mistaken. He really does not look like Fynn at all, though there was a hint of similarity from the back view. Her agitation subsides, and she is relieved to see that Paul has noticed nothing.

Paul has been looking at an elegant young woman who is seated behind Lizzie, reading a book. She is not as good-looking as his wife, but there is an enviable youthful freshness to her unlined complexion and regular pretty features which many a man might admire. He is aware of Lizzie's gaze directed across the expanse of the lounge, but is not curious enough to follow it. As his wife turns back, and at the same time he focuses on her familiar face, they both smile warmly and guiltily at each other. Paul is not one to lose a trick, so he suggests with a surge of genuine affection that perhaps they might now return to their cabin and have a little rest on their bunks. Rest, thinks Lizzie, is not what is on his mind, but she is happy to acquiesce. She can make up her mind about whether it will involve more than just lying down later on. Paul, her lovely kind Paul, will go along with whatever she decides. How lucky she is to have such a considerate partner!

When they are back in the cabin, Paul decides to have a shower, and Lizzie lies on one of the berths staring up at the ceiling. The image of Fynn is now lingering in her mind, and she casts herself back to the time when her pact of sharing everything with Anna took on a new dimension.


Lizzie recalls that she and Alan were living in Hampstead and both the children were at day school. At that time Anna was living in Fulham with Fynn in a small house that she was looking after for a married couple who were abroad for a couple of years.

By now Lizzie was aware of the philandering tendencies of her beloved husband, but she turned a blind eye because she felt that she needed him more than he needed her. In any case, she either could not or did not want to catch him out and precipitate a fracturing row. Slightly apprehensive and insecure, she realised that Anna's situation and hers had now become reversed and Anna was happy and stable in her new relationship whilst she had become the unsettled one. She had not yet met Fynn, but had heard all about him from Anna, who had told her that he was in his late twenties and beautiful. Lizzie again wondered at Anna's propensity to select and attract younger men. She herself often found them selfish and immature, but clearly her friend found in them qualities which outweighed these characteristics. It seemed that Fynn was not only 'wholly perfect' but 'wonderfully faithful' as well – he and Anna had been together for nearly a year. This was unusual because Anna rarely remained with her men for long. What Lizzie found curious was that Anna had not yet found time to introduce Fynn to her.

Alan had gone away for a month to work on the Continent, and Lizzie was feeling low and lonely. She phoned Anna and asked if they could meet up, and it was arranged that she would come over on Saturday for lunch with the children. No mention was made of Fynn, so Lizzie assumed that he would not be around. In fact, to her surprise, he was there after all, and he turned out to be a ravishingly charming young man who was delightfully kind to her children but, in contrast, quite reticent and distant with her. Anna was in good spirits at the beginning but became increasingly thoughtful as the afternoon progressed. Lizzie felt a little uneasy but enjoyed herself and tried to be amusing in the winning way that she had when she made an effort. After all, she was an actress and could cloak inner feelings and appear natural and relaxed. She did wonder vaguely if she had offended Fynn, but was not unduly concerned about his apparent aversion to her.

After that she met up with Fynn and Anna a few times – once when they went as a threesome to an old black-and-white classic film, and on another occasion when Alan had returned from Italy, and all four met up at a restaurant for dinner. Anna had undoubtedly influenced Fynn's attitude towards Alan as he exhibited the same antipathy towards him that she did, and the evening was not a success, though, to Anna's relief, Lizzie seemed to be getting on better with the younger man than she had on earlier occasions. Lizzie had been touched that Anna genuinely wanted her lover and her adopted sister to like each other.

Lizzie opens her eyes to see the cabin with Paul emerging from the tiny shower cubicle with a small towel round his hips, and closes them again to remember the first time that Fynn had come into her bedroom disarmingly unembarrassed by his nakedness. He had the naturalness of an animal but without the shyness.

That day had been her birthday, and the doorbell had rung. The children were at school and she was alone in the house. Expecting an extravagant bunch of guilt flowers from her errant husband who was away filming again, Lizzie had answered the door. There stood Fynn, with a curious enigmatic smile on his face and a rectangular package in his hand. He said that he was the bearer of a gift for her from Anna, and he had a card for her too, which he then pulled out of the pocket of his old brown tweed overcoat. He passed them both to Lizzie and wished her 'Happy Birthday'. He stood there expectantly so she invited him in.

Knowing quite well what was in the box – the same present she had been receiving from Anna and giving back to her for a number of years now – she put it down on the hall table and, standing at the bottom of the stairs, she took the envelope he had given her, tore it open and pulled out a card. Glancing at the black and white picture of Clark Gable looking dashing as Rhett Butler in *Gone with the Wind*, she opened it to read:

Fynn has a thing about actresses – he adores them. He has guiltily confessed to me that he has conceived an overwhelming passion for you, and I must also confide that I have become a little weary of his patient devotion and somewhat cramped by his constant presence, so I am giving him to you along with Adam – they do make rather a pair! I shall expect the beautiful bronze fellow back for my birthday in the autumn, but I leave it up to you to decide whether or not you want the one of flesh and blood to stay with you! "I wish you joy of the worm". xxx Anna.

Registering the quote from 'Antony and Cleopatra' because she had once played the part of Iras at drama school, Lizzie chose to ignore the context. Whilst she read the card which had accompanied the two young men, Fynn stood watching her, an uncertain but slightly audacious smile on his face. She looked up at him, her face betraying nothing of the confusion which this dilemma had aroused in her. Feeling a little awkward, Fynn asked, 'Why don't you open the present?'

'Because I know what it is.' But she nevertheless turned slowly and, picking up the package, removed the birthday paper, opened the familiar box and drew the softly glowing figure from some creased and tattered tissue paper. She turned her gaze on Fynn. 'He's beautiful, isn't he? We share him. We have done for years. The way we share lots of things.' She held the bronze up in front of her and then looked interrogatively at Fynn. He spread his hands and silently mouthed the words 'I love you'. Her face flushed slightly as she realised he did want her. And Lizzie, conscious of a faithless and absent husband who no longer valued or desired her, decided to accept Anna's gift. Faintly embarrassed by her need for some demonstrative affection, and still carrying the bronze, she turned and started to walk up the stairs. Fynn, who had noticed her blush, followed her.

When they betrayed Anna, they thought it was with her blessing. In a sense they were right, but the pain they caused her was real and the consequences damaging.

Back in the present, aboard a ferry bound for England, Lizzie, naked under a twisted sheet, is lying beside Paul, who has been successful in his endeavours to seduce his wife. She is feeling warm and content, but also slightly guilty because she feels she was more receptive to Paul's overtures because of her recollections of the first time with Fynn. She is ashamed that she was thinking of making love to Fynn whilst Paul was making love to her. Paul is now sleeping so she leans over and brushes a kiss on his shoulder blade as a token of her apology and as a way of trying to erase her unruly memories. She then turns on her side with her back to her husband.

But the mind is difficult to curb and as Lizzie lies in the dim cabin, with the slight rolling motion of the vessel beneath her and the soft breathing of the man beside her, she lapses back into her earlier train of thought.

There were two things that Lizzie realises she did not know until much later. The first was that Fynn was unaware of the exact message in the card. The second was that Anna had not been telling the truth. She was still in love with Fynn, but with a self-denying generosity which was out of character, she did not want to keep him if he did not want to stay with her. His devotion to her had waned as his attraction towards Lizzie increased, and it was he who wanted freedom and space, not her. With the inevitable death of the relationship, Anna thought, there was no one to whom she would rather bequeath Fynn than her sister, Lizzie – the other person whom she cared for most in the world. It was also honouring the sharing pact they had made as children and adhered to ever since. Though her sacrifice was made in the knowledge that her affair with Fynn would probably have finished in any case, it eroded Anna's peace of mind, and she regretted her selfless gift. It poisoned her relationship with Lizzie for over two years. The fact that it was she herself who had caused this, in a spirit of flippancy and bitterness, made matters even worse. But the crisis and the estrangement had eventually passed, and in time, when Lizzie had in her turn cast off Fynn, there had been a reconciliation between the two women. Anna had told Lizzie the truth, and they had forgiven each other.

The other casualty of Fynn's transfer to Lizzie and their resulting affair was the break-up of her marriage, which had already been shaky. Far less practised in deceit than her husband, Lizzie was unable to keep her lover secret. Alan took the moral high ground – something to which he had no entitlement – and sued Lizzie for divorce on the grounds of adultery. It was all rather messy and public. Lizzie was emotionally distraught, Alan unnecessarily harsh, and their children became insecure and unhappy; Lizzie broke up with Fynn over the stress of it all, and no one escaped unharmed. Anna, Lizzie recalls, had disappeared to India to avoid the fallout. Like stars in different universes, their spheres moved apart, and they did not come into conjunction again until they were drawn together once more over the death of Fynn.

One of the most painful experiences of her life was the dreadful scene when she and Anna met up whilst visiting Fynn in hospital. Because of the serious condition he was in, he had been put in a single room. Anna was sitting by his bed when

Lizzie came in. The women had only recently become reconciled, and had made a few tentative steps towards re-establishing their lifelong friendship. They had not expected to encounter each other here, and felt awkward. They looked at Fynn to see his reaction to their joint presence, and then at each other. Anna raised her eyebrows to try and give some warning to Lizzie.

'Here's my other guardian angel,' said Fynn in a sarcastic voice, having noticed Anna's hinted caution. 'Both of you look in blooming good health. Jealous? You bet I am.'

The young man's grace and physique were ravaged; only a hollow-eyed gaunt shadow of his vibrant beauty remained. Lizzie was shocked at the rapidity of his decline – she had seen him a month before and the deterioration in him was marked. It seemed as if his nature had undergone a change too – gone was his buoyant charm and impulsive high spirits, and now he oscillated between black humour and deep despairing gloom.

They sat there silently as he jeered at their caring expressions and mocked their genuine sympathy. Coughing and hoarse with morphine, and fully aware that he was dying, Fynn was angry – so angry. He was being cheated out of life and he would take his frustration out on the two women he had loved the most.

'You used me and discarded me,' he accused them vehemently. 'I was young and impressionable, and you both took advantage of that. You were selfish, greedy, frustrated women. I did so much for you both and you both did so little for me.'

'You seem to have a slight lapse of memory,' protested Anna.

'Why do you feel the need to desecrate what was once so lovely?' whispered Lizzie.

'Because you women devoured my youth, and now I'm not

to be allowed anything more. You used me and then left me high and dry. After you witches enchanted me and chucked me, I was so bloody miserable – you have no idea how awful it was. The stress and despair probably triggered this bloody cancer. I adored you and you left me. Both of you,' Fynn raved at them, his face contorted with fury. 'I hate you both now far more than I loved you.'

Lizzie and Anna exchanged looks of dismay which Fynn saw and reacted to even more violently. 'You and your girly pact. "We share everything,"' he mimicked. 'You shared me and then you dumped me.'

'You were not unhappy with the bargain,' Anna was stung to protest. 'I too suffered when I gave you up to Lizzie.'

'Not as much as I did when you both turned your backs on me. You were both older and should have been kinder. You took me into your lives. You offered me love.'

'You could have refused.' Lizzie was indignant.

'I had no choice,' he lashed out.

'You always have a choice,' Anna said, and immediately regretted her words.

'I don't. Not any more. Except to tell you both to go away. Get out. Leave me alone,' Fynn howled. He sank back against his dented pillows, exhausted by emotion.

Alerted by the noise, a small, very irate nurse ran into the room and threw them out.

Over a cup of bitter coffee in the hospital's austere cafe, Lizzie and Anna stared bleakly at each other, appalled at the scene they had precipitated and by what they had done.

'I feel miserably responsible – sad and sinful,' Lizzie began emotionally.

Anna was more rational. 'We are not responsible for his state of health. Cancer can happen to anyone at any age. We might have been a little to blame in the matter of his distraught state of mind after we both abandoned him. For that I'm sorry too. But sin is a concept I have a problem with.'

'Do you really think that we might be the horrible harpies that Fynn says we are?'

'I suppose that, under our sharing principle, we should be prepared to share in his vitriol as much as we shared in his love.'

'It's not quite that bad. We didn't really share him at the same time. You had him first, and then I took over. Were we too controlling?'

'Let's be honest – we were rather dreadful,' admitted Anna. 'We were very selfish, treating him like a piece of property, like the bronze, to be handed over from one to the other. It was inconsiderate and in bad taste – but let's not forget that he willingly complied and indeed wanted to make the swap. He's no saint either.' Anna stopped – she had just discovered an interesting fact. Though she felt very sorry for him, she found she no longer loved Fynn and could look at him in a more balanced and rational way than she once had.

'He seems to be blaming us for wrecking his life. And now he's dying.' Lizzie was near to tears.

'That can't be laid at our door. It's just bad luck. He's bitter about his curtailed years, but maybe that's because he lived too intensely and enjoyed his time too much. He doesn't have your faith in an afterlife and he's teetering on the brink of a huge black void.' Anna paused and then muttered, 'I know the feeling.'

'I shall pray for him,' said Lizzie earnestly. 'I shall forgive him for being so nasty to us just now. He is suffering, after all. But I do care. I'm very upset about his condition.'

'Not half as much as he is.'

'Why was he so angry with us, and so resentful?'

'Because we'll go on living. For the moment.'

Lizzie looked into Anna's eyes and said, 'I wonder how I would feel if I knew that I had only a short time to live. Would I rush out and try to do some of those things I'd always promised myself I'd do? Or would I be calm and accepting and try to end my days with grace and dignity? Would dignity be denied me if I was in too much pain? I suppose the truth is, we don't know how we'd react.'

'I'm not sure that I would "go gently into that good night," but I can't be sure. What I do know is that Fynn will "rage, rage against the dying of the light."'

Lizzie was as familiar as Anna was with Dylan Thomas – his poems had long been a shared experience. '"Though lovers be lost love shall not,"' she quoted in response.

And together they said, '"And death shall have no dominion."'

Lizzie sighed and then looked at her watch. 'I must go and pick up the children from school.'

In her car a few minutes later, Lizzie remembered a conversation she had once had with Anna, when the latter had speculated on what it might be like to be a mother, and whether children were a blessing or a burden. Lizzie always told her that it was only after having children that she realised that had she not been a mother she would have missed out on one of the greatest joys of life. She had willingly given up her career for them. Anna had said that she could not have done that, and then blamed her own selfishness. It was unlikely, Lizzie thought, that Anna would ever have a child. Fynn never would.

He died two weeks later.

It is almost as if, by recalling that distressing episode, Lizzie has finally exorcised it. She feels tired and, turning to face Paul, she manages to doze off.

# Chapter Eight

Anna's mind is in overdrive. She has never felt more mentally alert. But she is tired; she is physically exhausted. It has been a long day and she has been going for over twelve hours without pause for rest. She is hemmed in by a blurred moving mass of people as she exits from the Underground into the main concourse at Waterloo Station. She was in the doctor's consulting rooms for just under an hour, and afterwards she had walked for ten minutes to clear her head and tame her thoughts. She had forgotten about rush hour and had soon realised that a taxi would be difficult to find, and that in any case the Underground would be faster. She had hoped to catch a train at 5.30 p.m. which would have connected with the fast ferry to get her to the Isle of Wight in just over two hours. This would have given her just enough time to taxi across the island to the restaurant where her brother's fiftieth birthday party is to be held. The press of Londoners returning from their day's work is disquieting, like the echo of a past existence; she has forgotten how crowded the transport becomes and has miscalculated how long it will take her. She has missed the earlier train to Portsmouth Harbour and is now worried that the delay may mean that she will not catch the next one either, which departs in a few minutes, at six o'clock.

Anna realises she is too late to queue for a ticket – she will have to buy one on the train. She only needs a single, after all. She has that tight feeling of panic as she hurries through the throng of commuters going home, and tries to find the right platform. There are two minutes before the train leaves. Luckily a surge of people seems to be carrying her forward in the direction she needs to go. She has gained the barrier and runs onto the platform. The train is due to leave immediately and she is so agitated when she reaches the nearest door that she almost slips while stepping up into the carriage. A woman standing in the corridor catches her arm and steadies her. Anna glances at her gratefully and stumbles thankfully aboard.

A few seconds later, just after the door has closed behind her, the train starts to move. Anna, breathing heavily, is surprised and pleased to have caught it. It is then that she realises the impossibility of getting a seat. She enters the very full carriage, staggering with fatigue and dismay when she sees how crowded it is. She closes her eyes and tries to calm her mind and heart, which are both pounding from her exertion and panic. When she opens her eyes again a few people are staring at her with concerned looks on their faces. A tall man rises from his seat and she is handed into it, whilst someone else places her small bag on the rack above. She murmurs her sincere thanks as she sinks onto the seat which has been given up by someone who will now have to stand for at least forty-five minutes. She is feeling a bit faint and recognises that she may be in shock from the news she heard less than an hour ago. She leans back, takes some deep breaths and closes her eyes again to shut out the press of bodies and faces around her. She needs to think, to absorb the information she has been given. Later on she will have to make further decisions.

The doctor had started with the usual technical obfuscation in order to justify his advice based upon the medical facts and also to delay any bad news until he had found an opportune moment to say what needed to be said. He told her that the results of various tests done in France had recently been sent over to him, and after a few further preliminaries he had then briefly examined her. During his subsequent explanation, Anna had listened quietly with only the occasional interruption to ask him the meaning of some obscure medical terminology. Although she knew pretty much what it meant, it gave her a few moments' breathing space to adjust herself to the onslaught that was coming and which she had already predicted from the unusual gentleness of his approach. On her only previous visit, he had been abrupt – almost brusque – and though he was a careful doctor, he had not demonstrated a caring manner. Today had been different. So she knew.

Then, in order to spare him any further awkwardness on her account and to cut short any more protracted details, she told him that she had sought advice in France, and from her own observations, from the way she felt and the pains she had been having, she was aware that the situation had worsened. She was not going to have an embarrassingly emotional reaction to the shock of what was coming, so he might as well bite the bullet and tell her straight. So he did. There was no question of surgery as the tumour was now too large to operate on with any degree of safety and hope of success. It might even cut short what was left of her life. They could try chemotherapy again but he did not have much hope that this would now arrest the rapid growth. Indeed, the strength of the dosage required on the slim chance that it might make a difference would make her very unwell, and would probably not be worth undertaking. He regretted very much having to tell her that she had, at best, six months to live, possibly less and perhaps a little more. He admired her courage and her outspoken way of telling him that she already suspected as much, and he assured her that when her pain became too severe to cope with – probably in a month or two – she would be given all the necessary medication to control it.

He paused to give her time to speak or react, but she remained silent with an alarmingly composed set to her face. The room echoed with the unsaid. The doctor felt uncomfortable with this vacuum and cleared his throat. Was there anyone who could be with her this afternoon? She shook her head.

He then went on to describe what would be likely to happen, and told her that, depending on her wishes, he would either arrange for her medical care to be undertaken in England, or he would cooperate fully with the French doctors who would take over her palliative care, if she decided to return to France and remain there. Whilst he was saying this and telling her what drugs would be administered and when and what their side effects might be, her mind had wandered. To have suspicions and to have certainty were, she discovered, more vastly different than she had imagined. One might suspect that one was about to have one's employment terminated, but when one actually got fired and received marching orders, it was still a punch which left one breathless and reeling with disappointment. The absolute knowledge that two or more decades of her life had suddenly been stolen from her was a catastrophe, and the time remaining for her was shockingly short. But, she told herself sternly, you already knew that this was the case. This is no surprise, just confirmation.

The doctor had finished speaking and was asking if she was all right. 'Of course I'm not,' she felt like saying. 'You've just told me that I'm dying, so I must be quite ill.' But, realising that he felt concerned for her and was referring to her state of mind, she murmured that she would be fine, whilst thinking, 'What a stupid remark. Totally inaccurate.' She almost laughed at this idiotic exchange of words and the thoughts that contrasted with them. They both rose to their feet. He said he would write to her with all the necessary information. She nodded distractedly. Inwardly very agitated, she had given a grotesque smile, gathered up her wits and her bag, and quietly left the consulting room. She felt profoundly distanced from the rest of the world that was so healthy and vital. She went out through the large front door and raggedly descended the steps to the pavement. Her nightmare had just begun.

Now in the train listening to its rhythmic clattering beat, she tries to slow down her heartbeat by taking a few deep breaths. She is trying to exhale the memory of her initial horror when the doctor confirmed all the fears that had been eroding her peace of mind for some while.

Her initial reaction is to tell it all to Lizzie, and she has a mad idea of meeting her cross-channel ferry, which will be docking this evening in Portsmouth. She could drop her plan of going to her brother's fiftieth party on the Isle of Wight, and see Lizzie instead. She needs her chosen sister much more than her real brother at this moment. All day she has been aware of Lizzie gradually getting closer, together with Paul, in the driving seat of their car and of their lives together, coasting north along the French roads. They have been aboard the boat now for some hours, and she envisages them sailing sedately northwards, their elegant Bentley parked majestically in pole position on the car deck whilst they sip cocktails – or, more probably, a gin and tonic – in the shiny bar high up, overlooking the slumbering waves of the Channel. Lizzie is getting closer. Anna has a need to talk to her. They have always shared good news and bad, celebrated successes together and helped each other with problems.

Anna opens her eyes as her neighbour shakes open an evening newspaper, and then, finding it more restful to close out the pages of newsprint partially obscuring the standing passengers swaying uncomfortably in the moving carriage, she closes her eyes once more, and resumes her thoughts.

The possibility of phoning Youenn and telling him what she has learnt from the doctor does not even occur to her. He rarely takes telephone calls, and she does not know how she could break the news to him like that – even if it were a good idea to tell him, which it probably isn't. Perhaps she has the strength to keep it to herself until she has come to terms with it and worked out what attitude to adopt to this intruder into her life. Perhaps she can miraculously vanquish her foe. After all, Beowulf beat Grendel against greater odds. Myths and history are full of seemingly impossible feats being accomplished by heroic endeavour.

It is just that hope has never been a strong contender in her character's traits. She has very little hope that mankind will ever improve – suffering, wars and cruelty are as rife now as they ever have been. Goodness does not seem to be more powerful than evil. They merely balance each other out, so nothing gets much better or much worse. Hopes are generally unfulfilled. The trick is not to feel disappointment but just to accept that this is the way it is.

Why does it seem, she wonders, that whenever hope asserts

itself, immediately faith and charity seem to leap into the fray after it, staking their claims to be pre-eminent?

What about faith? She lacks this too. She has been horribly unfaithful to almost every person she has been close to – except Lizzie, of course. In respect of belief in a Deity, her intellect forbids it, though she admires such lofty moral convictions in others whilst at the same time mocking them as futile and self-deluding. Lizzie's faith in God is incomprehensible, irrational but touching, almost appealing, not quite enviable. It is one of the main areas of disagreement over which the two of them wrestle.

As for love – that sublime virtue, that eternal solace, that potent force – she has indulged in it, revelled in it and squandered it. She has been fortunate to find tenderness and passion within herself – to give it freely and instil it in others. Though foolish enough on occasion to turn away from those who have offered love, she has more often tried to retain it. For Anna, the highest love is unselfish, unconditional, uncritical. It is, she thinks, the only fine quality she possesses. Love has saved her from being self-centred and it has conferred on her the most intense happiness she has known. If she believed in God, she might even say she had been blessed.

Her pulse rate has finally returned to normal after her exertion to catch the train, and she now relaxes a little. She thinks that she might be able, after all, to keep her own counsel and not burden others with the perplexing knowledge of a situation which they can do nothing to change. What she has learnt is, anyway, no more than what we all know already – that life will come to an end. The difference is that hers is going to come to its conclusion rather sooner than she had thought or hoped. Let's not exaggerate or allow panic to set in, Anna says to herself. Though if she's honest and accurate in her recollections, in the last few months, wryly distorting Wordsworth's phrase, she has had a few suspicions and intimations of mortality. These have caused her some disquiet, though she has tried to ruthlessly repress her anxieties. She now needs to think clearly and coolly.

She opens her eyes and looks around, in an effort to focus on something else for a few minutes, and to try and control her billowing thoughts. She sees looking down at her the face of the man who has given her his seat, and she smiles up at him reassuringly, and says she is feeling much better and is very grateful for his kindness. He smiles in a smug, avuncular way – he is pleased with his good deed. It is the solace for his swaying discomfort. She then looks across her seated neighbour and out of the window to the bright sky of the late spring afternoon and the scenery flashing past to the repetitive tune of the wheels on the tracks. She is moving quickly towards her destination, whatever that may be. In her agitated state she feels that time, which always moves forward at the same pace, seems to be accelerating in sympathy with her mode of travel and her racing mind. She has journeyed far in this day and in her life up to this moment. She feels a bit cold. She has been dislocated by the bad news, but now her fear has subsided a little and she draws upon her mental fortitude to contemplate what she has just discovered. She must be rational, not emotional, in order to make decisions. She can be brave about it all – surely she can?

On the ferry, Lizzie is in that pleasant hazy state between waking and sleeping. Fragments of disturbing dreams drift through her mind, and even whilst she is aware that these are merely illusions, she is also unable to curtail them – they run amok and she watches them curiously as they cavort in her

154

mind, whilst at the same time she is conscious that she is in reality lying on a wide bunk in a moving vessel on an undulating sea. She makes an effort to either sink into full sleep or surface to total wakefulness, and she eventually manages to rouse herself. As she emerges from her reverie and her eyes focus on her surroundings, she register a flickering of warm sunlight on Paul's bare shoulder beside her. The late afternoon sun is filtering through the yellow-striped fabric of the partially closed curtain onto the sleeping man. His skin looks dusky golden and smooth. She moves her arm and places her hand on his shoulder, thus diverting the yellow bars onto her own paler skin. It now looks lemony and pearl-like, and she compares it to the texture of Anna's hands, which she had seen that morning in France, when the early light had shown up the bones covered with creased skin, the colour of parchment. Anna has never taken care of her hands, which look as if they belong to an older woman. As she contemplates her friend's appearance, Lizzie experiences a moment of extreme anxiety for her. Is Anna ill? She almost feels sick herself, because if Anna's health and well-being are affected, then so is hers – they are interconnected. They are in tune with each other and react like twin sisters if one of them is threatened. Then reason returns – or optimism – or blinkered vision. Surely all is well?

The mood of warm sunny afternoon contentment has evaporated and slivers of her uneasy dreams flit erratically across her mind. Surely she can ignore these now she is awake? She sits up and swings her legs onto the floor. She will phone Anna at Gavin's house tomorrow morning before she catches the ferry back to Brittany. She might even be able to persuade her to come back up to town and spend an extra day or two with them before returning to that dour, demanding Frenchman of hers. She would be able to take Anna out for a good meal and

was midway between her two marriages. Her former husband Alan had taken the children to Scotland for the autumn half-term, and she was at a loose end. Anna had recently ended an unsatisfactory short-lived affair with a musician whose devotion to his music precluded any deep relationship with women, who were for him merely a temporary distraction from his art. She was also temporarily unemployed, which was why she had decided to go away for a few days' walking in an area she had not visited before. The various friends who sometimes accompanied her on walking weekends were unavailable, so she contacted Lizzie, who, in any case, would have been her preferred companion. A few long hard walks, a few good deep talks, she knew, would set them both up and tone up their minds as well as their bodies.

They set off together in Lizzie's car, heading for Derbyshire, where they had booked into an inn in the village of Hope, and planned to spend a few days exploring the Dark Peak area of the National Park with its heather moorlands, deep valleys and sandstone escarpments. The first day they had walked along the attractive Hope Valley, admiring the autumn colours and absorbing the beauty and tranquillity, and the following morning they had hiked up to the walk along the Derwent Edges, from where they had looked down on the beautiful Derwent and Ladybower reservoirs under the crisp, clear late-October skies. The next day they drove a little further north to stay at a nineteenth-century inn high up on the Snake Pass, and spent a tiring day tramping along a remote stretch of the Pennine Way leading over the stony uplands of that isolated, windswept area. Both women were feeling that they had reached a parallel plateau in their lives, where the highs and lows of their now-terminated relationships had levelled out to a curious contentment at being single. In discussing their respective situations at great length, they came to many conclusions, including that all men were selfish and all women tolerant.

On the fourth day the fine weather gave way to incessant rain and a keen wind, so they drove on to White Peak in the Derbyshire Dales, where the undulating pastures were less wild and remote. Here they booked into a bed and breakfast and spent the afternoon in a quiet sitting room reading in affable silence. On the last day before they had to return to London, it was a turbulent but dry day, and they decided to set off on a circular walk of about thirteen miles, through low hills and rough countryside, that had been suggested to them in a guide book. Anna never liked to retrace her steps when walking, and Lizzie didn't mind either way, so this seemed like the best way to end their holiday.

Unfortunately, the unsettled weather seemed to have infected their cordiality. Their rapport of the first few days had been dented the evening before by an argument about morals and society. Lizzie had ended up by accusing Anna of arrogance and intolerance, and was criticised back for being complacent and 'pathetically irresolute'. Anna awoke the next morning still feeling resentful, and Lizzie, well attuned to her friend's changing moods, resorted to chatty conviviality over breakfast as her way of coping with the frostiness. This only succeeded (and it may have been her intention to do so) in irritating Anna even further. As they finished their toast, Lizzie finally said to her grumpy companion, 'Oh Anna, don't be so huffy! Last night's row is over – you shouldn't take offence so easily.'

The two women then got ready for their last walk before heading back to London, and told the woman at the bed and breakfast that they would be back for their luggage by mid-afternoon.

Anna went down to the car first with their boots and anoraks and a map which showed the route of the proposed walk. In an effort to please her disaffected friend, Lizzie was wearing a scarf which Anna had given to her the Christmas before – a long soft one in primrose yellow wool with an azure blue fringe. When she emerged, Anna, who was moodily wondering why she was being so pathetic and intractable, gave a slightly forced but cheerful smile when she saw the scarf and recognised it as a token of reconciliation. She silently resolved that the walk would blow away her ill humour, and they set off to drive to a point on the western side of the circuit from where they could join the main path. An old track led them from where they had parked their car uphill for about a mile. The trees arched overhead and a chill breeze funnelled up, rustling the dry leaves underfoot. When they reached the top and had traversed a field, they came to a wider, well-trodden path with a wooden sign pointing in both directions, indicating that this was the defined walk. After a brief debate they decided to go round in a clockwise direction, and to stop for a sandwich at a pub which their map indicated was half a mile or so from the path.

As they set off they chatted about uncontentious things such as how far the walk was and how long it might take them, and whether they would manage to locate the way to the pub from the map. As the gradient became steeper Anna pulled up the collar of her jacket and hunched her shoulders. She began to talk in a highbrow way about the symbolism of rings and circles and the rotation of the seasons and cycles of time and power.

Lizzie listened for a while, and then breezily announced that she thought spheres far more interesting than circles. 'They have density and volume and three-dimensional shape. Circles are so flat. The planets that orbit the sun are individually fascinating, whereas the paths they follow are just tracks in the void, abstract circles in space.' She was trying to contradict Anna in a light-hearted way, and also to mock her friend's pompous lecture. 'People can be both – rounded and flat,' she continued, 'And flat people are boring and their ideas inflexible. And pointless. Just like circles.'

Anna took the rebuke but decided not to react, feeling that she merited a bit of flak.

The wind was increasing, so Lizzie tightened her scarf around her neck whilst she prattled on, as yet with no response from Anna, about the 'music of the spheres, the orbits of the planets – and astrology'.

'You mean astronomy, of course,' Anna finally interjected sourly, buttoning up the front of her jacket.

'No I don't. I mean the astrological signs of the zodiac. Pisces, Scorpio, Cancer etcetera. Of course, as a Christian, I know its all garbage, but it's so appealing to many people – Destiny and Fate and what's in store for them? Astrology allows them to blame their bad habits on some sort of immutable astro-gene. They can take comfort about the future being mapped out from the hour and date of birth, which will exonerate them from any real responsibility for their actions. We all love navel gazing as well as star gazing.' Lizzie pointed to her solar plexus and then to the sky. 'What's wrong with wallowing in a fog of fantasy occasionally? It's fun.' She lifted her chin defiantly.

'No, it isn't. It's stupid,' replied Anna crossly, kicking savagely at a stone in her path and hating herself for being such a wet blanket.

'Well, once upon a time,' Lizzie continued ebulliently, 'everyone thought the earth was flat and that you could fall or sail off the edge. It must have been rather exciting and daunting at the time for those ancient voyagers in their tiny ships. Having an earth-centred universe was a way of giving importance to man's puny endeavours – the idea was promoted by the Catholic Church and was generally accepted, until Galileo came along and mucked about with it.'

'You're forgetting Copernicus – he came first, and was the one who convinced Galileo of a heliocentric universe, and knocked all the ancient Greek theories on the head.' Anna wanted to suppress what she considered Lizzie's facile attitude to the subject, and she also felt a petty need to demonstrate her superior knowledge. 'He disproved the Ptolemaic system, which had been based on Aristotle's theories centuries earlier.'

But Lizzie would not be deterred from her frivolous yet not uninformed approach to the topic. 'I always rather liked the Aristotelian idea of those celestial crystal spheres jangling away above the earth, with the sun and moon together with all the planets and stars circling eternally round the earth. It's much more comforting and cosier to put us in the centre of some sort of cosmic translucent onion and give our dear old familiar world some significance and importance. It's so daunting to think instead that we are just one tiny planet belonging to one small star which is one among millions of others in infinite and indefinable space.' She had been striding out ahead, and now turned to look at Anna with a wide confident smile which seemed at odds with the words she uttered. 'It makes me feel very small and lost.'

'And you don't like that,' Anna snapped back. 'You like to feel important – that you matter. That your God loves you. You're not humble – you're egotistical – typical of all you bloody self-centred actors.' She had to raise her voice for Lizzie, who was ahead of her, to hear, and even to her own ears she sounded shrill and unreasonable.

'Well done!' said Lizzie sarcastically as she turned round.

'You've managed at last to get back to personal insults. How pathetic!' Lizzie stopped directly in Anna's path with her hands on her hips, so that Anna too had to come to a stop facing her. 'What *is* the matter with you today? You're determined to be objectionable and dour. I can't be bothered any more with trying to lift you out of your black cloud. I don't want to spend our last day here arguing and sparring with you.' She looked around at the harmonious autumnal countryside enveloping their fractured companionship. It looked windswept, clean and wholesome. 'I'd rather be on my own.'

Anna suddenly realised that she too would rather be on her own. And she also felt a bit resentful that Lizzie had thought of it first. This was interlinked with feelings of guilt that she had been so lacking in humour and civility. 'So would I,' she said slowly. 'That's a good suggestion. Sorry, I know I've been a bit moody. A couple of hours of windy walking on my own will sort me out.'

'I hope so. I'm certainly not going to stay around and get infected by it. I've got lots of things to mull over, so some silence and good hard walking will do me good.'

Anna too was eager to be on her way. 'We're on a circular walk which normally takes about four or five hours to complete. Why don't we walk in opposite directions, and if we stay on the path, we'll be bound to meet up in a couple of hours on the other side?' The idea of separation and coming together again was rather appealing. It would be a cooling-off period, a choice, not an imposition.

From Lizzie's point of view, the plan was a good one because it meant that there would be immediate and increasing space between her and Anna's foul mood.

'Fine,' she said. 'I propose to keep on in this direction, so you'll have to turn round and reverse yours.' She considered this a fair proposal – since Anna was the one who needed to change her attitude, she should be the one to alter her direction.

Anna nodded, keen to show some accord. 'Who should have the map?'

'I'll take it. You already had a good look at it when you were planning the route. You said it was well marked, so just keep walking until we meet up again.' Lizzie held out her hand. With a reluctance she could not quite understand, Anna drew the map out of her pocket and silently handed it over.

Without another word, Lizzie took it from her and struck off up the path towards the top of a low hill, the blue tails of her yellow scarf fluttering over her shoulders.

Anna watched her. 'See you in about a couple of hours, then,' she called. Lizzie responded by waving the map over her shoulder without turning. There was a taunting springiness in her step.

Anna accepted this nonchalance as the punishment she knew she deserved. She stood still, her eyes on the familiar figure receding into the distance. She watched Lizzie climb over a stile into the next pasture, and then up towards the brow of the hill. 'See you later,' she shouted, but the wind whipped her words away and Lizzie did not turn. As Anna watched, her friend reached the top of the rise, and started to descend, her figure gradually diminishing before finally disappearing from view amongst the waving grass on the slope.

Anna felt an odd pain at Lizzie's lack of concern at their parting, though she had not expected anything else. 'Until we meet again, remember me,' she muttered. She knew the rule as well as Lizzie did – the one who walks away does not look round. The wind spiralled down the slope towards her and she shivered slightly before slowly turning and trudging back the way she had come.

Within a few minutes she was feeling somewhat chilled and isolated. Though the scenery was less bare and bleak than it had been on their earlier walks, it was devoid of other humans. She remembered a discussion from their past when they had talked about loneliness as a negative emotion because it was state induced by something which was involuntary, whereas solitude was a positive state because it was a usually a result of choice. She felt slightly deprived of fellowship and was experiencing a wistful feeling of having persevered in an unreasonable course knowing she would regret it but unable to deflect herself off it. Why had she let their camaraderie become debased by a futile point-scoring argument? She felt dispirited, knowing without a doubt that this sister whom she loved was at that moment striding out, glorying in the day and the elements, and elated by her temporary escape from the bonds of a suffocatingly close relationship. She hoped Lizzie would keep to the path and not be deflected by a sudden impulse to change the plan. The map had indicated that the path was well delineated, and there should be no obstacle to their encountering each other again on the eastern side of the circle they were following. Of course they would meet up. She shook her head to clear her misgivings.

Slowly Anna relaxed as she walked, and she put thoughts of Lizzie's sprightly progress out of her mind and started to enjoy her own. After half an hour, she met a couple walking the path in the opposite direction, and was at ease enough to bid them a cheerful 'Good day', which by then she meant and felt. After an hour, the clouds started to disperse and blue sky appeared between them. The wind decreased a little and Anna undid her top two buttons. She stopped her self-centred reflections and began to admire her surroundings and to see the colours of the heather and the grass, and listen to the birds, the sough of the autumnal wind in the trees, and the rustle of the fallen leaves as she walked through them. Time seemed to accelerate, and there were a few other walkers about now as she began to wonder whether she was nearly halfway round and when she would see Lizzie coming towards her. Her bad mood had evaporated and she was looking forward to their reconciliation. She would ensure that the harmony of their previous walks was restored.

Another half hour passed. She was determined not to feel anxious – perhaps Lizzie was tired and had stopped beside the path to rest. She imagined her sitting on a stone or a fence and losing time in her peaceful contemplation of the pastoral scene – Lizzie was always quoting that trite poem about having 'time to stand and stare'. After a few more minutes' walking, she admitted to herself that she felt a bit tired and decided to have a short break. She sat down on a slightly raised bank and glanced up the path ahead of her winding down a slight incline and passing through a thicket about a hundred yards from where she was sitting. No doubt she would soon see Lizzie coming towards her unaware that her delay might be causing concern. But for the present, the path was empty. Anna was hungry and felt in her pocket for the half bar of chocolate left from their earlier walk along part of the Pennine Way. She ate it slowly and looked back along the path she had walked, willing Lizzie to appear while her gaze was averted. She wondered which way they would take back to the car – which one of them would retrace their steps. She would magnanimously let Lizzie make the decision. She wouldn't mind. She glanced over her shoulder. Still nothing.

She turned back to face the south and the sun which was

now shining in between the clouds, and closed her eyes, willing herself to relax and dispel her uneasiness. She would not look again – all was well. It could only be about two o'clock. She became distracted for a moment by a buzzard wheeling over a patch of coarse ground where tufts of bleached grass were sticking up. Some poor little field mouse or vole was under surveillance. Then she heard a sound of distant steps on the stony path. Lizzie, at last. She exhaled slowly and decided she would not turn round yet nor give any hint that she was waiting or worried. But her relief finally got the better of her, and she stood up and turned round. A figure was indeed coming towards her, but it was not Lizzie.

She registered disappointment and then blinked and stared. A man in a black anorak with a small rucksack on his back was advancing along the path, and round his waist was a yellow scarf. As he got nearer, she recognised the blue fringe which hung down from the knot. She felt paralysed with apprehension – not for her own safety but for Lizzie's. How had he got the scarf? Where was Lizzie? The man was now fifty paces away and walking steadily. Anna was invaded by panic and a sick feeling of horror in the pit of her stomach. Her vision blurred as he approached her uttering an obscenely normal 'Good afternoon' as he passed and continued on his route. She gasped and swung round; his tall frame was already moving away and there was no longer any menace in his receding back. The figure with its yellow banner gradually grew smaller and was finally lost to view round a bend. The emptiness rocked around her. She knew now that Lizzie was not going to appear.

Anna stood on the alien path and quelled the urge to run after the walker and demand to know how he had got the scarf and what he had done with Lizzie. Her mind mushroomed with images of rape and assault and the possibility of her familiar body, broken and dead, pushed into the undergrowth. But there was no point – he would not tell her, would not admit to anything. He had had a pleasant, ordinary appearance. He had not looked guilty – but few murderers did. But he had worn Lizzie's scarf tied round his waist. He had no reason to hide his trophy – he would not think to meet anyone who might recognise it. And in her fright she had not got a good look at his face – so would she be able to identify him?

She dared not turn back, so stumbled forward instead, looking on either side for signs of the crime. She tried to tell herself that it might not be that bad – but she could not think of any reason why Lizzie would have given away her beautiful scarf to a complete stranger – it would have had to have been wrested from her. She had to get help, tell someone, find a telephone and call the police. After a miserable frantic few minutes, she came across a small path leading off to the right, and decided to follow it to see if it led to a road and any dwellings. Fortunately this part of the Peak District was more populated and she hoped she might meet other people along the way. She was filled with dreadful misgivings and her chest pulsated with panicky sobs. But curiously another part of her mind was telling her not to jump to conclusions and not to overreact. However, the faint idea that there might be an innocent explanation was irrationally rejected and Anna was soon running and gasping, overwhelmed by hideous apprehensions.

She then realised that in her haste and confusion she had lost the tiny path, and seemed to be on a wide expanse of rough open ground. She saw some trees in the distance and, for no particular reason, headed for them. At length, and just before she had reached a stage of utter exhaustion, she staggered across a field and burst through a hedge into a narrow lane. Looking wildly one way and then the other for any sign

'Lost your ticket, have you?' he asks in a bored tone. She suddenly realises that she had never bought one and again apologises before admitting this and asking him for a single to Portsmouth. 'You sure you want a single?' he says, and when she replies that she's going back by boat, he looks at her with that pitying sympathy he reserves for the kind of nutcases who think they can travel back to London by boat! She pays him and he hands her the single ticket with a curt nod, then moves on through the crowded carriage.

Anna slowly places the ticket in her wallet which she then puts back in her jacket pocket and lets her hands drop to her lap. Without difficulty she dives back into the past and the sudden confrontation on a windy day outside a country pub.

'Anna, what's happened?' Lizzie's voice had been full of concern.

'How can you ask me that?' Anna spluttered. 'I thought you were dead.' Within seconds the huge bubble of relief, which had enveloped her once she knew that Lizzie was alive after all, exploded into fury. 'How could you do this to me?' she shrieked.

Anna remembers her incandescent anger and the incoherent accusations she hurled at Lizzie. There was a lot of shouting and she knew that it was coming from her. She was aware of the two men standing silently watching the spectacle, whilst Lizzie kept quietly repeating: 'Listen, listen to me. Stop. Anna, will you listen?'

Eventually, drained of everything, Anna stopped, and promptly sank to her knees. Lizzie crouched down beside her and patted her rhythmically on her back. Anna was too exhausted to shrug her off.

An hour later, Lizzie and Anna reached their car. They had been given a lift by one of the customers from the pub. For half an hour after Anna's appearance there and the ensuing scene, the two women had sat at a picnic table in the rear garden, which afforded enough privacy for them to exchange explanations and recriminations. The wind blew round them as they sat with hunched shoulders and tried to reach some sort of equilibrium and truce.

Lizzie had listened to Anna's story and privately thought she had overreacted somewhat hysterically, although she was also touched that her adopted sibling had been so concerned for her safety. She had then insisted on Anna remaining silent while she told her side of things and explained why she was not at fault, and had not caused her so much pain out of thoughtlessness.

Lizzie had said that she had walked for about two hours, taking pleasure in the scenery and the exercise, and neither thinking about Anna nor dwelling on their quarrel. Then, having consulted the map, she had identified the path which led to the hamlet and the small pub which walkers often stopped at for refreshment. Some elder trees and thorn bushes partially concealed the entrance to this smaller path, and Lizzie was worried, since she had the map, that Anna might walk past the turning, so she had waited for a while on the main track for her to come by. But she was thirsty and had nothing to drink – Anna was the one who had carried the bottle of water – so she decided to drape her distinctive long yellow scarf over the bushes in an arrow shape. She knew that Anna would recognise the scarf and had no doubt that she would realise Lizzie's intention in placing it there, and would join her at the pub. After all, going there had been the original arrangement before they had had their silly row and gone off in opposite directions. How was she to know that some interfering walker would pass by and take the scarf? He probably hadn't even stolen it, but thought he might run into the person to whom it belonged and return it. It was hardly her fault that her sign had been removed, or that Anna jumped to such an over-dramatic conclusion.

Anna was extremely upset and still felt very aggrieved and resentful because she thought that Lizzie should have kept to the arrangement and stayed on the main path until she had arrived at their rendezvous. Any other course of action was selfish and irresponsible. Surely she should have realised that there was too much possibility for error – the scarf might have blown away before she got there, for example. She was convinced, quite irrationally, that it was because Lizzie was still irritated with her that she had decided to punish her by leaving her to walk alone. No, Anna was not to be placated. She had, after all, been thoroughly frightened and distressed by the other's total lack of consideration.

To resume the walk had clearly been impossible – Anna was too weary and emotionally exhausted – so Lizzie had got someone to give them a lift to their car. During the drive there, Anna remained silent to demonstrate her continuing anger and sense of being ill-used.

From their original starting point, Lizzie drove their car back to the bed and breakfast, and still Anna would not say anything. Together in their room, yet apart in mutual resentment, they changed, packed up their things, and got ready to leave. Since Anna was still upset, Lizzie decided she should do the driving home and they made their way south in strained silence. By the time they reached London, Lizzie was almost as angry as her companion. Their ill humour could not be dissipated and they parted in mute acrimony.

Neither of them felt inclined to contact the other for a couple of months, at which point Lizzie decided that it was silly to go on feeling resentment and wrote her friend a letter of reconciliation. Anna, whose rancour was also diminishing, had already tried to phone Lizzie but there had been no reply and she had left no message. She had wanted to make it up with Lizzie and tell her that she was off to the Continent on her travels again. Irritated once more by the fact that her sibling was not there for her, she left without trying to make contact again, and without leaving any forwarding address at the rented flat she was now quitting. Lizzie's letter was delivered to an empty hall and lay amongst other envelopes and circulars gathering dust.

After wandering through the Netherlands, Anna got a temporary job in The Hague, from where she soon gravitated back to her favourite European city – Paris. There, fluent in French, she always managed to find occupation and accommodation. The two women did not see each other for nearly two years, by which time Lizzie had met Paul and Anna had become involved with Malo. The painful memory of her agonised fear that Lizzie was dead and the bitterness of their subsequent rupture on that day of the walk haunted Anna for a long time.

And even now, Anna feels the tightness and terror that overwhelmed her when she first thought that Lizzie was dead. To banish this feeling and the pain of her over-emotional reaction, she focuses her eyes on the trees alongside the railway track on which the train is now slowing down to arrive at the next station. She has long since forgiven Lizzie – not that forgiveness is necessary in such a close relationship as theirs. They always come back together after every separation; after discord their unity is eventually renewed. It is like a law of nature – of their natures. Indeed, they are moving back towards each other at this very moment, Anna reminds herself.

The train shudders to a halt at a station. Anna decides not

to look out of the window. She does not want to know where she is. She finds the suspension of knowledge of time and place soothing and simplifying. She studies the backs of her hands – her knuckles are wrinkled and the raised veins and tendons show clearly in the translucent skin. Her knuckles seem over large compared with the narrower sections of her fingers. Carpus, metacarpus and phalange – a shred of memory from school biology brings the names of the bones into her mind. She hears a train door slam but ignores it. She will not allow her thoughts to be transferred from the contemplation of her hands to some action outside her enclosed capsule. Her hands are ugly but they are strong – or they used to be. Sometimes now her trusty right thumb lets her down and she cannot open jars and bottles that she used have no trouble with. She had once, indeed, prided herself on her ability to open with dexterity the stiff lid of any container. She knows that now she is physically depleted – but refuses to let her mind go down that path. She does not yet want to confront her inevitable decline. So Anna continues to concentrate on her hands. She registers the fact that her nails are short and uneven – and also that she does not care. There are some brown blotches on the skin near her knuckles – signs of age. In fact, the back of her hands look far older than their years. As the train draws out of the station – it's probably Guildford or Godalming, she cannot help thinking – she turns her hands over. With the palms upwards, they could be those of a much younger woman. They are exposed, soft and rounded, her fingers unadorned by rings, her thumbs splayed out to the sides. Some bars of light flicker over them, probably from the rays of sunlight filtering through trees the train is passing. The sun is lower now and its light is less intense, and its rays illuminate the subtle peachy colour of her palms. They seem vulnerable and almost beautiful. Slowly

173

# Chapter Nine

After waking up, Paul had a shower and he is now lying on the double berth, with a towel wrapped round his waist. The cabin is warm and he picks up the newspaper with a sigh of contentment.

Lizzie is sitting on the chair watching him. He has a good physique – for a man of nearly sixty; his skin is still smooth – not as firm as Alan's had been, and without the bronze sheen of Adam's. She is reminded that the loss of the sculpture coincided with her discovery of Paul's first bout of unfaithfulness. At that time she had been convinced that Anna was having an affair with her husband. This had sparked off a severe quarrel which had poisoned their friendship for a long time. Anna's rebuttal had been robust with self-righteous indignation at Lizzie's lack of justification for such an outrageous charge, and her accusation that Lizzie had 'stolen' the bronze was a savage counter-attack, equally unjust.

For Lizzie had been wrong. Though Paul was, as she later discovered, indeed being unfaithful to her at that time, it was not with Anna. A female friend had passed on to her the report that Paul had been seen leaving a night club late at night with Anna, on an evening when he had told her he was dining with some foreign business colleagues and had not returned until the morning. He claimed he had unexpectedly met up with Anna at the night club to which they had all gone after the dinner, and she had been having trouble with her companion, who was drinking heavily. Paul had excused himself from his associates and left to help Anna and her companion home as he was worried about the latter being troublesome and potentially violent. Back at her flat, he and Anna had sat up all night dealing with the drunk, who was threatening to commit suicide. Paul had phoned home but Lizzie had not answered the call, and the next day he admitted to her that he had been at Anna's flat all night and told her what had happened. Lizzie refused to believe him. She also refused to accept Anna's corroboration of the night's events, and felt, in her words, 'utterly betrayed by both of them'.

Paul's protestations of his innocence were rejected by his wife because Lizzie had for some time suspected that her husband was involved with another woman – his oddly tender treatment of her and his vague responses to her questions about what he had done that day when he got home in the evening didn't add up. Her patience and credulity had snapped when he stayed out the whole night. His unlikely explanation had in fact been the truth. But what was also true, though to this he did not confess, was that he also spent the occasional afternoon at a 'private business meeting' with a management consultant called Janine. Lizzie was entirely ignorant of this, so she made an understandable miscalculation in assuming Anna was the guilty one. The latter was outraged at the allegation that she and Paul were having an affair, and having denied it totally and truthfully, she in turn became very angry with Lizzie for not believing her.

*     *     *

Lizzie is now having a hot shower herself. She is still thinking about Paul and Anna and her misguided accusation. Her thoughts skip forward three years to the time when the two of them did embark on a brief sexual liaison. Quite by chance she discovered this. One day Paul had casually used an expression which Lizzie, with a sisterly knowledge, knew was unique to Anna, and on another occasion he had referred to an incident which had been a secret between her and Anna. She herself had never mentioned the matter to him, so the information could only have come from Anna. However, when she realised what was taking place in secret between her husband and her closest friend, she suppressed her immediate reaction to expose the deception, and with considerable self-control kept quiet about it and chose not to shame either of them. She had often wondered whether her earlier accusation had somehow lodged the idea in Anna's mind and made the improbable seem more possible. Also, her long-established habit of sharing everything with her friend seemed somehow to make the lapse less culpable. In any case, the episode was short-lived and Lizzie knew instinctively when it was over. It is odd that she has never told Paul about her knowledge of the affair. Perhaps back then she had been less secure about his attachment to her and had thought that exposure of his second act of unfaithfulness might open some irreparable cracks in their relationship.

She is towelling herself dry. The affair between her adopted sibling and her husband has been over a long time. So why does she now have the urge to tell him that she knows about it? Perhaps it is because their marriage bargain is now more firmly established, or because she wants to flex her muscles. She ought to resist the impulse to rekindle dead coals. It will serve no purpose. She leaves the tiny shower cubicle and walks back into the cabin. She puts on her underwear and then decides to make a cup of tea. She fills the small kettle from the tray and switches it on.

Paul is looking out of their cabin window. The sea has become a little more choppy since he fell asleep after making love to Lizzie, and there are some grey streaks of fraying clouds in the early-evening sky. He has always liked love in the afternoon – it feels illicit and naughty. He prefers having sex in the light – though Lizzie seems to find it oddly embarrassing – she prefers the dark. But she goes along with him – she is obliging and loving. He is a lucky man. He puts the newspaper down, leaning back against the pillows on the cabin bed and watching Lizzie in her underwear while she makes them some tea. Having a deluxe cabin means they can brew a hot drink when they want or have a beer out of the small fridge without needing to queue and then search for a table and seats. Lizzie doesn't mind mixing with the crowds on board, but he prefers to be self-indulgently private. He takes the cup as she hands it to him and smiles up at her.

'It's almost time for a drink,' he says.

'This *is* a drink,' she responds.

'You know what I mean.'

'It must be strange,' Lizzie says, settling into an armchair across the cabin from the bed, 'coming from a background where meals and drinks are habitually taken at particular times of the day. If parents have this custom it seems to become instilled in their children, who carry on the habit. Mine never did – meals were there, but not always at the same time each day. So different from yours, with your mother always having tea at four thirty and your father the first drink of the evening at seven and not a minute earlier. Patterns of behaviour are so comforting that people often continue with them and don't question the practicality of such strict routines.' Lizzie is enjoying airing her views and throwing in a few taunts. 'I often like to do things in a different order or to eat at odd times – it gives me a feeling of freedom and departure from convention. I think we should drink when thirsty or because we want some stimulant – caffeine or alcohol – and not because it is the "right" time to do so.' There is a very slight sneer in her voice.

'We're all different.' Paul utters the cliché intentionally. It is his practised way of defusing a potential argument. He has heard her expound on this theme before, and knows where it could lead. He drinks his tea placidly, and hopes that Lizzie is not in one of her critical moods. Sometimes she fastens on to a topic and won't leave it alone. Better not to catch her eye. He glances down at his bare chest and registers than he is feeling just a little cool, but is too lazy to do anything about it.

For the moment Lizzie is happy to be deflected. She recognises that her husband is using one of his easy-going remarks to steer the conversation away from anything that might be confrontational. It irks her a little but she goes along with it. For the present. She drinks her tea thoughtfully.

Paul's thoughts have moved on, as they often do, to contemplation of his arrangements for the next day. As far as he can remember, he asked his assistant to be sure to leave his first morning back at work clear of appointments. This is to give him time to catch up on the progress of various business projects, and assess how things are going. Then he can make any decisions which seem to be a priority. His absence – whether on account of business or pleasure – does not cause a problem: he has hand-picked his small team of employees, and he has learnt the art of delegation only to those whose skills he has astutely identified and on whose judgement he relies. He values these employees' contribution to the success of his business and he wisely rewards them well. Conversely, if one of them proves untrustworthy or lazy, Paul will dismiss that person without hesitation. He expects his staff to work with the same dedication and drive that he does. He is a hard man but a fair one. Happily, his philosophy seems to work well, and there is on the whole a satisfying camaraderie in the office, with only the occasional disagreement or bout of envy or pettiness. Paul does not tolerate discord and, though a business cannot always run smoothly, he is sensible enough to know that he should ignore trivial problems and concentrate on the bigger issues.

Tomorrow afternoon, for instance, he has an important appointment with a client for whom he does a large amount of business in Japan. It will be a tricky meeting at which he will draw on all his charm, skill and iron determination. After his ten days away, meandering through France with his wife, Paul is looking forward to resuming the gritty art of negotiating a lucrative deal. He smiles in anticipation of the tactics he will employ against his shrewd and powerful opponent. The best man will no doubt win – and Paul feels confident of success.

His thoughts return to the here and now – and what he needs next is a good meal. Preceded by a cold drink. He is hungry, and food is a pleasure. He has always been unashamed by his partiality for fine wine and his enjoyment of a well-prepared dinner at home or a sophisticated meal at a restaurant. He works hard. He deserves these things.

'We ought to have an early dinner at about seven, since the ferry arrives around nine,' Paul says, and then looks apologetic as he catches sight of his wife's amused expression at his need to be so regimented. 'Sorry, darling. It's become a habit of mine to have a leisurely dinner and drinks beforehand. You know I've spent so much of my business life dealing with irregular schedules and working in strange places and at odd times, but now that I'm nearing retirement I want a more ordered life. It's more comfortable.' He glances down with a look of slight surprise at the cup he is holding, as if it ought to be a glass.

Lizzie follows his glance and sees the well-kept fingernails of her husband's large, smooth thumb and forefinger which grasp the small handle. 'It's more comfort*ing*,' she says, amending what he has just said. 'All men want comforting – by the first drink, by a smiling wife, by regular meals.'

'You've hit it on the head,' Paul agrees amiably and without any trace of apology. 'No fuss, no bother, no nagging. That's the life all selfish males want.'

'You admit it so openly – you're almost proud of it.' Lizzie is nettled. She has finished her tea and is looking in their bag for her skirt.

'What do you want me to say? That I like disruption, trouble, or criticism? Of course I don't. Nobody does. They just put up with it if it happens. Sensible normal people try to avoid it. Both at work and at home.'

'Sensible normal people! Sometimes, Paul, you are so bland. I rarely have a good argument with you. We don't seem to get beyond platitudes. Why can't I have a serious discussion with you – about important things? The way I can with Anna.'

'Oh, so we're back to Anna again. Your "close" relationship with Anna!' The same sneering tone has now been adopted by Paul, whose patience is evaporating. Lizzie has finally managed to get under his skin, and he is disappointed that his self-restraint has been worn down. He gets up off the bunk and starts pulling on his clothes with irritated haste. 'Do you know, I'm surprised you two have never been accused

181

of being gay. When I first met you both I almost thought you were.'

'We did once have a conversation about the possibility of a lesbian relationship.' Lizzie is now dressing too, and neither of them is looking at the other. 'But we decided that it wouldn't work because although we love each other's minds, we don't desire each other's bodies. Which seems necessary for a full-blown affair.'

'Well I certainly couldn't love a man.' Paul's tone conveys the careless distaste of the prejudiced heterosexual male.

'If you did you'd probably call it friendship. You'd certainly love your brother if you had one.' She stops and looks out of the cabin window and into her mind. 'Anna is like a twin – she's probably dearer to me than blood siblings usually are. We've known each other so long and shared so much. She's almost my soul sister.'

Paul has long been irritated by the two women's intimacy and mutual affection. '"I can talk to Anna when I can't talk to you,"' he mimics his wife's voice, mocking a remark of hers that has just surfaced in his mind. He is now fully dressed and leaning against the cabin door with his arms folded in frustration. He does not recognise the savage feeling he now experiences as jealousy, but that is what it is, and Lizzie knows it. They have had similar exchanges before.

Lizzie is determined to be calm and unemotional. 'We talk about different things. And we argue too – we've had so many rows and separations and reunions. The way lovers do.'

'So you love Anna more than me.'

'I love her differently.' Lizzie sits on the chair to put on her shoes. She looks up at the irate face of her husband as he scowls from the doorway. 'She's a part of me. She's joined to me in a spiritual way. We orbit round each other.' Her face takes on an intent look as she tries to explain accurately the nature of her complex relationship with Anna. 'She and I move in our different circles, and they sometimes come together and sometimes move apart. When they do come together it's either blissful harmony or a collision which causes a miserable estrangement. It can be either – we don't know which until it happens. It can be very exciting and fulfilling or very painful. But it's so intense that we can't stay close together for long before we push apart again.' Lizzie is becoming almost lyrical in her song of sisterhood. 'Anna is my haven, my anchor, my confidante. But when it gets too claustrophobic, we have to break free again. We're in our own individual spaces much of the time, but I can't live fully without knowing she's out there somewhere moving towards me, thinking about me. That makes me feel cherished and secure – and her too.'

'Don't I do that for you? Isn't that what I spend most of my time trying to do?' Paul demands angrily. He loves his wife and feels humiliated and hurt by her description of a love which she obviously sees as a higher and purer emotion than anything she feels for him.

'Yes, you do. Physically you do.' Lizzie knows she has hurt him, but this is the truth and the truth is often painful.

'Bloody Anna. Fascinating Anna. Why can't she leave us alone? She drives me mad. What *is* so bloody wonderful about her?'

'You should know, Paul – you've been close to her too.'

Paul's overheated face drains of colour. The reference is too pointed – she must know. He is stunned that this has surfaced. Carelessly, he has driven Lizzie too far by ranting against Anna and she has managed to turn the tables on him yet again. Putting on his shoes as a stalling tactic to mask his confusion and give him time to think of a strategy to deal with this, he bends over and loosens the laces.

Talking to the back of his guiltily averted head, Lizzie calmly tells Paul that she has known all along about his affair with Anna a few years before. She knew it had happened when she was away in Greece working on a holiday brochure commercial. 'It was something you said after my return. You used a turn of phrase which only she and I use, said something about having no regrets and not looking back. And your oddly distant behaviour towards each other when we were next all together merely confirmed it.'

Paul is astounded to have been found out. He feels sorry, not because he had been unfaithful, but because his actions must have upset Lizzie. In his view sexual disloyalty does not score as a very bad vice – such behaviour is a transitory amusement or an irresistible challenge but, for him, inconsequential. He assures himself that this need not damage a loving marriage, and has prided himself on being very discreet with his affairs – most of all the one with Anna. However, he is sensitive enough to know that women – in particular his wife – see these things differently. 'Why didn't you tell us you knew?' he asks, addressing the remark to his shoes, relieved that he is occupied with tying his laces and does not have to look at his wife.

Lizzie thinks for a moment before replying. 'On an earlier occasion I had accused you both of having an affair when you were innocent, and that had caused a lot of pain all round. I wasn't going to go through all of that again even though the second time you were guilty.' She sits down in front of the mirror to brush her hair. 'Anyway, I forgave you both long ago. It seemed wise never to mention it to either of you.' She pauses and adds reflectively, 'Though I expect Anna realised I knew.'

At the time Lizzie had been upset, but now the memory of

their joint faithlessness does not bother her. She has long taken the view that she was just as happy to share Paul with Anna as she has been to share Adam with her. She had chosen not to say anything because she loved both of them and felt that by saying nothing she could retain their commitment to her. She had been right.

'It was a short-lived aberration,' mutters Paul, straightening up whilst looking down at his hands as if to check them, and thus avoiding his wife's eyes. 'I don't know what came over us. She felt as bad about it as I did.'

'I know,' says his wife soothingly, her back turned to him. 'I knew when it came to an end too. What a painfully guilty few weeks it must have been for you both.' She finishes applying her make-up and scrutinises her reflected face.

'It was dreadful.' He looks up and, seeing Lizzie smiling at herself in the mirror, continues more buoyantly, 'But a lot of water has passed under the bridge since then, eh, Lizzie?' He smiles awkwardly as she turns and smiles comfortingly back at him. It will be all right. He is relieved. 'Forgiven and forgotten?'

'Of course,' says Lizzie smoothly and emphatically. She clips on her earrings. Forgiven – yes, of course. Forgotten – no. She does not forget things – neither does Anna.

'Ready for dinner, darling?' Paul holds out his hand. He has come through unscathed. It feels almost as good as avoiding tax or securing a much-wanted contract. He can hardly believe it.

Lizzie rises to her feet, watching herself behave as an actress might – an elegant middle-aged woman about to dine with her erring but loving husband. She smiles and puts her hand in his. 'Let's go,' she says.

The train has been dawdling outside Havant, and Anna can

see the South Downs hazy in the dusk, and the calm waters of the Spithead beyond, with the Isle of Wight floating above them, its paler greys merging into the dusty blue early-evening sky. She remembers that as a child she used to go to the Isle of Wight for holidays in Shanklin with her family. Her father used to drive them all from Somerset, and Gavin and she used to chat, bicker and shriek in the back of the car until their parents could stand it no longer and one of them would shout from the front seat for 'two minutes' silence', during which the children would squirm, make faces and dig each other in the ribs. But as they came nearer to the coast, her mother would announce that soon, when they reached the top of the next hill, they would be able to see the sea – the glistening expanse of water which they had not glimpsed since the summer before. She and Gavin would crane their necks and peer over the shoulders of their parents, and then as they came up over the Downs they would catch sight of the view, which rekindled the excitement and freedom of their summer holiday, and all of them would laughingly shout out together the family joke phrase: 'Long time no sea'.

During the crossing on the old-fashioned car ferry from Portsmouth to Fishbourne, the children would scamper up and down the stairs and out onto the decks whilst their parents hovered nearby keeping a careful eye on the pair as they peered over the rails at the other boats on the water. Later, when they were driving across the island, if it was a sunny afternoon, Anna and her mother would happily sing together the Harry Belafonte song 'This is My Island in the Sun', and Anna would experience a sense of possessive warmth and well-being which heralded the start of their annual stay on the beloved island.

Gavin is there now. In his own way he loves the Isle of Wight more than his sister has and he chooses to return here with his own family year after year. He has many old friends on the island and so it was an obvious choice for him as a venue for his fiftieth birthday celebration. Some years after their mother died, the siblings' father decided to retire there, and when he subsequently died they had inherited his retirement home. Anna did not envisage revisiting Shanklin on a regular basis, so Gavin bought her out, and he now uses the small house as his holiday place. It is not far from the modest hotel in which they had always stayed for the last two weeks of every August during their childhood. He has a sentimental nature and it makes him feel connected to the past. Anna feels a little sorry for his wife, Ellen, who had been married previously to a man who had given her holidays in the Bahamas; she might feel that the Isle of Wight is a bit of a poor substitute, but says nothing – at least not to her sister-in-law. There are two daughters from her first marriage who used to like the Isle of Wight until they too grew up and grew out of family holidays. Anna is surprised that Ellen and Gavin have never had children, but she is not close enough to her brother to be able to talk to him about such intimate subjects. However, he seems happy enough with his home in Buckinghamshire and his holiday retreat on the island.

Anna has always felt a little guilty that her adopted sibling Lizzie has supplanted her brother in her affections. But it all happened a long while ago and, though no doubt Gavin has forgiven her, it has led to a lack of openness in their relationship. His exclusion from the inner realm of her life has put a distance between them which neither of them really makes much effort to diminish. In common with many brothers and sisters, they once shared a past but they do not choose to see much of each other in the present, nor will they in the future. Gavin is, thinks Anna, a kind and modest man who is conventional and hard-working, but he disapproves of his older sister, her lack of ambition, her itinerant life and her choice of men – many of whom have been embarrassingly young. He finds her friends too 'alternative', and she thinks his associates too dull. Rejected by the exotic Lizzie, he had found solace with the prosaic. Were it not for the bond of shared parentage, she knows they would never have kept in touch.

The evening ahead of her does not promise excitement – but there will be warmth, honesty and laughter, which her current life often lacks. She doesn't really know why she is bothering to go, when there seem to be much bigger issues about life and death for her to be contemplating. She would not be missed – Gavin would shrug and accept her absence in the same way that he has become used to her other foibles. Some years ago, she was meant to have returned from Paris for his wedding, but she had taken an assignment in the Middle East and was unable to return in time. She had sent a telegram, and Gavin in his gentle way had not taken offence at her absence. He has learnt not to expect me, Anna ruefully observes. She admits to herself that she is not proud of the casual and inconsiderate way she has treated her brother. Her devotion and loyalty have been given to others. And above all, and to the detriment of all her other relationships, she has consigned a large chunk of her soul to Lizzie.

She tries to visualise what Lizzie is doing at this moment. No doubt she and Paul are still on the ferry as it approaches the eastern tip of the Isle of Wight, round which it must sail to enter the Solent. Perhaps they are reading in their cabin or having an early meal. The vessel is to dock in Portsmouth, and it is to this port that Anna's train is also now heading.

The train judders to a halt. The reason cannot be leaves on the line because it is spring, not autumn. It is unlikely to have

188

been caused by someone jumping off the train – though she remembers that she was once held up on a train to Birmingham by a suicide. No one really knew what had caused the hour's delay but rumours of a tragedy involving a young man on the tracks near a railway cutting had eventually trickled through the carriages. Perhaps a problem with points or a red signal will be announced.

She stares out of the window and is confronted by the back of a row of terraced houses, their long, narrow gardens running down to the boundary fence of the railway line. She always thinks that there is something very intrusive about staring at the backs of houses. The front facades and gardens are on view to the public and show a smart, perhaps delusively confident face to the outside world. But the rear aspect shows the vulnerable and intimate side of the homes – windows with tatty curtains, crumbling paintwork and broken gutters contrast with new rear extensions, patios with plastic chairs and hanging baskets. Some gardens are scruffy with battered toys or discarded bikes lying around whilst others show a passion for gardening with small neat sheds and clipped hedges. She feels like a voyeur as she stares into these homes. A small memory tugs at her – it is of the time years before when Lizzie was plagued by a stalker who intrusively watched her house. The carriage jerks forward and jolts her out of this train of thought, and she looks at her watch. It is late and she is doubtful whether she will now catch the early catamaran across to Ryde – she may have to wait for the next one. The train moves on gradually down the track. Strangely, her day has slowed down, whilst her unruly introspections seem to be picking up tempo and dancing forward. But to what end? There may be a decision she will have to make. It is not clear yet what that will be or who will have to be involved. Need she consider anyone other than herself? Can she be so selfish as to not take into account those few human beings to whom she is close?

She suddenly thinks of Youenn, brooding in his French house, one hour ahead of her in time, a decade ahead of her in years. She should probably have stuck with Malo – why did she change a lifetime's habit of preferring youth and vitality to age and experience? Selfishness is inherent in both extremes. She knows her choice has been a mistake. Is it one that she has to live with, or is there now a chance to escape? She imagines her husband striding purposefully along the village street after taking his early-evening pastis at the Café du Centre, and arriving at the door of his Breton house. The house martins will be wheeling overhead but he will not hear their shrieks, nor will their darting swoops lighten his mood. She feels that by now he will be sitting in the *séjour*, staring at nothing, but focusing on her. She has a sudden sense of alarm, as if he is reaching across the Channel to her. Rabbit-like, she has got caught in the glare of his atten-tion, and she feels pinioned in the intensity of his gaze as she tries unsuccessfully to banish him from her thoughts. Will she be able to stay with him until the end or will she leave him? Can she really commit another selfish crime by abandoning this man, as she had done so often before with other men? She knows that it is easy to come and go – the hard thing is to remain.

Her stepson Malo must be twenty-nine now. She knows his address in Paris but never hears from him. Occasionally he is mentioned by his sister when she visits their father, but he has decided never to communicate with his stepmother – his ex-lover – again. He will not forgive her for leaving him for his father. She recalls the last time she saw him – seven years ago on the night when she told him about her defection to Youenn. Malo had been trying to persuade her to do some drugs with him. She had refused – not for the first time – and on this occasion, instead of being understanding about her reluctance to lose control of her mind, he had been angry and contemptuous. He had accused her of avoiding the excitement of risk-taking, of rejecting spontaneity and experimentation and of being incapable of letting go. He took her by the shoulders and put his face close to her and in a scornful tone said she was becoming boring and bourgeois. 'Boring and bourgeois,' he repeated as he shook her. She was upset, not by the pain he was inflicting on her, but by foreknowledge of the acute distress that she was about to cause him when she told him that she was deserting him. He mistook her tears, and then, in one of his quick mood changes, he had become ardent and aroused. Reluctantly and in confusion she had made love with him. The act was almost brutal and had reminded her of a sickening occasion earlier in her life when she had been coerced.

Afterwards, smoking a joint in bed, Malo, in a totally changed and lighter mood, had talked of where they would travel together. He did not mind what people said about the disparity in their ages, nor did he want to have children. With the confidence and extravagant optimism of youth, he talked of how they would live together for ever. She watched the smoke drift upwards and through its wreaths saw his serene young face. Then she told him.

At first he thought she was joking; then he refused to believe her, but when Malo finally realised that she meant what she said – that she was really going to abandon him – puzzlement turned to agony and the bubble of his happiness imploded. His anguish had been appalling, his anger frightening. All the young man's self-assurance and *joie de vivre* crumbled within seconds. His loss at an early age of his own mother had clearly scarred him more deeply than he cared to admit. His passion for Anna – the older woman, a maternal idol who was also his lover – had insulated and protected him from the outside world. He cried out that he didn't need others, that he'd abandoned his other friendships with people of his own age. All he wanted was her – her mind, her body and her love. He had not doubted her – he had relied on her and now she was forsaking him. For whom? he wanted to know.

For whom? Telling him that his successful rival was his own father was so hard – and he took it so badly. His rage was frightening. In an almost incoherent tantrum he damned them both to hell and spluttered death threats against his father. When he finally burnt out his fury, he lay on the floor face down like a bruised and exhausted child and refused to look at her. When she was sure that he was going to be all right and he had realised that the desire and resolve of her and his father were stronger than his, she felt she should leave. She did not want to wait for the sulky acceptance, the muted protests and misery which would eventually follow, and which would reveal to her the sad depths of his insecurity. Such a depressing tirade would make her dislike herself even more. Her beautiful, sunny, temperamental boy lover was to be discarded because she needed someone stronger and more mature. After momentary hesitation and under a cloud of shame and premonition, she slunk out of the attic apartment and never went back.

The next day she took a train down to Brittany and Youenn. A new life – or so she thought. Now, in another train at another time, she remembers the combination of shame and elation. And, at that time, hope.

*     *     *

Lizzie and Paul have booked their table in the ferry restaurant, and are having a pre-dinner drink in the bar looking out over the sea. The Isle of Wight is just visible ahead – a vague outline, pink and misty in the evening sun. Lizzie is seated on a high chrome stool – she has always rather liked bar stools which have a jazzy decadence about them, as this appeals to her self-confessed conventional image of romance and sleaze. She is watching the French barman as he deftly opens bottles and holds glasses under the optics. He pours out measures with a flourish and adroitly bears two glasses in one hand whilst he administers the mixers. His fingers are long, hairless and very clean; he has a ring on his marriage finger and another on his right hand. When he is looking for a particular bottle on the shelf behind the bar, he moves his splayed fingers along the row until he spots the right one and then his hand dives in to grasp it. There is a quiet, professional flamboyance in his movements that he may be exaggerating slightly for the benefit of an attractive female onlooker.

Paul is sitting on his stool with his back to the bar, watching a couple at a table who appear to be having a row. He enjoys watching confrontations in others – and he has seen many played out in real life and in plays over the years – but he does not want to be involved. His considerable organisational skills stop short of troubleshooting. He employs others to do that. Floating in this comfortable capsule in between holiday and work, lounging at yet another bar – a familiar occupation – he feels expansive, relaxed and stress free. He has already forgotten his embarrassment in the cabin half an hour before. He turns to the barman and orders a second drink for himself, and asks his wife if she would like another too.

Lizzie smiles at the young man as he raises his eyebrows interrogatively at her, and shakes her head. She has decided that she will accept his admiration of her, which he is probably faking, as doing so will enable her to glow in its warmth. She is only human, and enjoys soaking up adoration; she loves curtain calls, flowers or messages sent round to the stage door, and fan mail or letters asking for a photograph. But she draws the line at evoking jealousy and teasing victims – that is cruel, and she does not indulge in that. Though Anna, she reflects, is not always so considerate.'

She recalls a discussion on attraction and jealousy which she and Anna had some years before. 'At school you were far too pretty,' Anna had told her, 'and all the boys hovered round you like flies round a honey pot. I felt quite envious – and it's a tribute to my good sense that I didn't hate you for being so attractive.'

Lizzie had giggled at her friend, 'You looked after me and protected me from the envy of the other girls. And I covered up for you when you were wicked, and when you were found out. I softened up the teachers, defended you, and shielded you from their punishments. We were a mutually supportive team. We needed each other.'

She remembers Anna on another occasion asking in a genuinely puzzled voice why Lizzie seemed to crave the approbation of strangers. The conversation had taken place in a pub in Chelsea when Lizzie had been idly flirting with a swarthy man at the bar who was openly admiring her. Anna wanted to know why she wasted time fluttering her English rose petals in a feeble effort to attract drones

Lizzie, ignoring the note of pique in the question, had replied, 'If someone notices me, then I know I exist. I'm just an ordinary woman who needs friendship, admiration and someone who will love and look after me. I freely admit that

I want to be thought well of, and I can't see what's so wrong with that.'

Anna then said, 'I have needs too – I long to be loved. Just as you do, I want to have a soul mate I can talk to. But I don't mind being solitary and I don't care if I'm ignored by people I don't know.'

'But I am frightened of loneliness,' explained Lizzie. 'I want to be among people who like me. Most of us have anxieties even though we hide them. I attach myself to others to banish that feeling of insecurity.'

'So you admit to being vulnerable and pathetic,' said Anna stingingly. 'You clearly lack confidence in yourself and your abilities.'

'Maybe I do, but I never show it.' Lizzie was on the defensive now. 'I don't burden others with my problems. Most of my acquaintances think of me as supremely poised and self-assured.'

'Most of your friends don't know you and probably don't care as much as you imagine they do,' said Anna sourly.

'Then leave me with my illusions and my craving for approval. You're so purist and so judgemental. I sometimes wonder why I get drawn into these inner searching conversations with you. You run circles round me verbally in the same way that I could act you off the stage. You have a facility with using words and I have an ability to deliver them. With you it's always the dark night of the soul, the inner eye, the psychological thrust. You turn a conversation into an argument. I choose not to defend myself, so you end up insulting me. I feel hurt and unappreciated. You've a bad temper and you're not always so cosy to be with.' She stopped there. Anna was pale with remorse and chagrin.

They had bought another bottle of wine, made the inevitable

reconciliation, and then got mildly drunk together whilst they discussed plays that they both enjoyed and books that they both loved reading.

'A penny for them, my darling.' Paul is looking at her with a slightly puzzled expression and Lizzie realises she has let her face once again betray the fact that her mind is elsewhere. But she will mislead him – he will not want to know that it is again Anna who occupies her thoughts.

She says, 'I've been wondering if Roderick Case is right for that part Century have asked us to find an actor for – the charming bastard in their new TV serial.'

Paul thinks for a moment. He is not convinced that this is what she had been mulling over, but decides to take her response at face value. 'He might be very good in it. When are the auditions?'

'In a couple of weeks. I want to be sure I've rounded up enough good choices so that my director lands the job of finding the other parts.'

'I can see that you're already moving from holiday to work mode. As I will tomorrow.' He swallows the remains of his drink purposefully, and places the empty glass on the bar. 'How about a stroll outside for a few minutes, if it's not too cold? A bit of fresh air before dinner.'

Lizzie nods and uncrosses her legs before sliding off her perch, pleasantly aware that the man on the next stool is looking at her legs. She sighs softly at her own frailty, and on the arm of her attentive husband leaves the bar, walking with just a slight swing of her hips.

She remembers that he had said nothing as she left, but that is his way. She thinks of Youenn and his silences, which she now finds dispiriting and almost intimidating, where once she found them mysterious and fascinating. She recalls a walk with him on the north Brittany coast – a month after her defection from Paris and Malo. The Bretons call the coastline *sauvage*, which translates as 'wild', but she thinks 'cruel' is a more apt meaning. The seas pound mercilessly on the rocky cliffs along this shore, and the relentless years have seen so many ship-wrecks, so many drownings. And yet there is a stark elemental beauty to this region. And there was a forceful power emanating from Youenn too as he strode along the cliff path, his boots trampling the coarse grass on the hard ground and his large sunburnt hands half clenched at his sides. It was his combi-nation of silence and strength which she found novel and compelling. She linked him with the hard earth and cruel sea that both attracted and repelled her. He represented a novelty in her life – someone she could not manipulate or dominate.

A reticent, intelligent and informed man, he would occa-sionally talk to her about the history and character of the Bretons with a sensitivity and passion that she found intriguing and surprising. It is rare that he does this now and she wonders what has stopped him from confiding in her the love and deep affinity he feels for this region of France. He no longer shares his thoughts or shows his emotions. She wonders now whether he ever did, and thinks perhaps her love for him deluded her into believing that he had compassion and enthusiasm. Does he think that it weakens him to trust another person by revealing his innermost beliefs? Is that why he has withdrawn again into his private world? Youenn exhibits a taciturn exterior and has resumed a habitual assertive role on his home ground. Why does he feel that he needs to exert a husband's authority over her as well? Of his physical power and his superior strength there is no doubt.

Indeed, she still admires his energy and his intensity. He was always moody, but he loved her very much and she was mesmerised and flattered by his ardent desire, which she used to find magnetic, seductive and arousing. Their love-making had been passionate and beguiling. But she is weary of it now and feels guilty that this is so. It is ironic. After all her affairs and disloyalties, Anna is now faithful to one man, Youenn, though she is not sure if she loves him any more. She has chosen this path – but he is a jealous man and does not completely trust her. She still admires his steady adherence to his place in the world – his affiliation to the Breton landscape, its stern values and its joyful music. Anna, aware of her peripatetic tendencies, knows she has no real commitment to any job, home or culture. She has been just as content living in France as she has been living in England – and equally defensive or critical of both countries. She has never felt grounded in any one place, nor anchored in any one relationship – with the sole exception of her bond with Lizzie. She has resisted the shackles of duty and responsibility, fixed only in her resolve to keep options open. But now she is compelled to embrace her destiny with fortitude and resolution.

Recalled to the present and, looking outside her mind's window, she finds that the train has now stopped again and the doors are being opened. She gets off with her bag, and hears an announcement that they have arrived too late to catch the earlier catamaran to Ryde and that the next one will be leaving in just under half an hour, at 8.15 p.m. As she has time, she considers phoning her brother to say she will be later than expected. She has no mobile – Youenn deplores their use –

they are, for him, a nuisance, not a convenience – and she reassures him by stating that she too has never felt any real need to have one, preferring to communicate with those who are not present by the written word.

So she walks along the platform to the end, vaguely looking around her for a pay phone. She sees a porter and, mentioning that she has just missed the fast cataraman, she is about to ask him where she can phone from, when he says that if she wishes, she can catch the Fishbourne car ferry, which leaves at 8 o'clock from nearby Gunwharf Road.

'They take foot passengers. It's a slower crossing but it arrives on the other side at the same time as the next cat. It's a ten-minute walk but only three minutes by car and there are lots of taxis outside,' the porter says, indicating the main exit some fifty yards away.

The idea of taking the car ferry suddenly appeals to Anna. She knows it well as she has taken it many times in her child-hood, in an earlier life. Clutching her bag, she hurries out to the station yard and, climbing into the first of the waiting cabs, tells the driver to take her to the car-ferry terminal as quickly as possible.

Anna leans back against the scratchy tweed fabric of the rear seats and tries to relax for the short ride. Fishbourne is actually marginally closer to where she is going on the island. Had she arrived as planned at Ryde pier head, she would have had to take the slow island train to Shanklin, but now she hopes to grab a taxi where the ferry docks in Wootton Creek. She decides that to save time she will just go directly to the restaurant. If necessary, she could change into her party clothes on the ferry, but she already knows she won't. She recognises the onset of her 'I don't care' lethargy, and gives herself a mental jolt to snap out of it. Gavin is used to her just turning up – or not coming at all. He thinks of her as undependable, faintly unstable and very irresponsible, and she would not want to untarnish her image. Anna knows that Gavin needs and indeed rather likes to have such a wayward and perverse sibling – it makes him seem by contrast all the more unselfish and responsible. She has grown used to playing the part of madcap maverick and he has become accustomed to sighing over her unorthodox behaviour, whilst both of them are well aware that this impression of her character is incomplete and inaccurate. It suits them to inhabit these roles – it is like the continuation of a childhood game, and does not demand any complex re-evaluation of each other's characters. They know each other sufficiently well.

The taxi has arrived at the car-ferry terminal, and now she must hurry again. Paying the driver quickly with some loose change, she then darts into the building and buys a ticket. The ferry is about to depart, and she hears the announcement that the last foot passengers must go on board immediately, embarking by the ramp where the last vehicles are driving onto the car deck. As she crosses this ramp, Anna glances down at the narrow wedge of greenish-brown water between the pier and the ferry. A small trickle of apprehension seeps into her. Her legs feel leaden and reluctant to move but, pushing herself forward, she walks slowly onto the boat and across to the sliding doors which give access to the upper part of the ferry. Climbing wearily up the metal steps, she emerges into the lounge area. The tiredness she feels reminds her of her encroaching and deteriorating illness which will drag her downwards over the next few dreary months. It is a chilling prospect. Her former buoyant and carefree spirit is already becoming a state of mind that she once possessed and has now lost. She used to feel irra-tionally but joyfully that she would live for ever. She misses the optimism of that wonderful delusion and realises, as all humans eventually do, that her 'forever' has limitations.

Anna debates whether she wants to have a cup of coffee or a drink and sit down at one of the tables, but she suspects that if she does, she might be drawn in to chat inconsequentially to the woman who is serving behind the counter or to someone already sitting in the lounge. An odd feeling of reluctance to communicate with anyone at that very moment makes her decide not to bother. She will look for a seat in an area away from the main lounge and the other passengers.

The restaurant on the cross-channel ferry is far from full – the season is early and it is a weekday. The crew who work here are not very busy and thus have the time and inclination to be attentive and agreeable. Dinner commenced earlier and they will be docked in Portsmouth within the hour. A waiter has seated Paul and Lizzie on the starboard side of the boat at a table for four beside the large expanse of window which looks out over the sea. The sun is low in the pink sky visible from the other side of the vessel, and the vista from their side has already become greyer in the declining light. They have eaten their hors d'oeuvres and are waiting for their main course to arrive. Paul is sipping his wine and looks relaxed and genial. They have been talking but are now quietly and amicably occupied with their own thoughts. Lizzie has been watching those dining around them.

Seated at the next window table are a French couple who talk little but smile at each other. The woman has a very short haircut and is wearing a scarf knotted with painstaking care in an effort to look casual and chic. Something about the man wearing a dark shirt and with a moustache and gaunt features reminds Lizzie of Youenn, and she has a moment of apprehension on behalf of Anna, who will return home to him tomorrow. She cannot see what it is about him, besides his fidelity to her and the overt masculine power which radiates from him, that has attracted Anna enough to marry him. He is so different from her earlier boyish lovers. She does not understand it.

Slightly shaking her head, she shifts her gaze to a table of seven people who are seated in the centre of the restaurant. They are English – their features and clothes make this evident. There are three men and four women; they are all in their forties or fifties except for a young woman who may be the daughter of one of the couples. She looks sullen and makes no effort either to join in the conversation or to conceal the fact that she is bored. There is a hint of Katrina about her, thinks Lizzie somewhat sadly, feeling guilty that she has not given her daughter another thought since last night when Anna asked after her. Her children are no longer close to her, nor she to them, and this distance is echoed in their physical separation – they all live in different parts of the world. Lizzie knows that her mate has always assumed greater importance in her life than her cubs, and though she does not consider this unnatural, she nevertheless thinks it unusual and possibly reprehensible. She looks across the table at her man, and finds him looking discreetly at the same table of seven diners, with a smile on his face. Sensing her gaze, for he is a sensitive and intuitive man, he turns to face her.

'I wonder how it is we know for certain that those people over there are English. It must be their mannerisms and their body language we unconsciously recognise as familiar,' Paul says in a quiet tone of voice. He is well-mannered and would not want them to overhear any comments he makes about them.

Lizzie, for no particular reason, pretends that she has only just noticed them. She makes a show of focusing on them and then says, 'French people just don't dress in the same way as we do. They manage to look both natural and stylish – they just seem to have more panache. Most English people lack the French flair for looking compact and sophisticated – we always seem to look a bit more unkempt and loose limbed.'

'Not all of the English lack class. Some of us make an effort and some even succeed.' Paul's self-satisfaction irritates Lizzie, though she realises he is paying her a compliment too.

'I'm not talking about class – I'm talking about style. It's different. It's not better or worse – just different.' Lizzie hears herself sounding petulant and, erasing the niggling note in her voice, continues in a lower tone, 'I mean, take the man in the suede jacket next to the redhead. If he were French, he would be leaning back, slightly lounging, with one arm over the back of his companion's chair. But look, he is sitting bolt upright with his head craned forward with his hands in his lap. No Continental would do that at dinner – it's too intent, too stiff. We English don't always look relaxed even if we feel it.'

Paul has taken no offence at her slightly irritable way of correcting him, and deftly changes the subject. 'You know, Lizzie, he rather reminds me of Eric. Remember Eric? He used to poke his head forward and nod when he was speaking to emphasise the point he wanted to make. It was rather mesmerising.'

'Yes, I remember Eric – he was very opinionated and contentious, and liked to provoke arguments and stir up ill-feeling. He was horribly perceptive at identifying people's prejudices or weaknesses and then he would thrust in the barb, and sit back and wait with glee for the retaliation. I never liked him.'

Paul is often surprised by his wife's ability to sum up pithily what she thinks about someone in a few words, even if he does not agree with her assessment – which he is also prepared to tell her. 'On the contrary, I've always found him lively and good value. He's quite astute, and is always constructive at business meetings. On the social side, he always takes part in conversation and is an entertaining sort of chap.' Eric has been in the film business for many years and is a successful producer. Paul has known him for some time, and in Paul's case, as Lizzie knows well, familiarity breeds respect and toleration. Contempt he leaves to others, for he is a balanced, receptive man with fair judgement in his assessment of others. These are qualities that Lizzie admires and values.

Lizzie cannot excuse rudeness and insensitivity, and it is for this reason that she always found Eric objectionable. His habit of hunching forward was the physical echo of his personality, of which pushiness and aggression were the dominant characteristics. No, she did not like him at all. Especially after that last dinner party when he had caused such havoc, letting it appear as if it was all Anna's fault. She had never invited him back, and Paul, to be fair, had never asked her to. He accepted her aversion to his colleague. Lizzie casts her mind back to the evening of the fracas at the terraced house she and Paul had lived in then. It must have been about eight or nine years ago.

The walls of the dining room in the tall thin house were painted a rich ochre yellow, with dark green woodwork. The room was square, so Paul and Lizzie had bought a large round table for it. 'Round tables are more convivial and harmonious,' Lizzie had said, having recently read an article about auras and decor which claimed that sitting in a circle was more conducive to calm and meaningful social interaction. The same article had also had given her the idea of having a centre light suspended over the table. She persuaded Paul to go along with her notion, and so they had installed an expensive modern pendant light with a large mushroom-shaped shade. This reflected the light downwards, and could be raised up for meals taken in daylight, and lowered to a few feet above the polished wood for dinner eaten after dark. This had the effect of illuminating the table but leaving the faces of those seated round it in benign shadow. It also curiously lit up people's hands when they moved them into the arc of light shed from above. It was an interesting effect which Lizzie, however, did not feel quite comfortable with. She and Anna had always thought that the hands as well as the face revealed the character of a person, but this spotlight on the hands of her guests was a bit strange. She thought she might revert to candelabra in future.

But at the dinner party in question, she had still not got round to altering the lighting arrangements. It was winter, and Paul had built up a warm and welcoming fire in their sitting room, and Lizzie had prepared a meal with her usual flair and attention to detail. She gave few dinners because the long hours they worked in their respective professions meant that she and Paul rarely had time to do so, and frequently ate out. She enjoyed her work, which she undertook more because of the interest and excitement it gave her than out of any need to increase their already very adequate income. Although her job meant that she rarely had time to shop for food or to prepare meals, on occasion Lizzie liked to entertain at her elegant home and she considered herself a competent and inventive cook – unlike Anna, who, she reflected with affection, was hopeless in the kitchen even though she liked to eat well.

It was a dinner party to celebrate Paul's birthday, and also his landing a contract to supply equipment for a film production company. Eric had been instrumental in awarding the contract, so he had been invited along with his diminutive wife, a pretty woman who deferred to her husband on all matters and whom Lizzie found rather insipid. They arrived first, and while Paul put their coats in the study, Lizzie chatted enthusiastically with them, possessing the social graces to easily conceal her underlying dislike of them.

Ten minutes later, she was relieved to hear the doorbell again, and Paul went through to the hall. She felt a rush of cold air as the door opened and closed and then Leda, an actress friend with whom she had once shared a flat, appeared with her partner Danny, who was in the music business. After introductions a bland discussion of the wintry weather ensued, along with speculation as to whether there would be a frost during the night. Eric, his head jerking forward as he made his pronouncements, informed the others of the forecast he had heard just before coming out, and there was no doubt that the night would be very cold. He then maintained, first, that the subject bored him, and second, that weather conditions never caused him a problem. This, naturally, put an end to the subject, and Eric in a commanding situation from the start.

Next to arrive was Roland, a gay friend in his thirties who lived in the next street, and who was a struggling writer oscillating between poetry and fiction. He was a strikingly good-looking man with a gentle, wry sense of humour and an unassuming manner. He was introduced to Eric and his wife, with whom he shook hands, but he already knew Leda and Danny, and gave the actress a warm hug. The conversation had by now drifted onto the subject of muggings and theft, and Eric resumed his tirade, this time directed against pilfering on film sets and on location. Roland then happened to mention that he had mislaid his wallet that day and thought he had left it in an off-licence. Whilst the other murmured their sympathy, Eric stated that a pickpocket was probably to blame. Then, giving no one else a chance to comment, he immediately launched into a tale about carelessness versus culpability involving a witty story about a French politician who had lost his briefcase in a brothel in Paris. He positioned himself in front of the fire, leaning forward with his chin jutting out, and everyone in the half circle facing him felt obliged to listen and applaud. In this way, Eric began to dominate the gathering. Paul behaved in a more deferential way than was usual for him on such occasions, and was happy to allow the producer to assume control. Lizzie remembered that this same thing had happened when they had all been at a restaurant some six months before, and the man had monopolised the conversation – as if she needed reminding why she found him so disagreeable.

It was only a matter of time, she thought, before he started being spiteful or insulting. His peculiar talent was to humiliate with teasing humour and barbed precision. Leda was his initial target, with questions such as 'Have you been out of work as long as Lizzie?' and 'Is your agent doing his job or is he letting you down?' At first, the actress smiled with puzzlement at his lack of tact, and when she was given no opportunity to respond, she started to look embarrassed.

At this point Roland gently tried to divert Eric's attention with a comment about the proliferation of musicals in London theatres which contributed to a lack of good straight acting roles. Having just produced a popular but down-market musical in the West End, Eric then directed his venom on the young man. 'Are you unemployed as well as Leda? I seem to meet so many impoverished actors and writers – so few have any real

208

talent and even fewer make a success of their lives. How unfortunate it must be to be trapped in such precarious professions.' And so on.

Last to arrive had been Anna, who was invariably and irritatingly late. She usually managed to redeem herself by entertaining the assembled guests with a complicated and unlikely excuse clearly invented for maximum impact, though it failed to amuse her hostess, who was used to this ploy and had to suppress her annoyance of her best friend's habitual late appearance. She suspected it was intentional, as Anna had once pointed out that Lord Byron had made an art of arriving late, so implying that she would too. Lizzie had taken to designing her menus to accommodate the inevitable delay, since the ruse of inviting Anna earlier than the others did not seem to work.

On this occasion, Lizzie had almost given up on Anna, as they had actually gone through to the dining room and sat down and still she hadn't put in an appearance. Lizzie had become worried that another round of Paul's dry martinis would make her guests so inebriated that they would be unable to enjoy the meal, so she had shepherded them through. She liked to serve hot soup in the winter, and the home-made stilton and leek broth was already being consumed when Anna rang the doorbell. With a very small sigh of irritation at the bad manners of some guests, which he directed at his wife, Paul rose to his feet and went to admit the latecomer.

Anna appeared in the dining room with her profuse and disingenuous apologies and a convoluted tale of her neighbour's cat ('an exotic Persian blue with matted long fur that makes me sneeze') being stuck up a drainpipe ('horrid modern job – plastic, not metal'), which, when Anna herself had tried to climb up it, had come away from the wall ('crumbling plaster, poor fixings – wickedly dangerous'), throwing her into a convenient bush below ('my feat of derring-do reduced to bruised humiliation'). Her neighbour ('a woman with the troubles of the world and very greasy hair on her shoulders') had promptly had hysterics about the damage to her house, and, without enquiring as to whether Anna had any broken bones ('which I didn't, being very tough and ridiculously resilient'), she had gone to summon her husband ('a hopelessly impractical school caretaker') from the pub ('probably the Bunch of Grapes'). The cat had ('miraculously and inevitably') found it own way down off the roof and Anna had found to her chagrin that she was by then very cold and very late for dinner. To demonstrate the veracity of her tall tale, she indicated a tear in the hem of her long skirt where she had caught it on something sharp as she fell. There was general laughter at this monstrously improbable story while Anna, who had remained standing for better dramatic effect during her performance, sat down and cordially said good evening to Danny and Roland, who were seated on either side of her.

'Sometimes I wonder why Anna, with her theatrical talent for the absurd, isn't on the stage like us,' Lizzie remarked to Leda.

'She'd never get any parts because she would always turn up late and miss the auditions,' said Paul with a smile, as he placed a bowl of soup in front of Anna.

Anna had laughed acknowledging that his mild rebuke was fair. Paul, who had waited for Anna on many occasions, knew that she would not reform – it was not her way – she liked being 'out of tune' with conventional polite behaviour. That's what made her exciting and slightly daunting – her unpredictability.

Not everyone round the table thought Anna's social misdemeanour and her extravagant story amusing. Across the table from her Eric's antagonism was almost palpable. He had a tolerant but tight smirk on his face as he followed up Paul's remark by telling her that she would 'never be allowed to tread the boards with her unfortunate talent for histrionic overacting'.

Anna, who had not met him before and did not realise that he was involved in the film world, turned to him and said bluntly, 'Too right. The theatrical and film world would avoid me like the plague. Anyway it's not a scene that I'd want any part off – both too "luvvy" and too cutthroat. What do you do?'

'I'm a film producer,' said Eric acidly. 'I'm the merciless one who does the hiring – and the firing.'

'The producer is top of the pile – he has overall responsibility and bears all the financial strain,' said Paul swiftly, hoping to circumvent any further blunders.

But Anna and Eric were squarely on track to insult and argue all evening, sparring with each other across Lizzie's "harmonious" round table. During the main course, the topics ranged from politics to education to crime, and the two of them seemed to have opposing views on each subject, which neither of them shrank from airing volubly. The other guests, who were obliged to listen and witness this, were amused at first, but then felt embarrassed by the spectacle. Lizzie, whose polite, gregarious behaviour concealed her aversion to Eric, rather admired Anna for trying to deflate and defeat him, but eventually she found herself hoping that the pair of them would leave off as the atmosphere was becoming increasingly hostile. It was plain that, while Anna was enjoying herself, Eric was getting angry.

To him, here was a rival – someone who might hog the limelight and elbow him out of his usual deserved position of superiority. For her part, Anna resented and resisted the obvious desire of this bully to dominate the conversation at the table and to undermine any opposition. Although the verbal combat was to the obvious embarrassment of the courteous Roland, as well as to Leda and her partner, not to mention the host and hostess, from her expression of polite inattention, it seemed that Eric's wife was inured to this kind of confrontation.

Trying to deflect the acrimony and to change the subject to something less argumentative, Paul made the mistake of mentioning plays and literature – a topic of common interest. It was then that Eric started to expound the reasons why he and the large majority of people found Shakespeare's plays so unapproachable and alien. This remark was guaranteed to fuel the flames of Anna's righteous anger, and she protested vehemently at his anti-intellectual approach. She found unexpected support for her passionate and spirited defence of the bard from Danny, who was immediately accused by Eric of being 'another of those batty Shakespearean devotees'.

Lizzie recalls it was at this point that she had lost her cool and firmly asked her guests to have a truce whilst they ate the next course – a delicate and delicious pavlova that she had taken considerable time to prepare. Anna had subsided into silence, slightly ashamed of causing Lizzie such discomfiture, whilst Eric had gone red with vexation at being cut short when he thought he had been on the point of carrying the argument. The dessert was consumed in awkward silence as every person searched in their minds for something uncontentious to say and came up with nothing. Anna found herself covertly examining the hairy sinews of Eric's large hands that were clenched round his cutlery and revealed in all their ugliness by the overhead light. Lizzie, whilst recounting an amusing anecdote in an effort to restore normality and good humour, inwardly cringed with embarrassment.

\*       \*       \*

'Very pensive, darling. What's on your mind?' Paul has leaned across the table and put his hand on her wrist. She is jerked back into the present, though she can still almost feel her lack of composure. She sees that the waiter is hovering nearby, waiting to place their main courses in front of them.

Lizzie moves her hand to allow him to put her plate of grilled fish down in front of her. 'I'm thinking about that disastrous dinner party we gave.' She pauses.

'When Anna behaved so badly?' Paul is none too pleased to be reminded of it.

'You mean when *Eric* behaved so badly,' Lizzie corrects him.

'It was Anna you threw out of the house,' Paul reminds her. 'Before we left for the hospital.'

'I threw Anna out as a sop to your friend Eric, and to try to defuse the situation. He was the one who deserved to go.'

'You're right,' says Paul unexpectedly. 'Eric was dreadful. But given the situation at the time, with a big contract in the balance, I could hardly have kicked him out.' Cutting a slice off his steak and thoughtfully placing it in his mouth, Paul remembers how difficult and obstructive the man had subsequently been when there had been a delay in the delivery of some equipment which Paul was contracted to supply. Their earlier amicable relationship had never been the same after that evening. 'I always thought that my problems with Eric sprang from that awful dinner party.'

'But you were so nice to him all evening. It wasn't your fault the whole thing got so out of hand. It was the row about Shakespeare, when Anna became so tenaciously heated and Eric so thoroughly poisonous, that triggered the fracas.' Lizzie's usually crisp recall has been clouded by the memory of her embarrassment that evening.

Paul remembers very well that it happened during the latter

stages of that exasperating evening. 'Anna started to talk about her trip to Africa – she'd gone with that young Frenchman of hers . . .' Paul pauses, fumbling for the name.

'Malo,' says Lizzie too quickly, so she adds, 'I think.'

'Yes, that was it. Anna had been doing some research for an article she was writing about *Macbeth* and spiritualism, something about curses and jinxes, and she was relating some ritual she had witnessed in a central African country.'

'That set them off again,' Lizzie remembers. 'Eric roundly rubbished whatever Anna had been saying about black magic – something to the effect that only idiots believed in such superstitious nonsense.'

Both she and Paul lapse into silence for a few moments whilst they finish eating, and while they separately recall what happened next on that night some years before.

The discordant guests had moved on to the cheese course. Eric had not been drunk, though he had consumed enough alcohol during the evening to make him even more aggressive than he usually was. He had been over-exaggerating his dislike of Shakespeare and attacking *Macbeth* as a farrago of superstition and irrational behaviour in order to needle his opponents who considered the play a work of genius. Snorting with derision, Eric had then taken a large bite of mature cheddar on a water biscuit, and a piece of the cheese had become stuck in his throat, causing him to cough and splutter. Anna, watching with delight, had muttered that he deserved to choke on his words. Eric, infuriated and humiliated by his lapse of coherency and control, ignominiously hawked up and spat out the offending piece of cheese on to the table. At this point, Anna coolly said that some things left a bad taste in the mouth.

Further incensed by this remark, Eric thrust his chair back

214

and stood up, finally managing to utter that he had no intention of sitting at the table any longer with such a poisonous bitch. In his fury he was slightly off balance and, grabbing the edge of the table, he inadvertently pulled the cloth, causing his plate and Leda's next to him to slip onto the wooden floor and smash. 'Shit,' he hissed, compounding his social faux pas, and as he turned to apologise to Lizzie on his other side, he tripped over the corner of the tablecloth, skidded on the polished floor and lurched uncontrollably to his left. With a look of horror as he realised he was going to fall into his hostess's lap, he twisted his body backwards and, narrowly missing his own chair, crashed to the floor. He put out his hand to break his fall, and as he landed the snap of his wrist was almost audible.

At this point everyone rose to their feet, with the exception of Anna who, shaking with uncontrollable laughter on the other side of the table, was incapable of standing. Paul strode round to help his guest to his feet, only to be met with a howl of pain from the man whose fall had fractured his self-control as well as his wrist.

'You witch,' Eric shrieked across at Anna. 'You've broken my arm. It's fucking painful and it's your fault.' Eric was holding his injured limb to his chest with the hand dangling at an awkward angle, and was fending off his solicitous wife who by now was clutching his other arm.

Anna laughed even louder at this idiotic suggestion that she was to blame, but checking her inappropriate mirth, she managed to ask, 'How do you suggest that I've done that? By voodoo?' She turned to Roland, who was on his feet beside her. 'One shouldn't revile *Macbeth*. It's an unlucky play to produce, and clearly an unlucky play to slander.'

Danny interrupted her saying curtly, 'Do shut up, Anna. Eric has hurt himself and he's in pain.'

Anna could not resist the witty riposte, 'You mean that he's added injury to insult! Perhaps you didn't hear him, but he's called me both a bitch and a witch. Which shows he can rhyme if nothing else.'

Leda at that point had a fit of hysterical giggles and buried her face in her napkin. She was helped back onto her chair by Roland, who was also having trouble keeping a straight face. Mortified by his loss of dignity and swearing from the pain inflicted on him, Eric was reduced to a pathetically comic figure.

Lizzie, upset by her guest's painful humiliation and not amused by Anna's witty comments, looked over at her friend's red face glinting with guilty tears of laughter and hissed at her, 'Get out.'

She recalls with absolute clarity that Anna instantly stopped laughing, and after a pause quietly said, 'What?'

Lizzie's control broke and she recalls with deep chagrin that she shouted across at her adopted sister and lifelong friend, 'Leave the table and get out of my house. Now.'

There was so much noise and confusion that Roland was the only other one who heard this unreasonable demand. He realised that this was a bigger crisis than the one happening on the other side of the room, where Danny and Paul were fussing over Eric, who was trumpeting with pain and fury. He turned and watched the two women as they confronted each other across the table.

For a few seconds Anna, the colour receding from her face, seemed stunned. Then she rose to her feet with a strange look on her face, and in a deceptively calm voice asked Lizzie whether she was losing her sense of humour as well as her sense of proportion. Expecting no reply and not getting one, she quietly bent down and picked up her small bag and, giving her friend a final cool stare, walked out of the room.

Instantly regretting her lapse of poise and already horrified by what her angry outburst might have done to their friendship, Lizzie extricated herself from the gesticulating Eric, his fluttering wife and the soothing Paul, and hurried after Anna. As she reached the hall, she saw her framed in the partially open front door for a second before she slipped through the aperture into the night. The big door closed with a slam, pushed by hand or blown by the wind. Anna had left and not looked back. She had nothing to regret.

Shortly afterwards Lizzie's other difficult guest departed, taking Paul up on his offer to drive him and his wife to the nearby Accident and Emergency Department. Leda and Danny helped clear up the broken glass and crockery, and then they too left.

After the intense drama and its jarring climax the atmosphere now was one of concussed flatness, and Lizzie experienced a feeling of loss and melancholy. Roland stayed and drank a soothing cup of coffee with his hostess, and then walked home. As she handed him his coat, Lizzie saw the red cloak that Anna had arrived in still on the peg, and realised that she had gone without it. It hung there reproachfully – and Lizzie sighed.

Later on, when her anger over the fiasco and her disappointment with the disastrous evening had subsided, Lizzie realised she had broken their parting pact. She had ordered Anna to leave – it was unforgivable and unwarranted. It was the first time this had happened, but while it hurt her dreadfully, she would not admit it, nor would she apologise because she was still upset by Anna's wilful disruption of her dinner party.

She hears Paul speaking and, finding she has been staring at her empty plate for too long, she looks up at him as he says, 'Of course, Eric – and you know what a big man he is – nearly

217

fell on top of you, and it was because he twisted round to try and avoid doing so that he fell awkwardly and broke his wrist. If he hadn't, we might have had more broken bones that evening.'

'Well, it fractured my friendship with Anna for quite a long while. In fact, I don't think we've been as close to each other ever since.'

'Neither of you could bring yourself to apologise. She went back to Paris to her toy boy and we didn't see her for quite a while after that.' Paul omits to mention that this rupture between the two women was very welcome to him as it put distance between him and his recent indiscretion. But then he realises that Lizzie has just told him that she knew all along about his brief fling with Anna. This fissure in the marital trust between them had been smoothed over by Lizzie never disclosing her knowledge of it. Paul has long forgotten about the two women's pact of sharing, and is therefore unaware that this promise had been fulfilled once again by his and Anna's infidelity.

'No, we didn't speak to each other for a long time,' Lizzie says. 'Anna did send me a letter, but I was too angry to reply to it.' What she does not say is that it had upset her too much for her to be able to write back. She had realised with remorse that she had uprooted her life's support and cast it away. There had been a sense of loss so bitter that she was appalled by what she had wantonly destroyed.

Looking back on the episode, Lizzie now realises that it was then that she began to move away from Anna. She feels that something else happened that evening of the dinner party. For some reason that Lizzie does not understand, Anna changed; she lost her self-reliance and her *joie de vivre*, and subsequently became less dominant and less confident. Never again would they be so intimate or so open with each other. Never again did she accept Anna's behaviour so uncritically and so forgivingly. This made her feel disloyal, but more self-reliant, though the price she paid for her independence was no longer sharing in her friend's vitality and spontaneity. She remembers once, prior to that evening, saying to Anna at the end of one of their emotionally exhausting discussions, 'I don't know whether I'm happier when I'm with you or when I'm away from you. Being together is both wonderful and painful. Life apart is less intense and less colourful – but easier.'

To which Anna had rejoined, 'Who wants the easy option? Not me! I'd be bored to death. Sorry if I put you in such turmoil, but I just can't resist rocking the boat.'

Years before, when setting off for France – on her own individual path again – Anna had told Lizzie: 'We need our own space, our own circles. We rotate round in our own little orbits and from time to time we come together and our circles interlock, not without some clashes and confrontations, but sometimes blissfully and harmoniously. When things get too close, too intense, then we need to spin off into other worlds and other people, always knowing that there will be another conjunction sometime later, another period of intimacy. We need the separation in order to recharge and stand alone, until the solitariness gets too much and then our stars send us back to each other. Parting is always pain and loss, so let's not add to this by having any regrets. Let's keep to our bargain, and leave when we are ready to go but never send the other away.'

As these thoughts revolve in her head, Lizzie is staring out of the window at the grey coastline indistinct in the dusk and with a few early dots of lights quivering along it. Paul follows her gaze and says, 'Look, we've just entered the Solent – or is the eastern part called the Spithead? This must be Hampshire and that must be the Isle of Wight on the other side. Isn't that where Anna is going to be this evening – at some party given by her brother? I think she mentioned it last night.'

'Last night seems a long while ago,' murmurs Lizzie. 'We've both come a long way today. And now I feel her getting closer again. In fact, you're right – we're probably not far apart at this moment.'

'We should be docking at Portsmouth in about half an hour.' Paul is looking at his watch. 'Do you want anything more to eat?'

'No thanks. Perhaps some coffee though.'

'I might have an Armagnac.' Paul orders them from the waiter.

'The sun's going down,' says Lizzie, craning her head to look forward at the low sun just visible behind the bows of the ferry. There are flecks of pale gilt and reddish gold glinting on the small waves.

'It's been a very pleasant and relaxing journey today,' says Paul. 'Just a couple of hours' drive to London and we'll be home. It'll be good to get back. Though I must say that I've really enjoyed it.'

These soothing platitudes wash over his wife as she quietly says, 'Anna's long day is about to end too – her day in the fast lane. I hope it hasn't drained her too much. Last night, she looked thinner and more frail than I've ever seen her.' She looks across the table at the comforting substantial reality of her husband. Guiltily – but thankfully – she realises that she has switched her loyalty to Paul, who will provide her with the stability she needs for the future. She no longer has a taste for disruption and danger. Lizzie has an instinct for survival.

She shivers suddenly with an undefined premonition. She

knows Anna is not far away and senses that they are converging again. But this time it's unclear whether their trajectories will collide or whether they will pass as ships do in the night, and move on. She needs to voice her misgivings and uneasiness. 'About Anna. We meet up so seldom these days. I wonder when our paths will cross again.'

'Anna can look after herself.' Paul says this, but does not really mean it. He too had been surprised not only by her physical depletion but also by her submissive behaviour towards her husband – which was out of character for the woman they knew or had once known. 'And she's married someone – at last – who'll look after her.' Again, Paul is not saying what he thinks, which is that Youenn could destroy Anna. He's not really very anxious about this. They live a different life in another place, and he's happy that there is a watery rift between their country and his. He has long wanted to take Lizzie away from Anna, and he had not been keen to stop off and visit the couple on their way back up through France. But on the principle that confronting your enemy is a good tactical move, he had consented, and had decided to be amenable and agreeable. He was determined to charm his wife away from her soul mate. To have Lizzie, entire and undivided, to himself would be a prize worth winning – he loves her very much, and he needs her. He should not jeopardise this by committing tinsel disloyalties; he should focus on the jewel he has. Surprising himself, Paul silently pledges there and then that he will give up all other women when Lizzie renounces Anna. He is no longer uneasy because he senses that the other woman's influence has declined and he is confident of victory.

Lizzie leans forward and puts her small fingers on the prominent knuckles of Paul's right hand, which is resting on the table beside his glass of Armagnac. He smiles at her benevolently

## Chapter Eleven

There are few passengers on the car ferry – it is a late one
and most regulars catch the catamaran that she would have
taken if the train had not been late. It will take about forty
minutes to reach its destination at Fishbourne in shallow
Wootton Creek on the north coast of the island.

Anna has only just caught the ferry, and hearing the surge
of the engines as the vessel prepares to leave, she has decided
to quit the enclosed lounge where most of the passengers are.
The spacious accommodation deck, built high above the car
deck below which runs the full length of the vessel, is not
crowded, but Anna feels the need to be alone, and having just
spent two hours on a train, she wants some fresh air. She opens
the heavy door to the outside deck, where she leans on the rail
to watch the departure. She is assailed by the familiar salty
metallic smell and remembers the older generation of ferries
with their angled car ramps fore and aft lifted up like the semi-
folded wings of a giant insect. She used to travel in them as
a child with her family, voyaging across the green sea to their
island of summer holidays, adventures and freedom. She recalls
the throb of anticipation induced by the promise of two bright

weeks of fun in their special place by the sea under a sky that would always be blue.

Anna's day has oscillated between the fast and the slow. Stationary intervals – her appointments, her interview, and time spent in the restaurant – contrast with speed and motion – the flight, the limousine, the train journey and now the island ferry. The relentless momentum has been there throughout the day and parallels the tumultuous barrage of thoughts and memories that have assaulted her unceasingly. Her body is exhausted but her mind accelerating as if running on high-octane fuel; her will is strengthened by resolve; her imagination is in overdrive and she is unable to put the brakes on it or switch into a lower gear. This is the most significant race of her life. She has a feeling that the sprint is yet to come and she will soon have the finishing post in sight.

Her mental preoccupations have gradually taken over and pushed out the actual perceptions of her physical passage from place to place through the day. She has appeared in different scenes, travelled in time from present day to past episodes and back. It is as if she has been alternating the pause and the fast-forward buttons on the video memory of her life. What of the future? There is no vision here. She cannot contemplate it, nor does she want to. Since she has discovered that her cancer is terminal, the words 'rest of her life' have taken on a different meaning. The final act of her play has begun.

Her churning thoughts take on the feel of a grand nostalgic philosophical melodrama. She loves life: sensation and awareness. The prospect for her is grim – she will deteriorate – pain and drugs will obliterate her clear thinking. The act of dying does not frighten her – indeed, the moment of death is a vague curiosity. But, unlike her sister, she has no faith in a Deity or in a comforting heaven. It is all a blank, a nothingness into which she will negate herself. Shreds of the Anglo-Saxon stark vision of life permeate this fog. Sweet transitory life is a slender white candle burning quickly in the cool draught of eternity, with the wax running down wastefully and unevenly. It will not last till night. But unlike Macbeth in his agonising speech before his horrifying fate, she values the warmth and the glow of that luminous flame and is saddened that the heartless wind will blow it out sooner than she would have wished. The harrowing wind is coming. On this May evening in the autumn of her life, she confronts the desolate probability that she will not see the winter and the austere certainty that the world will not bloom for her again next spring. This is the unmitigated truth. She is comfortingly conscious of her self-pity and inflated mental imagery, and can inwardly smile at the seasonal cast of her grand sentiments. Her sense of humour is still alive and well even though the rest of her is falling apart.

The warm day is becoming chilly with a slight evening breeze and the camel jacket that she put on so many hours ago is not quite warm enough. It is now too big for her, she has lost so much weight. She is aware that Lizzie, who was looking sleek and well, had noticed this but was not given an opportunity to comment or question. The ferry is pulling away from the dock towards the main fairway. She looks back towards the inner part of the harbour and, through the tangle of buildings, masts and ships, watches the mottled bars of peach-coloured western sky fading upwards into a pallid smudged primrose. Lizzie has always liked pale subtle yellows which suit her dark hair and gentleness. Anna likes flamboyant red and orange tones, though she rarely wears these colours any more. She recalls a favourite crimson cloak she once had which she left behind in Lizzie's house that evening when her beloved sister had rejected her before expelling her from the warm house into a black nightmare.

Once again Anna wraps her past around her and brings those few hours back into sharp focus out of the blurred succession of events in her life around that time. She recalls the dinner – the taunting and teasing of that poisonous bully, the drunken producer who had been so rude to her, who broke his arm when he slipped and fell – but more poignant is the cutting memory of Lizzie's savage ejection of her. Perhaps her behaviour had warranted some disapproval, but to throw her out broke the rules of their friendship and hurt her dreadfully. Anna, however, remembers more vividly the horror of what happened afterwards. Following verbal abuse came physical abuse.

The instant she had closed the front door behind her, Anna was hit by a cold blast of wind and realised that in her haste to punish her friend by being gone and beyond recall she had forgotten her warm red cloak. Deciding to leave it behind as a beacon of her absence and of Lizzie's violation of their lifetime pact, she walked to the end of the road to try and get a taxi. But it was nearly midnight, and there were hardly any cars about, and no taxis at all in that residential area. She had arrived there by minicab, coming from the small flat she was renting for three months whilst working on her book and having a break from her life in Paris and the restricting intensity of her affair with Malo. She had hoped she might get a lift home at the end of the dinner party or at least be able to ring from there for a taxi.

She therefore found herself with the prospect of a long walk home on a cold night without warm clothing. She was upset and aggrieved by her situation and set off at a quick pace to keep the blood moving, still hoping that she might at some point be passed by a taxi cruising late. She decided to head towards a busier thoroughfare where there might be more chance of one. She was mildly concerned that some cars prowling in the late hours might mistake her for a female on the game, in her short dress and without a coat. However, at that moment, she felt more vulnerable to cold than to strangers. Her high heels clocked on the pavements and chafed her feet. She folded her arms round her chest, hunched her shoulders and muttered to herself as she walked, 'It's stupid, stupid to be walking around at night on my own like this.'

She had been walking for about fifteen minutes and was by now, she reckoned, over halfway home. She was still seething about being thrown out by Lizzie, and was grinding her teeth together out of anger and from the cold. It was dark – there were few street lights in this area – but by now her night vision had improved. She was impatient to get back to her small flat, so she decided to cut through to a better-lit main road which would take her to her street.

As a result, she found herself walking down an unlit unfamiliar road, bounded on one side by a row of Victorian houses and on the other by a low wall behind which there seemed to be some public gardens with some shrubs and a few trees. She then heard other footsteps, and glancing round, she saw a figure walking along some way behind her. She quickened her pace and resolved neither to panic nor to turn round again.

The footsteps seemed to be getting closer and all her latent fears of being attacked erupted. When her nerve snapped and she broke into a run, they did also. Thinking she was about to be mugged or robbed, and breathing heavily with her lungs hurting from the cold air, she decided to throw her bag at her pursuer. As she swung round, she realised with horror that he was right behind her, and saw a large white hand coming towards her. A second later her head was yanked back and a woollen garment was pressed over her face and held over her mouth. She struggled and lost her balance as the man dragged her along the pavement and into the gardens. Unable to utter a sound, she felt suffocated by the tightness of the cloth he was holding over her face. She writhed about, trying to kick and scratch him. 'I've got a knife,' he grunted, breathing heavily in his exertion. His voice and the smell of his sweat were a young man's. 'Struggle and you'll get hurt.' In the dark and in her terror she did not doubt this and went limp, hoping her acquiescence would protect her from being slashed and might preserve her life. She was pushed to the ground.

The rape was over quickly. Anna lay inert beneath him, her mind almost paralysed with fear of what would happen next. Something scratched into the skin of her stomach, and for a barbed second she thought it was a knife, but she felt no pain and later realised it had probably been his belt buckle.

When he had finished, he roughly turned her over and, still holding her down with one hand, he pulled away his sweater from her head and with the spread-out fingers of his other hand he pushed her face hard into the ground. Unable to breathe with her mouth pressed into damp leaves and gritty earth it was then that she completely panicked and thought she would die.

Then the pressure eased and, as his victim desperately drew in a mouthful of air, choking and scared, he stood up and, giving her a vindictive kick on her thigh, hissed 'Bitch' and was gone.

She lay inert, face down, her mind flooding with hope as she heard his running feet receding, and when she was sure he would not come back, she rolled over with a wail of utter distress and curled herself up into a ball, her dress twisted up around her waist. In the pitiless dark, clutching her knees, she rocked and moaned with disgust and shock. And also with gratitude for being alive. He was not a killer. He would not come back. She felt sick with relief.

She soon registered the cold fact that though she had survived the rape, she might succumb to hypothermia if she didn't move. She was among some bushes, and clutching at them, she stumbled to her feet, realising the odd fact that her shoes with their ankle straps were still on. She ripped her shredded tights off, wiping herself with them, and hurled them with revulsion into the dead leaves. Before pulling down her dress, she saw her scratched pallid legs and gave a shuddering sob. Emerging from the bushes, she staggered out of the gardens into the empty road. A few yards from where she emerged, she saw a bag – her bag – lying innocently on the ground. Only a few minutes had passed since she had dropped it. It was still there and so was she – but she was not untainted. A cold gust blew along the street and some dry leaves spiralled upwards. She crouched down and, with a single cry of impotent fury at the uncaring, unseeing houses opposite, she picked up her bag and started walking. Within a few yards she was invaded with panic and a desperate need to get away from the place as fast as possible, so she broke into a run.

Anna shivers as a gust of wind funnelling into Portsmouth Harbour catches her as she leans over the rail. She sighs and her eyes focus on the squat round tower which the ferry is passing as it steams out of the confined entrance. There are some gulls wheeling around the ferry and the waterfront houses adjacent to the narrows. But her churning thoughts once more revert to that night; it is as if she needs to follow it through to the end and finally exorcise it – and manage to erase it from the databank of her mind.

Trembling with fear and anger and cold, she ran the remaining distance to her home. She met no one, though a few cars passed her. It was as she stumbled up the stairs to her flat that she decided not to inform the police. She was bruised but not injured, and the prospect of the undignified examinations and intrusive questions she would have to undergo appalled her.

Safe behind two doors – the house front door and that of her tiny flat – Anna removed all her clothes and crammed them into the kitchen bin. Then she took a hot shower and washed herself all over using lots of soap, dispassionately noticing various bruises. She stood there for a long time, trying to make her mind go blank. She was alive – she clung to that one fact. The hot water failed to stop her shaking.

Over the next few days she had thought about the rape obsessively. It was chilling how unaffected she had felt by the sexual act – her terrified submission had been almost like assent; almost like an act of prostitution. She had been forced, but had she resisted enough? After all, he had not been much rougher than Malo nor much more urgent than Fynn. Just unknown and impersonal.

Clearly her mind had been violated more than her body. In her maltreatment, she had had no choice – her free will had been abused. In all her sexual experiences up to that point there had been a measure of consent. She also felt punished. Perhaps in the past and in different ways she had used men without their compliance, and now as some sort of retribution she has been misused casually and randomly. The stranger had seized his opportunity and she had been the unlucky victim. He had abused a woman, not her as an individual. Or so she thought. But she was not undamaged. She was disgusted with herself for not fighting and resisting him more strongly, and felt a coward for not reporting the incident afterwards.

Later on – after a week or so – she had sent a short letter to Lizzie. 'More has been broken than Eric's wrist and your plates,' she wrote. 'You have broken faith with me, and you have broken my trust in your integrity.' She did not censure Lizzie for putting her at risk by throwing her out. In the heat of the moment neither of them had given a thought about how she would get home. She herself had been unaware and uncaring of the possible danger to a lone woman walking home at night. She did not tell Lizzie about the rape, because on reflection she found that she could not lay that sort of guilt on her closest and oldest friend, whom she still cared for very much. She had not reported it because she had wanted to avoid any more distress and embarrassment and because Lizzie would have then found out about it. This was one secret she could never share with her sister. But by denying and concealing the rape she felt gutless, and she was miserably ashamed of her lack of zeal for justice.

Anna is surprised that after so long the horrible experience still surfaces in her mind. She has tried to suppress it, to forget it, but her relentless memory means that it crops up involuntarily at odd hours and in odd places, making her feel vulnerable and uneasy. And guilty because she has never mentioned it to anyone.

Anna is sure that if Lizzie had been attacked, she would have spoken about it – she would have brought it out into the open and got help. She recalls that when they were in their twenties, Lizzie had been frightened by a stalker who had hounded her for nearly a year. She had been in touch with the police on a number of occasions and had called on the support of Anna and other friends to help her cope with the constant harassment. When she and Lizzie had together discovered the identity of the stalker – a man Anna herself was seeing called Martin – he had stopped under threat of prosecution, and Lizzie had no doubt long since forgotten about the nasty experience. Wisely she has been able to lay it all to rest. Unlike herself, she thinks reproachfully, whose bad experience was more recent. The rape still haunts her; with the perpetrator unknown and unpunished, she has had no chance to confront her demon. Usually stronger in resolve and more resilient than Lizzie, Anna has tried to put the horrible nightmare behind her, but it remains festering in the recesses of her mind.

Perhaps this time she can let it go.

Up till now, Anna has always felt she could control wilful thoughts, but today they do seem very disorderly and turbulent. She wonders now whether her loss of libido can be blamed on the trauma of that night. Has it scarred her that much? It is as if the malignant memory is growing in parallel with her tumour. She had been violated, and its concealment has consumed her peace of mind. No, this time she must let it go. Though she is still infected with its poison – life is less sweet than it once was. She asks herself if this is so because she is losing Lizzie to Paul or because she is losing the battle with her cancer. The persistent warning of dull pain within reminds her constantly of what is to come. She shakes her head as if to clear away these insubordinate thoughts, and turns her attention to external matters again.

The car ferry is picking up speed now it has left the harbour and is heading out eastwards along the channel. She walks along the deck, holding on to the rail and staring as if mesmerised into the water below as it streams past the sides of the vessel, frothily green and turbulent. Feeling a stab of vertigo, she pulls her gaze away and looks up at the passing shore. Her gaze travels across the Southsea waterfront from the funfair to the thin pillar of the war memorial, and then shifts to the east, where in the dusk some way off she sees another larger vessel steaming in the opposite direction. It is a bigger ship and from the shape of its bow probably one of the larger cross-channel ferries which dock at Portsmouth in the evening. They seem to be sailing on course for each other. She watches with fascination as the two moving vessels gradually get closer together.

It suddenly dawns on Anna that this approaching ship bears a precious cargo. Without doubt there is a beautiful golden car sedately parked on a deck within the hull carried smoothly forward on the waves, and somewhere in a cabin above it are Lizzie and Paul, who have spent most of the afternoon sailing on this very ship from France to England. It must be their ferry – it was due to dock in the evening. It seems completely appropriate that she and Lizzie had been together in the early morning and that their paths should cross again in the evening. She accepts that this is destiny; this is what she has been moving towards all day. They will soon complete the full circle.

A surreal image balloons up in her mind, pushing out any rational thought. Of course, the ferries are destined to meet head on. She and Lizzie have been having collisions and partings all their lives. This will happen, but the difference will be that this time the parting will be final. One of them will not survive and it must be her. She is the weaker half now, though once she was the stronger. She is in the smaller vessel and it will be run down. This way out is the answer. She will not have to endure the slow and degrading disintegration of her mind and the invasive pain in her body. Who will be affected by her sudden death? Youenn is as hard and enduring as a stone – he will accept her absence – he will go on without her and will become independent again. Lizzie has found her rock and will cling like a limpet to him – she has made her choice and it has not been in her sister's favour. There is no one else who will care.

She would rather die with Lizzie close to her than fade and decline into death in lonely Brittany without the comfort of her nearness. She is straining forward, staring at the water between her and Lizzie. The gap is closing. This is the solution. This way, her twin will be involved in her departure and linked to her for ever at the moment of her going. Though freed of Anna's presence, Lizzie will always remember the final collision.

Youenn has never known of the force of her love and the intricacy of her bond with Lizzie. He would have been jealous. Yet he is a sensitive man and he has long suspected that although he has her body he does not have her mind. That is why he is so possessive. He wants more – he wants her soul. But Anna cannot give it to him – it has been bequeathed to Lizzie.

She has an urge to be nearer the water, the point of impact, and, abandoning her bag on the deck and turning quickly, she goes back into the lounge and swiftly down the steps into the car deck. No one is about; no one else seems aware of the approaching accident. She runs forward to the bows and stands under the raised car ramp, waiting. Irrationally, her rollicking mind tells her that there can only be a minute or two before the impact. She feels off balance, almost sick with exaltation and apprehension.

Anna thinks she must have had brushes with death a number of times through her life and been unaware of them. She knows of two occasions when she was lucky to escape. But now she feels close to it. This time – her third encounter – she hopes and feels will be the final act. Disaster will not be averted this time. She feels a cold thrill at her oncoming fate. Also relief that the decision has been taken from her.

It has taken over half a century for her to arrive at this point. This long day seemed to stretch out in front of her at dawn, but it has accelerated during the passing hours and now all that remains is these last few minutes. There had to be a reason why she has spent much of the day reliving the high and low points in her life. This is it. Her remaining time has now become compressed. Lizzie has been with her all day in her thoughts and is with her now. There is a moment of calm. A pause. Anna has the illusion that time has suddenly slowed down – the beguiling seconds seem to stretch out interminably. She closes her eyes and waits almost in a trance for the final cataclysmic impact.

Some minutes earlier, Lizzie and Paul left the dining room, and have been looking through the windows at the lights on the north shore of the Isle of Wight. Paul has suggested they have a quick breath of fresh air. Lizzie is willing to go outside if it is not too cold. Indeed, she is quite eager to do so because she is feeling slightly queasy and giddy – as if she has eaten too much or had one glass of wine too many. Paul reassures her that the May evening is mild, and he helps wrap her fashionable knitted jacket around her before opening the heavy door to the exterior. They step over the threshold and start to saunter along the deck in the cool evening air. They have emerged on the starboard side and are now looking across at the brighter lights along the Hampshire coast as their ferry nears its destination port.

Lizzie breathes in deeply to try and dispel her light-head-edness and the faint sensation of being off-balance. She rarely feels ill – and she is never seasick. It has always been emotional upheavals and rows that have made her feel nauseous. It is as if mental pain and anguish are transmitted to the centre of her stomach, where they churn and ferment. She recalls feeling sick during the whole day following that ghastly dinner party when Anna had been blamed and banished.

Lizzie remembers some of the quarrels with her sister and how they tormented her afterwards. Fond as they were of each other, their habit of sharing everything – whether it was secrets, the men in their lives, or the progress of their careers – caused rapport or discord in equal measure. Their closeness often resulted in disruptive and emotionally unsettling rows. The fracas over sharing Fynn had caused much distress and resent-ment, leading as it did to the permanent break-up of her marriage to Alan and the temporary estrangement between her and Anna.

Lizzie leans on the rails and, though she is gazing at the shore, her mind is on the past.

As a single parent, during the years following her divorce she had needed encouragement and companionship, and Anna had been loyal and supportive, even moving to a flat in the same area to be closer to her friend. Lizzie was struggling with two teenagers who were thoroughly normal in that they were demanding and selfish, and who, to Lizzie's chagrin, seemed to get on better with Anna than their own mother, and found it easier to discuss their problems with their adopted aunt. They also managed to retain a reasonable relationship with their father, and Katrina had even defected to stay with him for a few months following a period of rivalry and conflict with Lizzie. Ralph was a hard-working boy who would later study economics at university and go into banking. He seemed less vulnerable and less dependent than his sister and tried to steer his own path away from both his parents, eventually opting for university in the States and then a trainee job in banking in the Far East. Lizzie still feels that she has lost an opportunity, that she could have had a more fulfilling and closer relationship with her son and daughter, but the chance has passed forever, and though they are distantly fond of her, sadly they will never now be intimate with their mother.

She sighs, and to conceal this, she turns and smiles at Paul, who is silent and pensive beside her. He is watching the final splinter of sun descend below the horizon and sees, as she does, the black flecks of seabirds as they dart across the melodramatic yellow hue of the western sky ahead of them. What he is thinking about is unfathomable and Lizzie returns to her own reflections.

In her early forties, when she had given up hope of finding another partner whom she could love and respect, Lizzie had met Paul. Kind-hearted and considerate – although, like her, bruised by a fractured relationship and messy divorce – he was sympathetic and supportive. He was also amusing and attractive. Engrossed in his career, he was single-minded, but, unlike other men she had met, he was capable of giving a part of himself to her. They spent a lot of time together, and inevitably she had less of it to give to her friend. Anna had been outwardly enthusiastic about Paul, professing to be delighted that Lizzie had found another man to love, but Lizzie had suspected that the other was carefully concealing her wounded feelings that she had been put aside.

Lizzie's Catholicism had meant that she felt very guilty about her divorce, but her need for a happy, stable relationship and

Paul's persuasiveness overcame her doubts. After their marriage, which had been a short, stylish event with a few good friends, it became apparent to Lizzie that Anna was once again jealous of her husband. The difference was that this time the two of them actually liked each other, which had not been the case with Alan. They laughed together over frivolities and jokes and discussed serious topics with an earnestness which sometimes Lizzie herself found disconcerting. But Anna was envious of Lizzie's joy in her new husband, and Lizzie was wary of Anna's ability to stimulate Paul's intellect.

Matters came to a head over lunch when the two women were at a small Chinese restaurant in Gerrard Street. They both enquired about each other's work – Lizzie was busy with her new career as an assistant to a casting director, and Anna was preoccupied with a series of articles she had been asked to write for a magazine – but neither was really interested in the answers. Anna had seen little of Paul and Lizzie because she had been having a pleasant but unimportant fling with a journalist from Melbourne who was employed by the same magazine. She had been telling Lizzie that she found her writing more satisfying than her affair, and was rather cruel in her dissection of the ingenuous and inexperienced young man. Watching Anna take equal enjoyment in eating her Chinese dumplings and belittling her Australian lover, Lizzie had snapped, 'I feel rather sorry for the poor bloke. You think too much, and don't feel enough. You're always telling me you live on the periphery – well, get involved. There's an emotion called love out there and you should try to find out what it means.' She took a gulp of red wine and banged her glass down on the table.

Anna choked slightly with surprise and retorted with asperity, 'You're a fine one to talk! You've almost destroyed *our* love and wrecked our friendship. I've always felt that you and I were more than sisters, but you've decided to reject our pure spiritual relationship in favour of the prosaic physical compromise of a husband-and-wife team. You could have us both, but you elbow me out. You're unworthy. You're disloyal.' Her voice had risen and she was oblivious to the curious stares of those around them. She felt betrayed and she didn't care what outsiders might think.

Stung by the accusation of unfaithfulness, and at the same time knowing there was an element of truth in the allegation, Lizzie leant forward and said in a low but vehement voice, 'That is not fair. I was always true to you – I've always cared. You like to think of yourself as the cool intellectual and me as the butterfly brain, but at least I'm real and I have feelings. You tell me about your wretched affairs with no hint of warmth or involvement. You simply don't care about your lovers. You aren't capable of real emotion. You're cold.'

Anna leant back in her chair against this onslaught but said nothing more. Out of the corner of her eye, Lizzie could see the incurious immobility of the two Chinese waiters at the back of the room, and feeling sick with embarrassment, she hissed, 'For God's sake let's pay up and get out.'

Looking back on this quarrel, Lizzie realises that it must have taken place around the time of Paul's infidelity with Anna. This would account for Anna's agonised and guilty counter-accusations. Lizzie would never know precisely why it had happened, though it was clear that not only were Paul and Anna close friends, but there was a frisson between them and they were sexually attracted to each other. Perhaps more significantly, they had a common bond – they both loved her. This superior love had probably also been why they decided to quickly put an end to their illicit affair. Genuine in their desire not to hurt Lizzie, the object of their higher love, and dreading discovery, the guilty pair would have felt wicked and immoral in their deceit of her.

Some weeks later, without any reconciliation between the two women, Anna moved back to Paris, where she found a part-time job teaching English, a cheap apartment in the Marais, a new young lover, and time to work on her never-ending book on Shakespeare's tragedies. Lizzie missed her, but not enough to get in touch until nearly a year had passed, by which time both of them were yearning for appeasement, for reunion and for the balm of their sisterhood. So they made contact, and arranged to meet up once again, but this time Lizzie went to Paris, where she met Malo, who was Anna's latest amour. That they would share everything was again promised. But inherent in a promise is the possibility of transgression. "'Without contraries there is no progression,'" Anna had often said, quoting Blake. "'Attraction and repulsion, reason and energy, love and hate, are necessary to human existence.'" And so the cycle of broken trust would be repeated once more. Like shattered spokes in a wheel.

Almost unconsciously, Lizzie fingers the small pale scar on her hand. It has all but disappeared but there still is a small raised hard patch to remind her of a bike accident long ago in her childhood. She used to think that her life was incomplete without Anna but she is not so sure now. Lizzie acknowledges that Anna is her link with the past, but feels that from now on they must take their separate paths.

Lizzie vaguely registers some lights approaching up ahead and suddenly focuses on her conversation with Anna the previous evening. Her sister had been surprisingly distant at first. Almost reserved and withdrawn – which was most unlike

240

the Anna she knew. When Lizzie had confessed about her brief indiscretion with Malo, Anna had hardly reacted – and seemed quite unusually quiescent and accepting. She seemed to lack her usual spirit and energy – which Lizzie had guessed was being sapped by the sulky but intense Frenchman she had married. The immature Malo had been subject to mood swings too, but these had been part of his charming extravagances and enthusiasms. Youenn would have been a more difficult proposition, but she knew that Anna would have wanted the challenge. Maybe she had made the substitution because she didn't respect Malo, whom she could easily control, and knew that taming Youenn would be impossible and undesirable. Perhaps she finally felt the need for someone stronger than herself.

It seems that Youenn has proved simply too strong, and Anna has shrunk in stature and spirit. She had not looked too well last night and was far too thin. Lizzie feels anxiety. If there is a serious problem with her health, Anna would surely have confided in her. She has always done so before – it has been the core principle of their sibling-like relationship. She was certainly open about the problem in her relationship with Youenn. Was she hiding anything, though? There had been a time when they had shared all confidences and problems, but Lizzie can see that this era is over. There is something that is missing, a fastening that has come undone. She speculates about when they will next meet, and shivers when a cold wave of apprehension washes over her, whispering to her that 'when' might be 'if'. Another coming together is inevitable before they finally spin apart. Surely.

But her unease is short-lived and she suppresses the vague premonition of disaster. She knows why she feels more secure, why she is more positive and fearless about the future: She has

241

# Chapter Twelve

Disorientated by the motion in the bows of the ferry, distracted and almost hypnotised by the prospect of her own impending annihilation, Anna has miscalculated the distance between the two ferries, both of which are steaming slower in the channel outside Portsmouth Harbour. Following its usual route, the Isle of Wight ferry is approximately abeam of the Southsea Memorial and begins to turn away from the course of the incoming Channel ferry, to leave Spitbank Fort to port before steaming across to Wootton Creek. The sun has sunk into the grey and yellow clouds in the west and darkness has begun to spread over the waters, the waves glinting in the last of the evening light. A few seabirds soar on the fading winds of the dying day.

Anna, shivering with awed anticipation, feels the movement and the slight tilt of the ferry turning in a slow sweep away from the path of the oncoming ship, away from the collision she hopes for. She opens her eyes and, distraught with disappointment, staggers across to look over the side by the raised ramp. The bigger ship is still a few hundred yards off, but her ferry is passing in front of it and will steer clear. She emits a sob of utter vexation. What a fool she has been! Of course ferries do not collide these days – technology, efficiency and training do not let that happen. She must be deranged to have imagined that they would. For a few seconds she stares in horror at the realisation that there will be no collision, no easy way out, no avoidance of pain, no curtailment of degrading decline. She is ready to die; she wants to die; she needs to die. Now. Her sun has set.

The ferry has altered course but she cannot do the same – her path is fixed and the idea of drowning will not be dismissed. She has a choice – her death will be a deliberate act of self destruction. Has this course of action been submerged in her sub-conscious since early this morning? Her 'adieu' has welled up and has now burst upon the surface of her mind. There is still time, she thinks, as she begins to run down the length of the open car deck, passing below the accommodation super-structure, weaving in between the cars to get to the other end of the small vessel. It is nearly dark; there are no other passengers on this level; it is unlikely that anyone will see her go.

With the exertion of running, her habitual dull cramp becomes an acute spasm. She is in a state of panic lest she miss the final chance of coming together with Lizzie. Reaching the stern, she jumps onto a bollard and then onto the edge of the raised metal gunwale, and leaps off into the boiling wake.

In the sea, hearing the booming and thudding of the engines receding behind her, and stunned more by the coldness of the water than by the impact of hitting the waves, Anna surfaces, kicks off her shoes, and starts to swim. She has always been a good swimmer and does the crawl – it's faster. She wriggles free of the jacket, the weight of which may slow her down. She has one more task – to get there, to meet Lizzie – one last time.

Her life is fragmenting into a kaleidoscope of ragged thoughts. All day she has been floundering in her past. Now she must concentrate on the fugitive fleeting present. These are the final minutes of her long day's journey into night. She talks inwardly, wordlessly.

'My God, it's cold. Keep going – I can do it. I won't be cheated. I chose it. It was meant to happen. The ship looks so big from down here. It's coming on. I must aim in front of the bows if I'm to meet it. If I'm to meet Lizzie. Keep going. I'm still in control. It's getting darker. I am for the dark. The water's colder. But I can make it. Not far now. It will be oblivion. Suppress doubt. Life has been good. Death is only a word. And death shall have no dominion. My garden will live on.'

The woman is getting tired – she is much less strong than she used to be. The waves are slapping into her face and, trying not to choke or swallow water, she tries to ignore the pain in her stomach, feeling panic that she might get cramp and not reach her goal. A sudden irrelevant thought strikes her – she has left her book on the boat – it will be found and then they will know. She smiles inwardly – a dead author sells better. And her suicide will help. She sees the ferry looming up – a gigantic black shadow – a drumming noise.

'It's so huge – I don't want it to pass without taking me with it. Oh God, don't let me miss it. Why do I call on a Deity I don't believe in? Lizzie will pray for me, but I'll be beyond prayer. I'm getting tired … keep going. I can do this. I ache … This is to avoid worse pain. I'm here! I can stop swimming. Lizzie's up there. She knows I'm near. She'll miss me but not for long. She doesn't need me now… I don't need her any more.'

The wall of the ferry is sliding past in front of her. The

huge bow wave is washing her away from the side, preventing her touching it. Reaching out an arm she sees her pale hand – it looks beautiful, ethereal – through the water.

'Oh Lizzie, the gap's widening between us. Paul is drawing you away, driving you in a golden chariot. My influence has waned, dimmed. Darkness is about to pass. Love passes. Yes. It's all right between us, Lizzie. I can sink and you can swim. But you'll remember me. No more secrets. Secrets die with us. No more sharing … except this moment … I am going down – stretching up to you. No more partings. No regrets. This is permanent. For eternity. I can't keep the water out of my mouth. Oh God, I can't breathe. I'm suffocating … sliding … falling …'

Lizzie is watching the failing light on the waves. Paul is close to her, and has put a proprietary but comforting arm around her shoulders. She is shivering a little, but inhales the keen fresh salty air and savours its taste and tang. She glances down. The waters below are dark and frothy as they sluice past the sheer side of the hull, gleaming wetly before darkness extinguishes the light.

The long day of travelling is almost over. She feels a calm exhilaration. She silently thanks her Creator. The peace of God transcends her understanding. It is night and tomorrow will be another beautiful day, full of hope. Lizzie has been set free. Her twin has bequeathed her the courage to face whatever comes next. She can embark on a new path and make new tracks. Anna has been close, so close, but now she is gone. She has slipped away quietly into the darkness and will settle in the comfortable recesses of her sister's memory.

To banish a slight sensation of vertigo, Lizzie raises her head. She looks up at the sky, seeing a few stars shining through

the ragged moving clouds. The gulls have gone, flown to wher-
ever they go at night. She knows with unutterable conviction
that she has lost Anna. Forever. But she remembers the rules
– no turning round, no looking back.

# *Acknowledgements*

For their help and advice, my love and thanks go to Fizz and Adrian Rowbotham, Marie-Noëlle Gerard-Knight, and Charmian Ryan. For their encouragement, love and support, I shall always be grateful to my family – Michael, Julie and Jack.